KATY BARNETT

THE EARTH BELOW

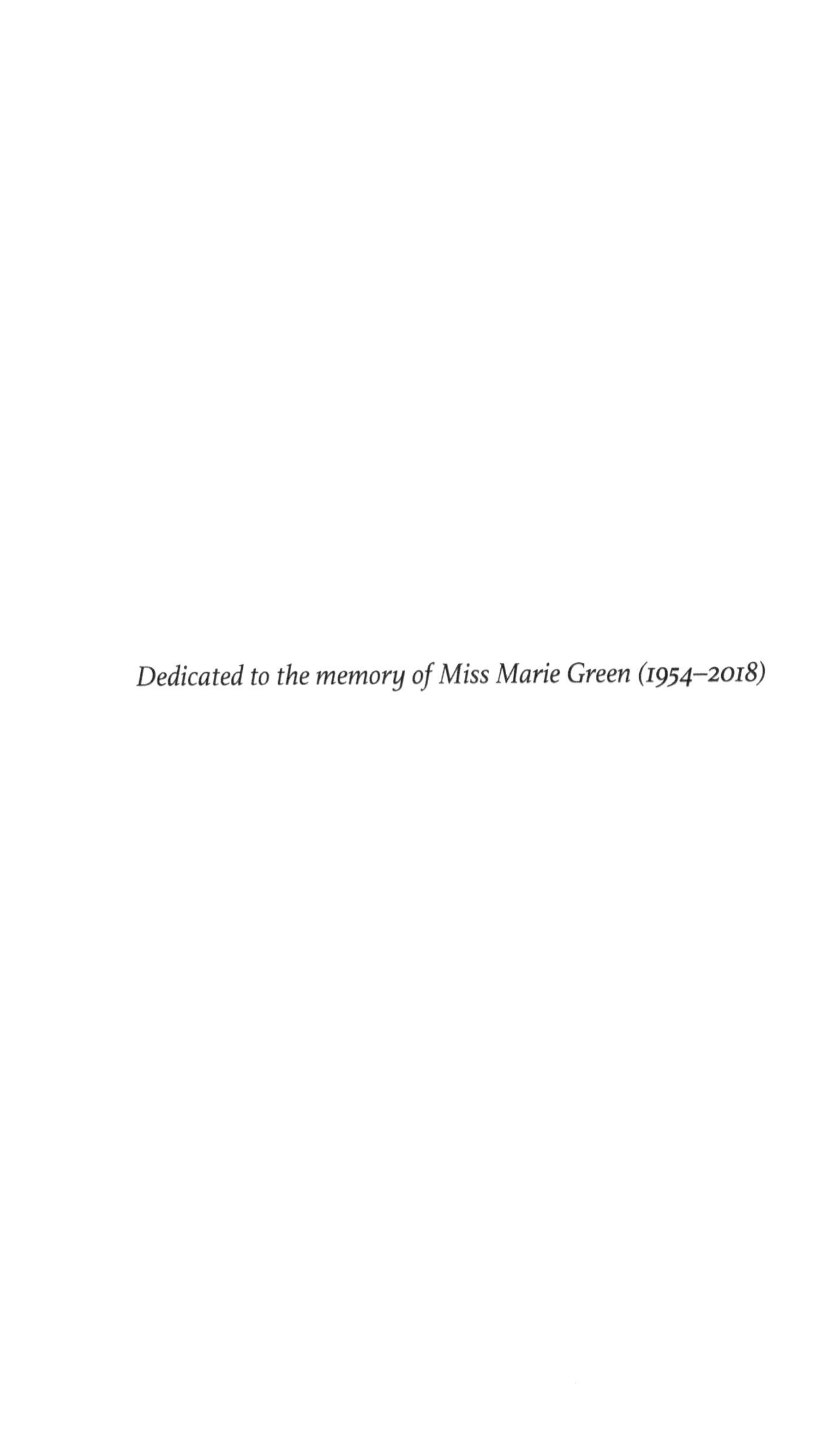

Dedicated to the memory of Miss Marie Green (1954–2018)

CHAPTER 1

Toc toc, toc toc, toc toc. The noise reverberated through the floor and into my ear, waking me.

I sat up on the grubby mattress, my heart beating fast, and scanned the windows. I couldn't see anyone yet, but I was sure someone was coming.

The noise got louder, like buzzing in my skull, and I began to shake. *Oh no. Not this again!*

I lay back down on the mattress and forced myself to breathe, then tensed my toes as hard as I could, then relaxed them, tensed my feet. I continued on up my body until I got to my neck and face: *tense ... relax.*

Then I stood, but my hands still shook. I clasped them together to stop them, but it didn't work. So I started my pacing routine, counting my steps in my head.

One two three, turn! One two three, turn! One two three, turn! One two three, turn!

I couldn't go further than three steps in either direction because my left leg was chained to a metal pole in the middle of the carriage room. They'd gutted the carriage down to its metal outer casing, and sawed away any horizontal poles so I couldn't hang myself. I'd discovered the chain around my leg wasn't long enough to use for that purpose either, and my blanket was too thick and tough to be torn or shredded.

Would I have gone through with it? I didn't get the chance to find out.

As I paced, I sang under my breath to keep time.

'We are all one happy family.
A parent to one is parent to all.
We love each o-o-o-other.
We love and share, we love and care.'

The footsteps kept getting louder. I grimaced and won-dered if they belonged to the limping Barren who usually brought the breakfast porridge. I'd developed an irrational hatred of the poor man. I'd even thought about what it would feel like to punch him in the face until the bones crunched ... *stabbing his meaty chest ... no, don't think, don't think, don't think.*

I'd never had these thoughts before being sequestered. I wondered what I was turning into. I felt my face. Yes, still two eyes, a nose, a mouth.

It sounded like there was more than one set of footsteps, and I couldn't hear the *shuffle, thump* of the limping Barren.

Two people stopped outside the dusty windows, dark silhouettes behind the bright lantern they held. I cowered against the back wall, peeping through the cracks in my fin-gers. In my hurry to flee, I had knocked over the toilet bucket, and the smell of urine filled the room.

'What? What is it?' My voice sounded loud and croaky to my ears.

One of the shadows unlocked the doors and slid them open. He sighed, and tapped his foot. 'I told you, Chief Coun-cillor. Look at her.' I recognised the whining voice of Marvin, the sequestration overseer.

Another familiar voice, deep and resonant, said, 'Yes. I see.'

I froze at the back of the room. *Chief Councillor?* I wasn't sure if this was another hallucination—they had come to me in the darkness, shapes and shadows, coloured lines inter-twining and curling about, like the old pre-Catastrophe maps of our home.

The second figure approached. As my eyes adjusted to the bright light of the lantern, I saw that it was indeed the Chief Councillor, his green eyes grave. He touched me on the shoulder and I flinched.

'Marri. Your sequestration period is over.'

I stared, my mind a fuzzy blank.

The overseer fiddled with the chain around my ankle. Finally he managed to turn the key and removed the rusty, ancient padlock. The chain dropped to the floor with a clatter. It hurt my ears, and I winced and put my hands up again.

The Chief Councillor frowned. 'Come on girl, stand up. You're free.'

He was wrong. I wasn't free. I was still weighted to the floor by something heavier than that chain.

Marvin took my arm. The shock of his touch made me yelp. 'Marri, get out.'

He pulled me out of the carriage room that had been my cell for the past three weeks, and down the steps onto the tracks. I tripped on the edge of a concrete sleeper, and sat hard on the rocky scree. I hugged my knees.

Marvin whistled. 'Jared! Do something useful and take this one back to the unpartnered women's rooms.'

Shuffle, thump. It was the limping Barren to whom I'd taken such an unreasoning dislike. He grasped my right elbow gently and pulled me up.

'You're not the only one to be like this after sequestration,' he said in a soft voice as we walked past the other sequestration carriages, most of them empty. We reached the bricked-in entrance to the sequestration area, and another Barren opened the heavy metal door to let us out. Then we climbed up wooden stairs to the platform, past the sinister gallows and up an old, steep metal staircase, encased in a metal tube. I was so weak that I had to use the decayed black handrail, wet with years of dripping slime. I shuddered as I touched it. My legs ached and my lungs burned by the time we got to the top. Despite my pacing, the occasional visits to the Lights, and the daily exercise run down the sequestration tunnel, I'd become unfit. I barely recognised the pale arm gripping the handrail.

The Barren took us down Selwyn North, one of the wider tunnels with a patterned blue tiled roof. The smell of morning porridge wafting down the corridor made bile rise in my mouth. I tried to stop, but the Barren steered me through the main eating area, as it was the only way we could get to the unpartnered women's quarters.

As I entered, everyone turned towards me. The whitewashed walls were almost too bright to look at. I gasped, overcome, although I'd known the people at the tables all my life. *The eyes!* My breath came quickly and my hands began to shake.

'Keep your head down. Just walk.' Obediently, I looked down at my grubby feet stepping over the cracked tile floors. I concentrated on the texture of the tiles and the filthiness of my toenails, and counted in my head again.

Eventually we got to the door of the unpartnered women's room. The Barren opened one of the double doors. 'There you go.'

'Don't leave me!' I grabbed his arm. He must have known that I'd hated him. 'I'm sorry—'

I saw pity on his face. 'On your own now, girl.'

He pushed me through the door and walked off, *shuffle, thump, shuffle, thump.* The heavy door swung closed behind him.

I sank to the ground and curled into a ball, my head on my knees, and rocked back and forth for a while. It was comforting and dark there. A few people stepped around me, gingerly. But with my strangely enhanced hearing, the whispering watchers wormed into my consciousness anyway.

'She's been in sequestration—'

'They took the baby off her, didn't they?'

'Earth Above, look at her *arms*—'

'No, don't feel sorry for her. She was stupid—'

The last words stung as if someone had pelted me with stones, and I groaned with the truth of them.

I flinched as I heard someone come near. I felt a gentle touch on my shoulders, but couldn't stop myself from flinching a second time.

'Marri, it's Suze. You remember me?'

I stopped rocking. I put my head to the side and peeked through the crack between my arm and my knee. Yes, there was Suze's smiling, round face and crazy, curly hair. She was still talking.

'We met when you were pregnant with your first and I was pregnant with—Earth Above, it must have been my eighth?'

I hid my face again, not sure how to respond.

After a long pause, Suze said in an even brighter voice, 'Why don't we find you a free bed? And then, maybe, after you've had a sleep, you can shower.' I could almost *feel* that she was wrinkling her nose.

She slid her arms around my shoulders and hoisted me into a half-standing position. 'Did they not feed you? There wasn't much of you to start with, but there's less now!'

Then she steered me towards a bed. I kept my head down as we walked. I flopped onto the bed, and Suze opened the folded blanket and put it over me. I got into a foetal position and pulled the blanket up above my head.

Suze peeped under the blanket. 'Isn't that better than the floor?'

'Thanks,' I whispered.

'You've done your time,' Suze said loudly. 'There's no cause for you to be punished further.'

My heart sank as I realised that she wasn't just speaking to me. *How much more do I have to take?* Tears leaked out onto my pillow and I pulled the blanket back up.

I lay silently until the chatter ceased and I could only hear my own breathing. Soon I fell into a black and dreamless sleep.

I awoke with a sense of foreboding. In the moment of disorientation between sleeping and waking, I thought I was still sequestered. But when I rolled over and saw the intricate tiles on the curved roof above my head, I remembered where I was. The gaps in the tiling were as familiar as the pattern of lines on my own hands.

I yawned and stretched, and an uninvited thought entered my head. *If they've released me ... what have they done with Macon?* I buried my head in my pillow, grinding my teeth. *Don't think about him.* The taste of betrayal was still bitter.

I sat up and looked around. Most of the unpartnered women were on rostered duties, apart from a few slumbering bodies humped under blankets. I was glad I didn't have to deal with anyone.

Someone had put a new set of clothing and a towel at the end of my bed. They'd even guessed at my foot size for some fabric undershoes and wooden overshoes. I'd been dreading the Communal Store on the Upper Level, so close to the Strikeforce Common Room. I gratefully scooped up the clothing and padded to the bathroom at the end of the dormitory, head down and shoulders hunched.

The bathroom had been painted yellow, probably before the Catastrophe, but now the paint was peeling, black spotted mould spreading down the walls like fingers, bubbling through the paint. The musty smell of the mould fought with the sewage smell from the toilet cubicles. The few fluorescent lights on the ceiling barely penetrated the gloom. One of the light bulbs buzzed, about to fail.

In the shower cubicle, the sputtering water on my skin was almost too much to bear. I had to turn it off and breathe deeply for a while. But then it became pleasurable to wash off the grime of sequestration. My breasts and belly hung flaccid and empty. I wondered what had happened to my baby. Hot tears mingled with the lukewarm water, and I choked back sobs: I knew I couldn't ask. Then I noticed that my upper arms were still yellow where I had been held down. I scrubbed at the bruises but it was no use. Finally I tried to untangle my hair. It had become matted and filthy over my three weeks of sequestration.

I dried myself and changed into fresh clothing: drawstring trews, baggy top with a drawstring tie at the neck. I had to pull the trousers very tight. Then I left the cubicle and stared into the flyspecked mirror. I always look terrible under that light—my pale skin turns green—but I barely recognised the bony, hollow-eyed face staring back at me. I tried to comb out my wet hair with my fingers, and pulled out a great chunk of coppery strands.

The light bulb flashed and hummed intermittently behind me, visible in the mirror over my shoulder. My head hurt. *Why hasn't the bulb been replaced?* My mouth was dry and furry.

A large scavenged bucket holding drinkable water had been placed at the end of the row of chipped enamel sinks. I scooped water into a mug, took a sip, swished it around my mouth, and then spat it out. *Ah, that's better.* Then I drank the rest of the water.

Someone spoke behind me. 'Hey! Marri!'

I dropped the mug into the sink with a clatter, and turned quickly. It was Suze again. Her face dropped. 'Sorry, I didn't mean to scare you.'

'It's okay. I'm ... jumpy.'

She held out a wide-toothed comb. 'I've got a free shift right now. I saw you struggling with your hair.' She laughed and patted her own unruly curls with her other hand. 'Did you want to borrow this?'

I tried to smile, but the expression felt unfamiliar and stiff on my face. 'Thanks.'

I took the comb and dragged it through the tangle. Another knotted chunk of hair came out. I plucked it from the comb and dropped it into the bin. 'Sorry!'

Suze frowned. 'You'll have to cut it. What a pity, such an unusual colour!'

Macon had loved my hair. 'I don't care if you shave my head.'

Suze blinked at my tone, but then assumed a cheerful face again. 'Wait here while I get the scissors!'

She trotted off. I tried again to untangle the ends of my hair, but I had to stop because I was sure the brittle plastic comb was about to break. It was a precious pre-Catastrophe relic, and I'd hate to destroy it.

Suze puffed back with a rusty pair of scissors. 'Here!'

She got me to sit on the edge of a basin while she hacked at the knotted red-golden-brown clumps. The basin cut into my buttocks and thighs, but I kept still as she chopped. As the hair fell, I felt a weight falling from my mind, as if I was finally throwing off the chains of sequestration.

'There!' Suze cocked her head critically. 'Better than before, I guess.'

I turned and looked in the mirror. My grey eyes stared out of purple hollows. Suze had cropped my hair savagely short, almost in a masculine style. It looked brown rather than red or gold at this length. I'd spent my childhood wishing for nice black hair, brown skin and brown eyes like everyone else. We're not supposed to look different, and I'd always felt that my appearance reflected badly on my character. My colouring didn't even have the decency to be *certain*: it looks different in different lights.

'Thanks.' I patted my shorn head. 'A new start.' We cleared the clumps of hair from the floor and put them in the bin.

'It's almost lunch bell,' Suze said, back in the main dormitory. 'Want to go down?'

I hugged myself and nodded. 'Before everyone else gets there.'

We left for the communal dining room. I didn't have anything to say, but Suze kept up a steady patter of conversation: about how bad her sleep had been—Jessie in the bed next to her snored—and how she hoped they'd find new partners soon, for both their sakes.

An uncomfortable question bubbled into my mind and I grasped Suze's arm. 'When's the next Month Party?'

Suze grinned at me. 'Two weeks. I bet you can't wait!'

I tried to smile back, but I suspect it was a grimace.

Suze didn't notice. 'You've missed all the *news*! Did you know, Rich is going with Fion again! That's the second time they've been registered, can you believe it? Mind you, they didn't have a child, so I guess it's okay—' She froze as she remembered what I'd done. There was a pause before she picked up again. 'Oh and Neena just found out she's pregnant ... so she won't be going. Isn't that nice?'

I didn't want to go to the Month Party; I wanted to be by myself. But that wasn't an option after everything that had happened. I tried not to listen to Suze's chatter, although I made polite noises at intervals: 'Ah. Really?' 'Oh.'

We turned down Selwyn North and the stench of porridge hit me again. I leaned against the wall for support, accidentally putting my hand on an old rusted map of the tunnels from before the Catastrophe, coloured lines criss-crossing. I remembered my hallucination in sequestration and removed my hand.

I took a deep breath and walked in. The eating area was large; they'd dug out and merged two existing tunnels to expand it. The walls were whitewashed, apart from the mural of the Chief Councillor. He stared down at us, his dark hair immaculate, his face benevolent. One painted eye was slightly smaller than the other—the perspective was slightly wrong.

The assault on my senses was overwhelming, even though the dining room was far from full. Suze kept chattering loudly and people called to her, but I put my head down and folded my arms around myself, moving as quickly as I could to the lunch queue.

I stood behind Rich, one of the Strikeforce men I disliked the most. My heart sank, but I greeted him politely as we collected scavenged plastic cutlery. He was no more pleased than I was: his lip curled with contempt, and I ducked my eyes.

'*What's your problem, Rich?*' I thought I'd spoken under my breath, but I hadn't spoken quietly enough.

'You don't deserve what we have here,' he hissed. 'Our survival depends on obeying the rules. You don't appreciate the chance you've been given.'

I hunched my shoulders and put my head down, my eyes filling with tears. It was all I could do to stop myself from crumpling to the ground. 'I've learned my lesson. I know I did wrong.'

Fortunately, before the conversation could get any worse, we reached the service area. The Barren put a scoop of lumpy porridge in my bowl. At least it was warm, unlike the food I'd received in sequestration. Of course the Barrens would only get our cold leftovers, so I was also grateful I'd produced three offspring.

As Suze and I settled on the hard benches, the woman sitting opposite me stood and moved further down the trestle table. I tried to still my face: Seana was a known tattler. The grey porridge blurred, and I forgot to start eating.

'*Marri?* Is that you?' I jumped as I realised there was someone behind me. Then I recognised his voice and a small but genuine smile came over my face.

'*Felix!*' I turned to the man behind me. 'Yes, it's *me!*'

Felix had been my best friend since we were six, and my accomplice in childhood mischief, including our efforts to explore the furthest reaches of the tunnels, hoping to find a way to the surface. Our expeditions had ended in failure and notoriety: when we were twelve, we'd been caught by a Strikeforce patrol.

'I wasn't sure ...' Felix patted his curly hair and raised his eyebrows. I put my hand to my head as I remembered my haircut.

'Why don't you join us, Felix?' boomed Suze.

Felix slid into the space next to me, a rare smile spreading over his thin face. 'When did they let you ... ?'

'This morning.'

Suze clucked her tongue. 'They didn't feed her enough, Felix, make sure she eats!'

'They gave me the same amount as always. I just ... I didn't feel ...'

Felix glanced sidelong at me, concern in his brown eyes. I looked down at my porridge and dug my plastic spoon into it to avoid any further questions. I chewed a lumpy mouthful mechanically, swallowing with effort.

Suze kept eating, and gossiping in a friendly way about who had partnered up lately. I was so grateful for her kindness earlier, but Month Parties were the last thing I wanted to hear about. I tuned it out again, and stared at my bowl.

Something Suze said caught my ear. *That name.* 'What did you say?'

I sensed that Felix had frozen beside me, with his spoon halfway to his mouth. He put up his hand, but Suze was unstoppable.

'I was just saying that Macon's with Rilla, and she's pregnant—'

A lump of porridge seemed to have lodged in my throat. 'He's with *Rilla?*' *Dark-haired, tall, curvaceous. A popular girl ... As different from me as you can get.*

Felix glared. 'Suze ... Can you *think* before you open your mouth?'

'I forgot!' Suze said, half lifting her hands.

I tried to shrug. 'About what?' It didn't come out right. My lips felt like cardboard. Their expressions showed my attempt at nonchalance had failed.

Suze looked pained, but she brightened. 'You need someone to take your mind off things. Someone *new!*' She gave Felix a sly look. 'There's a lovely man sitting next to you. Have you noticed?'

I rolled my eyes. 'Of course I have! It's just—he's never—'

Felix squirmed in his seat, his cheeks reddening.

It was all too much. I stood and invented an excuse. 'I've just remembered—I have to see the Duty Master.'

I put my dirty bowl in the washing-up pile, my panic rising as people surrounded me. When a Barren glared at me, I realised I'd put the bowl down with a smack, almost breaking it. I forced a smile and paced towards the exit.

'Wait for me, Marri!' called Felix. He shovelled the final spoonful of porridge into his mouth, and rose. I knew he'd be eager to escape Suze's attempts to set him up with someone.

Perhaps she'd offer herself to Felix at the next Month Party? I winced. Some people shouldn't share with each other.

As I stood waiting for him, Rilla walked in. She scowled as she saw me, and put her hand over her belly in a familiar protective gesture. I blushed to my hairline, and jerked my eyes away. A murmur passed over the other diners. The old saying came into my mind: *Think of the Monster Rat and he appears.*

Felix shepherded me out of the meals area before I could make more of a spectacle of myself.

We took the back way to the Upper Levels, the tunnel few other people use because it's steep, and smells like old socks. Felix went first, and I followed, clutching the damp metal handrail.

As we climbed, I said to Felix, 'Sorry you had to put up with Suze. All she wants to do is set people up into productive partnerships.'

Ahead of me, he shrugged.

'Out of curiosity, though, are you—?'

Felix stopped abruptly and faced me. 'Not you too!'

My heart stopped at the expression on his face. 'Felix, what's happened?'

The only sounds were the clunk and whine of the pumps that kept the tunnels from flooding, and the slow trickle of water from the pipes lining the roof. Green slime grew over the tiles, and tiny stalactites hung from the roof like strings. Felix looked at his feet.

I put my hand on Felix's arm. 'You're not in trouble, are you?' If you went too long without partnering or producing offspring, you could be declared a Barren—or worse. But surely it hadn't been that long? '*Earth Above*, why didn't you say?'

He looked up. 'You've been sequestered for the last three weeks and recovering from childbirth before that. There was nothing you could do.'

'I'm a woman ... you could have—'

'*Marri.* You've been partnered, pregnant or with the babies since we were fourteen. It's not like I had a chance with you—'

The words burned. I took a backwards step, and my breath huffed out. 'I *tried* to let you know I'd be your partner, you remember, at *that* Month Party? But you didn't seem to notice, and then that's when I ...'

I couldn't go on. Felix's face filled with regret. 'Don't blame yourself. It's *my* fault.'

I hit my forehead with my fists. 'I shouldn't have drunk so much that night. If I'd just stayed with you—'

Felix pushed my fists away from my face. 'Please. Stop. Look at you, you're a skeleton—and your eyes! What did they do to you?'

When I didn't answer, Felix continued to rant.

'They should have sequestered that spoiled piece of shit instead. But they'd never do that, his sire wouldn't allow it—!'

'*Shh!*' I shook Felix's elbow, and looked up and down the corridor to check again that no one else was there. 'I'll be your partner. You know that!'

Felix stared at the green runnels of slime. Eventually he said, 'I knew you were making an offer—that night.'

I'd suspected he'd been pretending not to understand my offer, but it stung to hear it confirmed. 'Why didn't you accept it, then?' I couldn't keep the hurt from my voice.

Felix's voice was flat and toneless. 'All my partnerships end in disaster.'

'What about Neena? You seemed happy with her.'

Felix's face twisted. 'She reported me. To the Council.'

'What? She ... *what*—?'

'I was drinking a lot then. It was the only way I could get through it, but I couldn't do my duty.'

'You know we're not supposed to drink except at Month Parties ... did you get it from one of those Strikeforce idiots? Not from *Leo*?'

He turned his back to me. 'Why do they have to *force* us into partnerships? It makes me sick.'

After a long silence, I put my hand on Felix's shoulder. 'I'm still here, if you'll take me.'

The fluorescent light on the walls of the tunnel reflected in his eyes as he turned; unshed tears hung on the edges of his eyelashes.

'You're a better friend than I deserve.'

We were standing so close to one another that I thought for a moment he was going to kiss me. Did I want him to? Why wouldn't I? My heart skittered in my chest, and thoughts ran through my mind in a panicked cascade.

To my secret relief, Felix turned away. 'We'd better go now. We don't need any more trouble—either of us.'

I trudged off down the Selwyn Common corridor, only to be told by the Duty Master that I still had three more days off.

'I'll make sure the Council hears of your devotion,' he said wheezily, winking at me.

I returned to the unpartnered women's rooms to cower in the safety of my blankets for a little longer.

CHAPTER 2

Over the next few weeks, as I returned to my duties, I did better. I still found it difficult to remember things, and to speak normally with other non-Barren adults, but I fell back into the routine of regular shifts caring for the children.

The Chief Councillor's weekly speeches had also helped me, reminding me what was important: we had to live and love together to make a better future for our offspring. I recalled that I'd felt particular joy when I saw my own two daughters while on Parental Duties, and I scolded myself. *A parent to one is parent to all.*

Still, I felt proud, despite my flaws. A part of me was even looking forward to the next Month Party, although I was also still anxious.

I had tried to speak to Felix after the conversation we'd had in the back corridor. I wanted to be clear that I was going to make an offer to him. He'd said he was busy, or dashed away before I could talk to him. Fear nibbled at my mind, but I dismissed it—I knew I was overly sensitive after being ostracised and sequestered.

But I wondered whether I should think about approaching other men, or if others would approach me. Then, like a drop of black ink diffusing through water, a dark thought spread across my mind.

What if he comes tomorrow night?

Surely the Chief Councillor wouldn't allow it, even after what I did?

A cold fist clenched in my stomach. I stood rigid, holding

my breath. My jaw hurt, and my hands knotted so hard that my nails dug into my palms. *I still want to kill him.*

My earlier feeling of resolution had fled. I tried to focus on my morning duty: tending the hydroponic gardens. I took a deep breath of the musty corridor air to calm myself. It was no good.

He manages the Barrens; that takes up his time. He won't come.

I knew I was deluding myself.

A scream was about to force its way from my constricted throat. I tried to loosen the muscles by swallowing twice. Then I closed my eyes, and chanted in my head: *Don't think, don't think, don't think, don't think,* until I drowned out the bad thoughts. I'd come up with this technique in sequestration. Eventually, it worked.

The hydroponic gardens were on the Lower Levels, down several sets of steep metal stairs. I had to walk past the sequestration tunnel on my way, and shuddered as I passed it.

The limping Barren—Jared, I remembered—stood outside the tunnel gate. I raised a hand to him. He twitched with surprise, but nodded back.

The hydroponic gardens smelt of manure and wet earth. One of the least pleasant Barren duties was to gather human ordure from the cesspits in the Barren barracks and turn it into useable soil. I asked the supervisor what I should do. He frowned. 'Tomatoes, Marri.'

I knelt to pick the tomatoes, dark dirt covering my knees. I'd forgotten the peculiar, pungent smell of crushed tomato leaves. I felt oddly satisfied when some tomatoes simply fell off the vine into my hand when I touched them, without the need to yank them from the stalk.

I started to relax, until I noticed that the supervisor's eyes followed my every move. I knew that he'd report on my behaviour today.

After lunch, I was on duty in the kitchens. The kitchen was a small room on Marsham Branch, off the Blue Line corridor. I made sure that I went the back way, up the steep metal steps, so I could avoid walking past the Strikeforce Common Room.

The smell of smoke, food and rubbish wafted down the corridor. Only three or four people could fit in the kitchen during each shift. Everyone complained, but it had to be here because there was a large ventilation tunnel above, with an electric fan to draw away fumes. There had been talk about expanding the kitchen since I was young.

A bitter thought arose: *Maybe the Council should fix the kitchen, instead of watching everything we do.* I pushed the unworthy thought back down. *Don't think.*

Ramala was a short, round older woman with black springy hair. She was chopping mushrooms, but raised her head to call hello as I walked in. She directed the activities of the kitchen and made our meals palatable. Unfairly, she wasn't allowed to eat until all of us who were not Barren had eaten our fill. She also had some of the worst duties: gutting animals, disposing of cooking rubbish.

The smoke from the ovens caught in my throat and made my eyes water. The junk we used to fuel the fires didn't always burn cleanly, and the fan couldn't remove all the fumes.

I blinked when I saw Felix stirring a pot of stew. Steam and smoke wreathed around his head and made gorgeous whorls in the air. I hadn't realised he was on kitchen duty today; his primary duty was to teach the younger boys to read and write. Mine was Parental Duties, looking after the three- to five-year-old children before they were segregated into girls' and boys' groups at six years old.

I studied Felix's thin, serious face before he noticed me. If he accepted my offer and I produced a child, would it have dark curly hair and olive skin like him? I hoped so: it would be easier on the child if it looked normal. But what if it ended up with a double dose of our desire to explore, our tendency to get into trouble? What would happen to it then?

I narrowed my eyes, but then checked myself. I shouldn't invent problems for this poor non-existent child when I wasn't even sure whether Felix would accept me. Still, my own thoughts reassured me; I was getting used to the idea of my friend as a partner.

Felix turned and saw me, and for a moment his eyes lit up with an unalloyed smile. Then his smile dropped and he turned away. The wreckage of my own smile was stranded on my face for two or three heartbeats before I could remove it.

With an effort, I turned my mind to my duties. 'What do you need me to do?'

Ramala was oblivious to the tension between me and Felix, her back turned. 'This pot is almost useless. Why do those Strikers never get me the pots I want?' She put her head up. 'Chop the root vegetables, please, Marri.'

As I put on an apron and gathered up the vegetables, Ramala made polite conversation. 'How have you been? You know, since ...'

'It's good to be back with everyone again.'

'I bet it is.'

'It was very noisy and bright at first, but I'm almost used to it.'

There was another silence as I chopped, Ramala lugged large pots around and Felix stirred the stew under her direction.

Ramala spoke again. 'You must be excited about the Month Party tomorrow.'

Felix had dampened my enthusiasm, and I let a little of my true reluctance show. 'Guess so.' As soon as I'd said it, I wished I had spoken with a different tone.

Ramala's brows drew in. She put the spoon down on the bench with a crack. Her hands were on her hips. 'You should be grateful! All that nice food—*I'd* swap with you in a heartbeat. Half a heartbeat!'

The pile of sliced vegetables blurred and wobbled as my eyes stung with tears. 'I'm sorry.'

We worked in miserable silence for some time.

Eventually Ramala snorted. 'Fetch the dried meat from the larder for me, there's a girl.'

I left the kitchen, glad to have an excuse to escape. The larder had been built after the Catastrophe, at the end of a long corridor. It was poky, cold, and dark, but at least it was *dry*, which was why we had dug out the area and stored our food in the earthen room at the end.

Only one of the light bulbs in the larder was working, right by the entrance. My mind went to the flickering fluorescent light in the communal women's toilets. I was almost accustomed to it now. Things always seemed to be running short these days.

Shadows lay in the corners of the larder like heavy blankets. I couldn't remember where the dried meat was stored, and I peered at the darkened shelves. In my preoccupation, I didn't notice the other person standing at the shelves with his back to me. I bumped into him as I moved sideways.

He was taller and broader than me, and he turned and grabbed my shoulder. *No, no, no!* I hit out, punching his arm and chest. *Don't touch me!* I was unsure whether I thought it or said it aloud. I kicked at his knee, and he grunted with pain. He let go.

'Stop, it's *me*—!'

I stopped struggling, but I couldn't stop panting.

Macon's reddish-brown hair was still cropped short. He

was unshaven and pale. There were dark shadows under his eyes. Joy, anger and despair rolled into one in my chest.

I drew a breath. 'You scared me! What are you doing here?'

His eyes shifted, and the one remaining light caught the green in them. 'Taking an inventory for the next scavenging run. Light bulbs.'

'Oh.' I looked away at the shelves, dismayed and furious to realise that a small part of me still longed to be held by him. *Your lips on my neck, your hands ... No! Never again.*

I clenched my hands into fists and put them by my side. 'We need a new fluorescent light in the unpartnered women's toilets. Put that on your list.'

Macon picked up a pencil and piece of paper from the shelf. Reflexively, we both checked the corridor. It was empty, although Ramala's singing echoed from the kitchen, interrupted by her racking cough.

Macon and I hadn't spoken privately since I had told him that I had been called up by the Council. We had said inexcusable things to one another.

I stared at the ground. We shouldn't be speaking at all, but I couldn't move. The thick, uncomfortable silence of things left unsaid had trapped me here.

Macon broke first. 'For the Earth's sake, what did you do to your hair?'

I looked up. 'I cut it off, obviously.'

'It makes you look ... gaunt. Are you ... okay?'

Rage boiled up, bubbling like a stew pot. 'Why should I give a rat shit what *you* think about my hair?'

'Calm down.' Macon crumped the paper list in his hand, his voice still quiet. 'You don't understand. The Chief Councillor is very disappointed, and—'

'Whose fault is that?' I clenched my fists. 'It was *your* idea to meet, but I'm the one who paid—!' I turned away. 'Your sire wasn't going to let his offspring be sequestered, *no* ...'

'Keep your voice down, for the Earth's sake!' Macon glowered. 'You could have said no to me. And I was punished too—'

I swallowed, and managed to keep my voice to a hoarse whisper, but I was shaking all over. 'They stood you down from the Strikeforces—that's all. You have *no fucking idea* what my punishment was like—!' I choked.

Macon blinked when I swore. 'I'm sorry that things have been bad. They haven't been easy for me either—'

I scoffed. 'Your life is perfect compared to mine.' I couldn't resist a dig at him. 'How's Rilla—bearer of your next child?'

'That partnership's over.' Macon turned away from me, but not before I saw pain constrict his expression. 'Nothing came of it, in the worst way.'

My anger drained away as quickly as it had risen, and prickling cold horror replaced it. *Another miscarriage—her fifth or sixth? No offspring carried to term.* I put my hand to my face as shame consumed me.

'Oh ... I'm sorry, Macon. I didn't know! Shit and piss.'

He sighed. 'Worse for her than for me.'

'Not something I'd wish on any woman.' I put my hands on my hips, remembering something. 'Do you understand *now* why I got upset about Tomas?'

He blinked. I could tell that he didn't know who I was talking about, and my voice rose again. 'The child they sequestered me for bearing! *You're* his sire, remember? That last time we met, you hoped that he wouldn't *take*.'

I winced as I remembered what I had said to him then: that it wasn't the child's fault that we were its progenitors, and that I'd rather Macon died. After that, I had thrown a small rock at him, and stormed off.

In sequestration, I'd realised that I'd lost my temper with Macon because he had spoken my own shameful hope aloud.

At times during my pregnancy, I had wished that poor Tomas would go away, against everything I'd been taught in Motherhood Studies. I closed my eyes and recited the words in my mind. *The life of every child is precious. Parent to one, parent to all.*

I opened my eyes when someone coughed. Macon and I turned.

Ramala was in the doorway, her hand pressed to her gaping mouth. 'I was worried Marri had fallen off the shelf and hurt herself; Frankie always puts the meat too high.' She frowned, disapproval radiating from every pore, and looked us up and down. 'You two aren't carrying on *again*, are you?'

I recoiled. 'He's the last man I'd—!' I swayed as the blood left my head. 'He's doing a lightbulb inventory. I didn't mean ... I bumped into him and screamed.' *Shit, shit, shit. I should have walked away.* Acid rose up in my mouth and I swallowed it.

Ramala's eyes were narrow, and her mouth was tight. 'The meat?'

Macon took a packet of meat from the shelf and handed it to Ramala. Then he picked up his list, turned and left.

I knew the rhythm of his walk like I knew my own heartbeat. I touched my shoulder where he'd held it.

'Foolish girl,' said Ramala.

I was mute, pleading with my eyes. I wouldn't blame her if she reported me: she might be moved out of the kitchens or get better food. My shoulders slumped. *If they sequester me again ... I'll kill myself before they get me. I'll do it this time.*

Felix didn't look up as we returned to the kitchen. He stirred the stew, staring into the swirling, hot liquid. I was glad Ramala didn't mention what had happened.

I unwrapped the salted dried meat and began to chop it, trying not to cry. It was hard to cut because my hands were shaking so much. Misery burned in me.

Knock knock! I jumped and almost cut my finger at the rap on the door lintel. It was a Strikeforce Patrol. Leo, one of Rich's cronies, looked in, and his small eyes narrowed as he scanned the room. 'Anyone seen Macon?'

Felix looked up, and gaped at Leo with suspicion. 'Why would he be *here*?'

Leo's eyes shifted from Felix to me. 'I don't know—'

I kept my eyes on the meat, making the slices as even as possible. My heart was racing and sweat poured down my face. *Someone must have reported Macon's movements—they're watching him too.* Leo strutted around the room, a smile on his face. He lingered behind me, watching me slice the vegetables. I could feel his breath on my neck. I had to repress the desire to pull away from him.

Ramala rested her spoon on her chin. 'Now I think of it, I *did* see him hanging around the larder when I got the meat before.' She caught my eye for the briefest moment and I smiled internally, hoping that Macon was long gone.

The other Strikeforce man, older and balding, grabbed Leo's arm. 'Let's check it out.' Leo glared at me again. After he'd left, the room felt less cramped. He wasn't a large man, but he always took up a lot of space.

We listened as they searched the larder, and then came back past the kitchen. Once their footsteps had faded, Ramala reached out, took the cutting board, and scraped the sliced meat into Felix's pot. She touched my quivering arm.

'Sorry I snapped at you about the Month Party, Marri. You hit me on a sore spot. I can only imagine what it's like to have all those children—*pop, pop, pop*—like peas out of a pod. It must be hard for you too.'

I shrugged. 'It's not like either of us have a choice.' I'd always known childbirth was dangerous: my own mother had died birthing me, and I'd almost died with Cady, my second offspring. But that's just the way it was. We had children until we died or became Barren.

I rubbed my thumb over the blue-black tattoo on my inner left wrist, a habit I'd developed in sequestration. My birth mother's symbol was a series of concentric circles. I could feel it without looking; it was slightly raised from the rest of my skin, twice inked, once when I was a baby, and then again when I became old enough to go to Month Parties. Then I touched the triangular tattoo on the other wrist: my sire's mark, also double-inked. I had thought that the second inking was one of the most painful things a person could experience, until I went through childbirth.

Ramala dumped the vegetable scraps in the compost box. 'You know, I heard from some of the old women when I was young that girls used to have a choice.'

I stared. 'You knew people who were born *before*! You can't be that old?'

Ramala laughed, causing the lines at the edges of her eyes to crinkle. Her face was made to laugh. 'Ah, stop it, girl, you're too kind!'

I would have loved to ask more, but Frankie interrupted us. He was another Barren, younger than most and very strong. He was lugging a container of wood, paper, and cloth junk on his shoulder. 'Hey Ramala, got some oven fuel for you! I'll put it in the big box. Hi Felix, hi Marri!'

Everyone knows Frankie. He carries all the heavy stuff from place to place. He's also one of the few Barrens allowed to attend Month Parties, because he helps the drumming team when it's short-handed. Of course, he's never allowed to eat our food, or interact with the women.

Ramala and I greeted Frankie, but Felix ignored him. I stared at Felix's stiff back, astonished. I'd never seen him treat a Barren badly before. It was true that Barrens were different to us, but I'd always been aware that, if I survived birthing children, I'd end up as a Barren too.

I couldn't resist admiring Frankie's muscular arms as he pushed past me. I'd always thought he was handsome, with his high cheekbones and his ruffled black hair. I'm not the only woman who has admired him. *Such a pity he got that disease when he was a boy.* Frankie noticed me looking and smiled, his left cheek dimpling. I blushed.

He stopped in the doorway, the empty sack over his arm. 'Felix, are you on the drumming team tomorrow?'

Felix didn't turn around. 'No.'

We waited for a further response, but there was none. Frankie made a rueful face, then shrugged as he left. 'See you all round.'

I looked at Felix. 'Frankie must be a relief drummer tomorrow.'

Felix just grunted.

I could put up with Felix being rude to me, but this was another matter. 'Felix, he didn't deserve to be spoken to like that!'

'Leave me alone!'

Ramala raised her eyebrows. I shrugged and made a face: *I don't know what's wrong.* This wasn't quite true. I'd realised that both Frankie and I had tried to talk to Felix about the Month Party.

Felix's bad mood hung around him like an unpleasant smell. He didn't speak for the rest of the shift.

I resolved not to let my big mouth get me into any more trouble. *Maybe it would be best if I stayed silent.* Unfortunately, my mouth often overrules my best intentions. Fortunately, there was a lot to do, so I couldn't brood. Sweat ran down my face as steam filled the small kitchen, and I pushed up the sleeves of my shirt. Dried, salted rat meat can be chewy, so we had to let it simmer for a long while. Sometimes the

Strikeforces get other meat from supraterran animals, but it's not always available. The rats are rife down here, particularly in the kitchen, so that's what we eat most of the time. We learn how to use slingshots from a very young age.

We had to swat Sir away from the meat. Sir is a big black-and-white wall-eyed tom who prowls the pantries. He is the patriarch of our cat clan, and has broods of yellow-eyed kittens. He often sleeps next to the ovens, and sometimes gets so warm that his black fur smokes. Then we beat out his smoking pelt, and he looks at us balefully with a half-open yellow eye for interrupting his slumber.

Eventually Sir abandoned his attempts to get at the meat. He curled up into a neat circle and slept. He chose to sleep by Felix's oven because Felix ignored him.

Finally, the stew was ready, and we passed the pots to the Barrens who serve the meals. Felix and I went to dinner separately, without speaking.

In the communal dining area, Leo stopped Felix as he collected his bowl. They spoke briefly, looking over in my direction. My breath caught. *Oh crap! Felix wouldn't tell on me to save himself—would he?* Until his strange behaviour today, I would never have considered the possibility. Tears prickled the corners of my eyes, but my stomach fluttered with fear.

As I tried to force myself to eat, an older man, Ralph, sat beside me. He smiled as I glanced at him, showing his missing teeth. I had difficulty smiling back.

'Month Party tomorrow,' he said.

'Mmhm.' I turned to my stew, avoiding his gaze.

'You'll need a partner. They'll be watching.' His hand wandered to my thigh and squeezed it.

I didn't answer. Ralph's hand climbed further up my thigh. I shifted as far from him as I could. I was sure that other people at the table could see what he was doing, but no one said any-thing—even though physical contact between non-partners is forbidden.

My heart beat faster, and I gobbled my stew, my leg pressed away from his groping hand.

When I left the dining area, Ralph followed me into the corridor leading to the unpartnered women's dormitory. I squeaked with fear and tried to dart away, but he pushed me against the corridor wall, his breath stinking.

'You watch, Marri. You can't be so choosy now. No more handsome young Strikers for you.'

'Leave me *alone*!' I slapped his horrible spider-like hands.

He laughed. He was stronger than me and we both knew it.

Jessie turned into the corridor, and took in the scene with a glance. 'Cut it out, Ralph, you filthy old sleaze.'

Ralph assumed an injured expression. 'I was just trying to help her.' He leered at me. 'Mind my words, you'll be happy with the likes of me.' Then he walked off.

'Thanks Jessie,' I said.

Her gaze was flat and cool. 'Why did you let him do that to you, Marri? Why do you let any of them?'

It would have hurt less if she'd knifed me in the stomach. As it was, I couldn't answer: my voice seemed to be stuck in my throat. She stalked away.

I went to the non-partnered women's bathroom, and stood under the sputtering shower to wash Jessie's words away. *Please, let tomorrow be better.*

As I lay down to sleep, I tried to remind myself of the rea-sons I had to be grateful. Others had it worse. Ramala pre-pared the food with such care, but didn't get to eat anything but scant leftovers. Frankie had to put up with rudeness. Even poor Rilla's situation was worse than mine. I should be grate-ful that my offspring were still alive.

CHAPTER 3

The next day at breakfast, I sat next to Pia, one of my few friends, and listened to the cheerful chatter at our table about the Month Party that evening. I couldn't join in. I'd spent the night worrying that I'd be sequestered again. I felt like I had been run through a laundry mangle, and my eyes were scratchy and dry. The painted eyes of the Chief Councillor bore into my back. *He knows I talked to Macon yesterday.* I tried to cheer myself up by reminding myself that I was on three-year-old Parental Duties that morning. I didn't dare think about my afternoon duties.

The children's area was on the Upper Levels, along the Selwyn South line and then onto Selwyn South Station. I stepped as quickly as I could over the rusted rails and crumbling concrete sleepers. Finally, I reached Selwyn South Platform, and skirted around the dormitories built from adapted train carriages. I went up the stairs to Selwyn South Mall, where the children played and learned their lessons. Like our communal eating area, the children's area had been a thoroughfare with open rooms off to the side. There were faded and incomprehensible signs above some of the rooms: I didn't know who 'Fast Mart' might have been, but he'd left his name in a few places. Barriers built out of scavenged materials separated the thoroughfare into sections, dividing the children into age groups. Raised concrete and wooden platforms kept them safe when the tunnels flooded.

I was disappointed to see that Fred was on duty in the three-year-old play area. He had sired one child, but it had died.

All the women knew he was an inconsiderate sexual partner with an explosive temper. I resolved to keep my distance. To my relief and delight, Suze was standing in the kiosk, and I greeted her warmly.

Some children were playing with communal toys: dolls, wooden blocks, and wheeled vehicles like the ones we find abandoned in tunnels, all crafted from scavenged material. One little girl, Priscilla, raced up and grabbed my hand to show me a complex game she'd invented. As far as I could work out, it involved putting rocks in a line.

As I admired the line of rocks, a boy ran past, chasing three other children and shouting, 'I'm the Monster Rat! Run, run, run!' The sound echoed in the curved roof above. I smiled to myself. As a girl, I was terrified of Monster Rat. It was huge, with glowing red eyes and horrible fangs, and was said to appear when someone was going to die. Various people on overnight Parental Duties had had to reassure me that it *wasn't* under my trestle bed.

It occurred to me now that someone had probably invented the Monster Rat as a means of keeping the children under control, so that they didn't wander into decrepit old tunnels filled with water and rubble. *The real monster in those tunnels doesn't have glowing red eyes and horrible fangs. He's human,* I thought. *And I couldn't run ... No—don't think.* I wrapped my arms around myself.

A boy called Jay fell over while running from the 'Monster Rat'. He wailed, his mouth a big red square of distress. I picked him up and held his curly dark head to my chest, kissing him. He flung his arms around me and said, 'I love you!' through sobs.

'I love you too, Jay.'

I carried him to the side room where we stored medical and cooking equipment. I patted his curls, touched that he remembered who I was after three months. Suze was cutting up precious hydroponically-grown fruit. I stole a strawberry and popped it into Jay's mouth, and Suze grinned and pretended to swat me with the knife. Then she gave me a strawberry too, a rare treat which we usually only get at Month Parties. The sweet tartness burst in my mouth, and I tried to make the taste last. Jay's sobs slowed as he chewed, and soon he was better.

As I watched the playing children, I tried not to look at Cady, but my eyes were drawn to her because, like me, she didn't look like anyone else. She smiled at the little dark-haired girl she was playing with, holding her hand. I hoped that Cady got into less trouble than I had as a child. My eldest, Lilah, seemed to be taking after me. Someone had told me that, while I was sequestered, she had been caught trying to creep into a forbidden area. I felt a pang of guilt that I'd passed my undesirable characteristics on to her.

Then I shook myself. I owed it to these beautiful children to give them all equal attention. I was still holding Jay, and I hugged him again to make up for my selfish thoughts. He squirmed from my arms and joined the other children. The time for affection was over.

I turned to Suze to ask if the fruit was ready to serve. For a heartbeat, the lights hummed, and then there was a flash. *Blackout.* One of the solar generators had failed again; an engineering Strikeforce team would have to connect a backup generator. It had been happening more often lately. Some of the children started to cry.

Fred called out in the darkness. 'Get the torch, Marri!'

I groped for the faintly fluorescent emergency torch fastened to the wall. It had been painted using a kind of mushroom that grows in the tunnels. I used it to find an oil lamp in the cupboard, then lit the lamp and put it in the middle of the grouped children.

'*Don't* touch it,' I said. 'It burns.' I pretended to put my finger near the flame, then pulled my finger back quickly and put it in my mouth. 'Ow!' The children looked at me with round, serious eyes, the orange lamp reflected many times over in their gazes.

I laid out more lamps as Suze brought the fruit platters. Fred told the children a comical story about someone who fell into a toilet during a blackout. The children laughed. Poo never fails to cheer them up.

Buzz. The lights came back on, and the pumps whirred into action again. I sighed with relief. I don't know how the generators work; they don't teach the women about it, any more than they teach us how to read. I hadn't known they existed before Felix tried to explain them to me, but his explanation left me with more questions. I should have asked Macon how they worked.

Too late now.

Fred and I blew out the nasty oil lamps as quickly as we could, and then returned them to the cupboards in the kiosk.

'So, Marri—' Fred started, as I put away some lamps. 'Month Party tonight.'

I hadn't thought it was possible for my heart to sink any lower, but I was wrong.

'Yeah.' I moved away, my body tensing.

'Looking forward to seeing you there.' He gave me a look he seemed to think was seductive. It made him look cross-eyed.

'Ah ... it'll be nice to see you too.' I inched away further. 'But I'm sorry: I've got a prior arrangement with Felix.'

I had come up with the lie in the middle of the night, after replaying the incident with Ralph in my head. I'd realised the only way to keep men like that from approaching me was to say that I was with another man.

Fred gave a scornful laugh. '*Felix*? Even you can do better than that.'

I shrugged and returned to the room, leaving Fred to put away the rest of the lamps, but any serenity I'd been granted by my time with the children had gone. I closed my eyes and hoped that the afternoon shift wouldn't go as badly. I'd been looking forward to it since the day I had been released.

After the bell went, I ate lunch. I could barely eat fast enough, fear and excitement warring in my belly.

Then I went back up to Selwyn South Platform and turned down Selwyn Southbound to the babies' area. I could never go down this corridor without being reminded how Macon and I had met here by accident, while I was on duty with the babies after birthing Cady. That was when he'd whispered we should meet again. I shook my head to dispel the memory, and walked briskly to the babies' rooms.

Like some other larger areas, the babies' rooms had been dug out beyond the tunnels and platforms since the Catastrophe. Wooden cribs lined the walls, women hovering over them.

It was feeding time, and the women with milk were breast-feeding the babies, sitting in the chairs set aside. Sorrow filled me: my milk had dried up while I was sequestered. I had always loved watching the concentration on babies' faces as they suckled, the way their little hands grasped at your shirt or your hair. One of the women, Jenn, held a newborn, and I felt a twinge of intense jealousy.

I remembered when I had first fed Lilah, just after she was born. She had looked at me curiously, wondering about the world around her. *Did I look like that at the woman who birthed me? Did she see me before she died?* I would never know.

The Barren midwives were sitting around a table, holding

babies and drinking moss tea. As I approached them, I heard one midwife whisper, 'Do you think they know? Will they arrest her?'

I kept my eyes high, but stumbled as I walked. I had to stop and compose myself. I managed to ask them what help was needed. They told me to check the sleeping babies. I nodded. Not all babies live through those first two years, the most dangerous time for our children. Some develop a terrible croup-like cough, perhaps because of the dampness. Sometimes epidemics go through the nursery. We try to scavenge medicine made before the Catastrophe, and to use the right cures for the right illnesses, but so much knowledge has been lost.

I paused as I passed Tomas's crib, pretending that I was tucking in the baby next to him. He was easy to find among all the dark-haired babies. Mine have always been bald, with a little covering of blondish-red fuzz, like a peach. I knew I'd be reported if I paused too long, but I couldn't help myself. He no longer looked like a newborn. I wondered if Tomas's name would suit him, or whether he'd have to grow into it. I hadn't named him: the Council allots names to the newborn children.

Tomas shifted in his sleep. His left hand escaped from his wrapping, my tattoo on his wrist: three interlocking circles in a triangular pattern.

My fingers twitched as I moved down the row. I yearned to kiss Tomas's fat, creased thighs, and to rub my cheek on his velvety head. I had done that once or twice with my other babies when I was on duty with women who wouldn't report me. Most of us give each other leeway with the newborns, but there were a few tattlers. Naturally, I spread my affection around. It's selfish and unfair to the other babies not to cuddle and kiss them too.

Another baby started to cry, as if to remind me of my duty.

I changed him, and put the dirty nappy in the washing basket. He was still crying, so I jiggled him, patted him, and sang to him until he burped. Such a large burp for a small person, no wonder he'd been unhappy! I kissed his head and told him he was a good boy, and he fell asleep. I began the careful manoeuvre of transferring him back to his crib without waking him.

A loud knock woke the baby and he wailed. I looked up, but immediately suppressed an irritated protest when I saw the four Strikeforce men at the door. Blood beat in my temples and I froze to the floor.

A Barren midwife stood up, disapproval written across her face. This was a *women's* space. But her words were careful. 'Welcome to the nursery. Can I help you?'

'We're here to make an arrest,' said the balding man I'd seen on patrol with Leo yesterday. I half-choked, and held the baby to me. It felt my distress and wailed louder.

The men shouldered past the midwife, towards me. My breath came in panicked bursts, and I thought about putting the baby down and running. My legs wouldn't work at all.

'*Move*, woman,' said the bald man.

I stared at him uncomprehendingly.

One of the other men, a tall, lanky man, shook his head. He was one of Macon's friends: Phil?

'Are you crazy, Marri? Get out of the way!'

Phil shoved me aside roughly, and stomped into an inner room. He came out holding the arm of a stout white-haired Barren midwife.

The woman was crying. 'I haven't done anything!'

'What shit!' said one of the Strikers. He slapped her face and they dragged her away. The baby in my arms screamed in a crescendo to match her cries, his face red and crinkled, his gummy mouth wide, and his tongue curled with rage. There is nothing worse than a baby's cry. It pierces you under the ribs and crawls up into your brain.

The grey-haired Barren midwife who had greeted the men took the screaming baby from me and patted him.

'What did she do?' I asked.

'They're saying she ended the lives of offspring before they were born.'

I drew in a shocked breath. 'The life of every child is precious. Parent to one, parent to all.'

The midwife nodded at my orthodox response, and sat with the now-calm baby. 'Have a seat, Marri. You don't look well.'

Another midwife bustled out with a cup of moss tea and showed me a seat at the table. 'They always get spooked after sequestration,' I heard her say to a feeding mother.

I was settling another baby when Jenn, the woman with the newborn, touched my shoulder. 'Don't you have to get ready for the Month Party?'

'You're right!' I forced a smile. 'Looking forward to it!'

My lack of enthusiasm must have showed, despite my efforts to hide it. Sympathy shone in her brown eyes. 'I hope it's okay—'

'Thanks, Jenn. Me too.'

To my surprise, she hugged me. 'Good luck, Marri.'

I grabbed a clean set of clothes from the communal stores. Then I brushed my hair with a gap-toothed comb, washed my face, and headed to the Month Party. *Can't be late.*

I had to go to the communal dining room, take a side tunnel up to the Blue Line, and walk down the tunnel until I got to Colwell Road Platform. The metal rails had been pulled up and melted down, so it was an easy path. Oil lamps had been set out, lighting the way, just for this event. I saw other people and couples in the distance and hung back. I didn't want to have to talk to anyone yet.

I could just hear the hypnotic noise of the drums in the distance, growing louder as I made my way down the tunnel.

When I reached Colwell Road Platform, I climbed the rough steps that someone had hewn into the edge. Then I dragged myself up the metal stairs and came to the Month Party hall, puffing slightly.

Fires burned in big drums placed at intervals around the circular, high-ceilinged room, sending golden flickering light onto the beautiful wrought girders holding up the roof. On the edge of the room, couches and beds had been curtained off for those who were shy. I puzzled over the sign saying 'TICKETS' on the old building near the beds. I've always wondered what it means.

I kicked off my overshoes, making an effort to remember where I'd left them, and walked across the floor in my cloth undershoes. It's easier to dance without overshoes, and this room was not as damp as some of the others. The floor was paved with beautiful white stone flecked with black, so closely cut that you could barely see the joins, unlike anything we could make now.

I passed the drummers on my way to the food table. Frankie winked at me, his bare arms glistening, brown, muscular and distractingly sweaty. *Yes, such a pity he's Barren.*

The table was laden with hydroponic fruits and non-rat meat, pierced by skewers: a real feast. I savoured some orange fruit, and fantasised about stealing a piece for Ramala, as an apology for my thoughtlessness the day before. But I risked sequestration or worse if I was caught stealing Month Party food and giving it to a Barren. It wasn't worth it.

As I turned away from the food, I bumped into Rilla. I hadn't seen her since my release. *What is she doing here? Surely her body needs time to recover?* Then I realised. *Poor girl, she wants to try again.* Our eyes met. A spasm passed across her face.

'Hi Rilla,' I said, as neutrally as I could.

She looked at me, and turned away. I didn't take it personally. But as I tried to join another conversation, Elena glared at me, and Rich and Fion shuffled away. Were they punishing me, or trying to protect themselves? I closed my eyes and took a deep breath. *I need a drink!*

I went to one of the cauldrons next to the food table, grabbed a mug from the pile and pushed through the crowd to scoop up a cupful. After the drink, I felt more relaxed. I don't know what they put in it, but it works.

I peered into the flickering shadows, and spotted Pam standing beside a fire drum. She'd slept in the bed next to me when we were eight or so. We'd compared tattoos and discovered that we had the same sire, although Pam has the usual dark hair, dark eyes, and brown skin. We went on a mission to find him. Eventually, the Registrar took pity and showed us a grumpy-looking Strikeforce Vice-Commander called James. James must have been aware of the two girls following him, but he gave off a very strong sense that he didn't want to be approached.

I went to Pam, feeling more like I was floating than walking. A smile spread across her face.

'Marri! How nice to see you!' She hugged me tightly. *Thank the Earth. Maybe tonight will be okay after all.*

We started to dance. The drummers struck up a chant, and the beat of the drums buzzed in my breastbone. The rhythm of the dance took over my body, and I was untethered from my worries and concerns.

People poured into the room. As I crossed the room to get another drink, men tried to catch my eye. The look on their faces reminded me of Sir stalking a rat. There have always been more women than men down here since the original groups were trapped during the Catastrophe; because males seem to be more susceptible to the flus that sweep the population every two or three years. But because many of the women are breastfeeding or pregnant, there are always more men than women at the Parties. I'd forgotten how great the disproportion was.

I accidentally caught Ralph's eye as I moved through the crowd. He beckoned to me, leering. I forced a smile, shook my head, and kept moving. *Ugh.*

Before I knew it, I'd finished my second drink. As I wended back across the room, faces flickered in front of me. I had a moment of panic as I realised how strange they looked— caught in mid-gesture or mid-dance, their skin reddened by the flames.

Suze was dancing with Peter. She winked at me. In the light and shadow, the fine wrinkles around her eyes were more obvious. *I wonder when her time is up?* I hoped she had a few years left before she became Barren.

Pam was kissing Charl passionately on the dance floor when I returned, and he already had his hand up her top. *Probably a prior arrangement.* You're not supposed to do it, but everyone does. They've given up trying to prevent it because it's better than not partnering at all.

Over the other side of the room, I caught sight of Macon standing with Pia. He leaned over to kiss her cheek, and she slipped her arm around his waist. Hot jealousy stabbed through me, and my heart turned over in my chest. *I hate him. How dare he make me feel like this.* I couldn't hate Pia, though. I shouldn't hate either of them; they were both behaving correctly.

I had a third drink to erase that feeling. *Why can't I be more normal? The Council was right, there's something wrong with me.* The room was alien and unwelcome; familiar faces loomed ominous in the red light. I bit my lip so hard I tasted blood, and wiped my eyes with the back of my hand.

I turned, looking behind me, hoping to see Felix. I found the Councillors instead. Attractive young women surrounded them, as usual. One man turned—Councillor Conor, his thick, reddish face leering in the semi-darkness. Rilla hung off his arm, her smile an imperfect mask that didn't wholly cover her terrible desperation.

Acid rose in my mouth, and I pushed through the crowd, my heart beating fast. *Run. Get away.* I went back to the cauldron, downed a drink, and then another. After that, everything seemed distant, as if I was floating on the ceiling. I wandered in a daze, not caring as I bumped into the thrashing, pressing dancers.

I don't know how long I wandered aimlessly before I spotted Felix standing alone at the edge of the room, his arms folded. I shook my head at his stupidity. *He should at least* pretend *to look more comfortable.*

When Felix saw me, the sullen look dropped from his face and he smiled. Relief flooded through me as I hurried over.

'Hey Felix!' I lurched at him and tried to hug him. A small part of me was aware that I was grinning widely. He gently pushed me upright and away. He was stronger than I would have thought.

'Marri!' His brow creased. 'Earth Above, how much have you had to drink?'

I brushed off his comment with a wave of my left hand and kissed his cheek. 'I'm fine, I'm *fine*. I've been looking for you. Dance with me!'

I grabbed Felix's wrist and pulled him onto the dance floor. *So far, so good.* He moved a little closer, and gingerly put his arms around my waist. It was weird to be held by someone close to my own height and build. But even in this odd attenuated state, it felt good—*really* good—to be held by someone I trusted and liked.

'So ...' I said after a time. 'Should we—?'

'You're the only woman I want to be with tonight, Marri.'

I'd never noticed how dark brown his eyes were until that moment. I tried to hold back tears. 'I should have done this years ago—'

I put out my hand.

For a terrible moment Felix paused.

But then he took my hand in his, his palms slick with sweat. 'I accept your offer.'

I sighed with relief, and put my arms around him. Then I kissed him, finally.

To my surprise, it wasn't that great—a little formal and stiff, even though we'd known each other forever. I was disappointed until I remembered how he hated showing emotion in public.

'Let's go somewhere more private.'

I dragged him away from the press of sweaty, dancing bodies to the edge of the dance floor, aware of interested eyes following our progress.

We found a curtained area at the edge of the room. I drew the curtain, plunging us into semi-darkness, and sat on the bed. 'Sit down.'

He slowly sat. I took his hand.

'You're with me now! There's nothing to worry about.'

We sat for a while with our arms around each other, and I pushed his dark curls away from his face and smiled at him.

We kissed again. *Still not great. He's so tense!* I closed my eyes and imagined I was kissing Macon. I was in an abandoned tunnel, consumed by urgent passion. *It was always over too quickly, but oh! in that moment—!* My body responded, warmth filling me. *That's better.*

I lay back and pulled Felix onto me. He half-fell, and we became a tangle of awkward limbs.

It'll be better next time, when he's more comfortable.

I removed my top, untied the waist of my trousers, then went to undo Felix's trousers.

Abruptly, Felix pulled away from my fumbling hands and stood up. 'This isn't working! I can't do it!'

I sat up, and put my arms around myself. 'What's wrong?'

He sat on the end of the bed, and put his head in his hands. 'I hate being forced—'

My body ached for comfort. It had been so long since I'd had a pleasurable—even tolerable—experience with a man. *Don't think. Don't think about that.*

My lower lip trembled. 'I thought you *wanted* me to offer myself to you. I was trying to make everything right.'

'I'm sorry, Marri, *I'm sorry.* I meant what I said, I promise. If it's not right with *you*, what can I—?'

For a terrible moment, I thought I might throw up. The room spun as I lay back and stared at the iron girders.

Then I sat up again, put my shirt on, tied my trousers up. 'For once, I've done what I'm supposed to do, and you don't even want me.' Tears of drunken self-pity ran down my face.

Felix put his head up. 'It's not your fault. There's something wrong with *me.* Can I explain properly tomorrow?'

My mind conjured up terrible afflictions: tumours, wasting diseases, lung problems, infected wounds. The kind of things that leave you Barren if you're *lucky.* My heart smote me, and I flopped back on the bed.

'I'm sorry. You should have told me—I won't tell, whatever it is.' I sighed. 'I just wanted to be held by someone ... *kind* ...'

Felix looked at me quickly. 'Who hasn't been kind?'

All the fear, hurt and worry I'd tried to drown bobbed to the surface. 'Something happened. Something bad—'

'What bad thing? Who? Was it Macon?'

'No—' I put my hands over my mouth to muffle the terrible high cry which escaped my mouth. 'The Council ... Councillor ...'

I couldn't continue, and buried my face into my pillow. I shook my head when Felix tried to ask more.

'It *was* Macon,' he muttered. 'You got involved with him and they noticed you. He's one of them, you know. The Chief Councillor's going to appoint him to the Council as soon as there's a vacancy. Stinking Councillors and their offspring!'

I stared at him through tears. 'Don't say that about the Chief Councillor! He saved us!'

My final memory was of crying into the pillow, while Felix patted my hair.

When I woke, I had a terrible sick taste in my mouth. I wasn't sure where I was.

I rolled over in panic, and found Felix sleeping next to me. A lock of curly hair had fallen across his forehead, his mouth was partly open and he was breathing heavily. I had pulled the blankets off him. He didn't look unwell. He looked perfect.

I wasn't sure what to do. I didn't know what to say either. I avoided the issue. I snuck out without waking him.

CHAPTER 4

I was at a loose end. Non-Barren people have a free day after a Month Party. I wished I had duties to distract myself, because my mind was drowning in self-pity.

You can't do anything right. You've ruined your friendship with Felix. Macon is happy with Pia, just as he should be. He's normal, but you can't make a partnership work with anybody. You deserve everything that happens to you.

Then I worried about Felix. *He's in trouble with the Council and he has some kind of disease or condition. Is he Barren? He could be dying! How can I help him?*

I was too unwell to eat. I went to the communal bathroom to get some water, but my breath came quickly and shallowly, I couldn't get enough air into my lungs, and my heart pounded in my chest, *bom, bom, bom, bom, bom*, quicker than a Month Party drum. Pain speared through my guts, and sweat dripped down my face. I sat doubled over on a toilet, then retched over a hand basin, but nothing came up. I wondered if I was dying too, like Felix. Eventually it passed.

I went for a walk, despite my throbbing head, hoping to find Felix, and to get him to explain what was going on. I went to the hydroponic gardens on the Lower Level, where Barrens were tending the plants under bright electric lights. The green growing things were soothing, but Felix was not there.

It wasn't just the plants that needed light. One of the founders of our community had been a medic before the Catastrophe, and he had scavenged and rigged up special lamps—still known as 'Lionel's Lights', even though Lionel was long dead.

If we didn't stand under them regularly, we got brittle bones. It was one of the rostered tasks for everyone, even Barrens.

I decided to visit the Lights, even though I wasn't due for a session. They were on the Upper Levels, next to the storerooms, so it was a climb, but I thought it would do me good.

When I got there, I found some Barrens and two Strikers preparing for a scavenging run later in the day. They looked at me strangely when I joined them, but they accepted me into the circle: no one can be excluded from the Lights.

I linked arms with a Barren and a Strikeforce man on either side, and we sang the happy family song. *We love and share, we love and care.* Afterwards, I stood in the warm light with my eyes closed, thinking. It occurred to me that the Lights were the only place where the song was true—Barren, Striker, and bearer of children, standing hand in hand. Then I remembered what Rich had said about my bad attitude. *I should be grateful. Don't question the song. Don't think.*

I checked the children's areas on the Upper Level, then tramped down again to the communal dining room on the Middle Level, but Felix wasn't there. The lights went out—the main supraterran solar generator must have failed again. Someone came by with an oil lamp and we trooped onto the Selwyn Common platform to wait. Barrens ran to bail out the lower corridors and undo the water locks which channelled water into another area when the pumps weren't working.

As I thought about the Lower Level, I had a brainwave. *Our reading cave!* Felix and I had met there when were younger, and he'd spent hours teaching me how to read. They say women don't need to read because we'll be looking after babies for the rest of our lives. But I had been desperate to learn, for reasons I can't articulate even now. Felix had traced words and letters on the floor with a stone, and sometimes he had smuggled precious books out for me.

The cave had been created when the earth shifted, possibly around the time of the Catastrophe. To get there, I had to squeeze through a crack in a tunnel near the Laundry, which was more difficult now that I was an adult woman who had borne three children—though my recent weight loss during sequestration helped.

A pool of water lay on one side, suffused with a blue glow. Water gushed down rocks into the pool with a constant tinkling splash, but I'd never seen the pool overflow, so it must drain. Blue luminous twinkles on the roof gave everything a dim and eerie light. When we were children, Felix had boosted me up to investigate the source of the glow. We were intrigued to discover that the roof was covered with tiny worms, all dangling threads of blue glowing liquid.

My eyes were still adjusting to the dim glow, so I didn't notice at first that someone was seated by the edge of the water, his legs drawn up and one arm around his knees. As I peered at him, he moved, and I squawked with fear.

It was Felix. He was chewing the nails on one hand.

I laughed despite it all, and it echoed.

'Hey,' he said, his face long and melancholy. 'Did I ... *frighten* you?'

I tried to grin. 'No, well, yeah, I mean—I was looking for you.'

I sat down and, like him, drew up my legs and put my arms around my knees, listening to the water fall. Finally, Felix spoke.

'I'm sorry about last night—'

'It's okay.' I put an arm around his shoulder and squeezed him. 'I'll get you a medic. Some of them are all right, I'm sure they'll be able to help with ... whatever you've got.'

Felix looked confused. Then his brow cleared.

'I'm not ill. Not like that.'

I frowned at him. 'What's the problem, then?'

He said quietly, 'I don't know where to start.'

I waited.

After a long time, he took a deep breath. 'They've forbidden you from seeing Macon—again. I know it didn't work the first time, but what about this time? Did being sequestered help you forget your feelings for him?'

I answered him swiftly. 'I hate Macon. *Hate* him—'

'But I bet you still felt weird when you saw him last night?'

It's easier to be honest in the dark, when no one can see your face. Darkness encourages the revelation of secrets.

I ground my teeth. 'I saw him with Pia last night. And I was ... actually ... maybe ... upset. I'm *weak*—'

I felt rather than saw Felix's nod. 'I understand. Believe me.'

A small sting of jealousy pierced me as I tried to imagine which girl had managed to attract Felix's interest. I rubbed my forehead. I couldn't picture what she would be like.

'Who is she?' Then I wrinkled my nose as a possibility occurred to me. 'Oh crap, she's not a half-sib?' There are some rules that even I would never break.

'If only,' said Felix.

For a moment, I was flummoxed. What was more unacceptable than a partnership with a half-sibling? Then an insight struck me, as luminous as the dangling beads held by the worms. 'You don't mean ...?'

Felix sighed. 'Yeah.'

I didn't know what to say.

As if to fill my silence, Felix continued. 'I realised there was something wrong with me a long time ago. I've tried to ignore it, and for a while—like when we were children, exploring the tunnels—I even forgot about it ...'

He stole a glance at me, to gauge my reaction.

'Whenever I've been with a woman, it just—it doesn't *work*

for me. I love you, and I'm so grateful that you're trying to help me, but—'

I closed my eyes. The afterimage of the glowing dots on the roof left orange patterns behind my eyelids.

'—But I'm a woman,' I finished for him.

'Yes.' Felix's shoulders tensed again. I didn't remove my arm.

'Right,' I said, opening my eyes, the orange afterimage persisting in the gloom. I was shocked, but at a deeper level, the pieces were falling into place.

I remembered how sad he'd been after a boy had died in the flu epidemic when we were nine, along with about one third of our settlement. I was surprised by Felix's sadness, because the boy hadn't been a close friend—in fact, he'd always seemed a little wary of Felix—but I hadn't thought about it further.

Felix slumped. 'Please don't report me.'

'Earth Above, Felix, I never would! I don't want you sequestered or exiled. Or ...' I couldn't mention the most likely possibility aloud.

'Aren't you freaked out?'

I thought about it. 'If you'd told me when we were younger, I would have been,' I confessed. 'Right now, I'm glad you're not dying.' I stared at the water, thinking further. 'And I'm kind of relieved that it's not my fault you're unhappy.'

We sat in silence. Eventually, I had to ask. 'Who is it?'

'Someone on the drumming team.'

I smiled. 'A drummer ... not Frankie? That's why you were rude to him!'

Even in the dim glow, I saw Felix's blush—and the fear in his eyes. 'It's not *that* obvious, is it?'

'No. You just looked like an arsehole.' I glanced at Felix and grinned. 'He *is* gorgeous—those arms! No wonder you're always so keen to get to drumming practice.'

Felix laughed too. 'I'm only on the team because of him. The drumming is kind of repetitive, you know.'

I chuckled, but was struck by a sudden concern. 'Does Frankie know you like him?'

'We've been ... ah ... getting together—for the last two years.'

'You're *joking*?'

Felix gave me a teasing look. 'When you were secretly meeting Macon—didn't you wonder how I knew about all those places? The ones I told you about?'

I shook my head. I hadn't considered that his knowledge came from personal experience.

Then I put my chin onto my knees. 'I used to think everyone else kept the rules, and I was the failure. Now I'm starting to think that everyone breaks the rules. It's just I'm more stupidly obvious about it.'

Felix was grim. 'On bad days, I think there's something wrong with us. But on good days—there must be something wrong with the rules. They just don't fit us. You can pretend for a long time to ignore your feelings, and try to deny them—but it kills you inside.'

I hunched into my knees further. 'Giving in to them isn't much better. It still leads to disappointment and pain.'

'It can't have been all bad. At least you and Macon were productive—!'

I refused to be diverted. 'I'm fertile. I'd be honoured to bear your child too. I don't care if you prefer Frankie. We can try again—!'

Felix laughed.

'I'm not joking!' I paused. 'And if it would help if he was ... um ... there too ...?'

Felix's laughter died. He shook his head. 'You *must* be

joking about that?'

I shrugged. 'Not totally. At least he's cute!'

'And you think you know everything about someone—!' Felix shook his head, dismissing the thought. 'You should keep away from me. You're under enough suspicion as it is. I'm going to end up hanged.'

Felix's words caused a terrible memory to unfurl in my mind. *Petra*. Her face swung before my eyes. Swollen. Bruised. *Tortured*. When I was a child of about seven years or so, she had refused to choose a partner. After six months, they had allocated her to someone, and she had refused him too. We'd been forced to watch her execution. It had haunted my nightmares for a year. I shivered as I remembered her final words. *'This is my choice.'*

I had only recently realised that Petra must have preferred women. Most girls, including me, had experimented together when we were young. But once we reached adulthood and had our tattoos reinked, it had to stop.

'Thinking of Petra?' said Felix.

I jumped as if an insect had run up my arm. 'How did you know?'

'That woman who disappeared afterwards must have been her lover. They never found her.'

I grimaced. 'What was her name? Tina? Sheena? She was always really lovely on Parental Duties.'

Felix looked away. 'Do you remember when we were hanging around on the Green and Yellow Line, and that *thing* approached us?'

My stomach lurched at the memory. 'That growling skeleton thing! All rags and dirt. I thought I must have imagined it.'

'Marri, I think it was *her*.'

I covered my mouth. 'I wish we'd realised. We could have

helped her.' Then I sighed, putting that horror aside, although I was sure that it would haunt me forever. 'Don't end up like Petra. There must be a better way.'

'Even if I sire a child, it might not be enough. I'm worried I'll be reported and hanged anyway.'

'For what? Has someone seen you meeting Frankie?'

Felix grimaced. 'This is *strictly* between you and me.' His voice was so low that I had to lean in to hear. 'After you birthed Lilah, and you were with the babies, I was in a bad way. I wanted to die. One of the Councillors found me trying to pluck up courage to jump off a walkway—the one that goes above the gardens?'

I grabbed his arm.

Felix ignored me and continued. 'So, he and I ... he's lonely and sad. Sometimes I still meet him.'

Guilt and shock left me poleaxed. I remembered the time he was talking about. I'd been preoccupied with the babies, and still grieving what felt like the arbitrary end of my first partnership—with Macon.

'Thank the Earth he stopped you!' I paused, realising what he'd said. 'But Felix—you don't mean ... with a *Councillor*?'

Felix gave me a smile that was mostly guilty—but not entirely. 'Yeah.'

I thought about the substance of what he'd said. 'But nobody knows you've done anything, other than Frankie and this Councillor—who've, uh, done the same thing? And now me?'

Felix looked anxious. 'Someone saw me leaving the Councillor's room two days ago. That's why I was in such a bad mood on kitchen duty. If ... that person ... tells the Council—I'm already in trouble. The pro-Conor faction will use me to bring this Councillor down.'

I shuddered.

'*Who*? Which Councillor is it?' I'd never paid attention to the machinations of the Council, and I was regretting it.

Felix shook his head silently.

'Go on ... you can tell me—'

'They'll execute me, just like Petra.'

He might be right. They'd make an example of him, and maybe this Councillor too, if there were factions set against him. *Throb, throb, throb,* went my left temple. I put my head in my hands.

'What now?' I said, once my head stopped pounding. 'What do we do?'

A tear reflected blue light as it ran down Felix's face. 'I can't see any way out. I keep circling back to the same place—the walkway ...'

'Don't even think about it!' I shook him. 'You're *not* to do it, promise me. *Promise!*'

'I'd rather do it myself than be a spectacle—in front of all of you.'

I grabbed his arm. 'You can't give up. I thought about it too, when I was sequestered. I wish we'd found a way out, when we were children, exploring those tunnels.'

Felix threw a small stone into the pool. The *plop* echoed around the cavern, and ripples spread out in glowing blue circles where the stone landed. He threw another stone. *Plop!* The second set of ripples spread across the earlier ripples, making a fascinating pattern.

'We still could,' he said.

I pulled my short hair nervously, wishing it covered my face. 'We thought we'd find other settlements and people. We didn't find anything, we never made it close to the surface. It's lucky we didn't kill ourselves.'

'We did get close—we went further than anyone, other than the Strikeforces, and we were only children.' Felix's eyes were shining. 'All those rumours about the surface, other people surviving—we can find them.'

'What if they're only rumours? The air is poisonous up there, remember? There are diseases.'

Felix snorted. 'Those are rumours too. They're meant to scare us, control us.'

'The vomiting blood disease is real. My sire died of it, just before Lilah was born—'

I put my chin on my knees and tried to forget what they'd told me about my sire's death. He'd been quarantined and had died alone, raving with fever. I'd never known him, but the stories had been horrific. And we'd been told about the poisoned plants and animals and water Above since we were very small. Maybe they were exaggerated, to keep us grateful and compliant. But surely they weren't invented out of nothing.

'The Strikeforces have to take special medicine, and wear masks,' I said. 'Macon told me. There are places they can't go, it's too dangerous.'

Felix frowned. Then he perked up again. 'Then they'd have maps, so they can scavenge. Maps to the surface, maps *of* the surface. Some areas must be less poisonous than others.'

I didn't know where he was going. 'That doesn't help us.'

Felix looked exasperated at me. 'Frankie can let me into the Strikeforce Commander's office! I'll steal a map and some medication. We can do this.'

This was starting to feel less like a dream and more like a plan, and that scared me more than the vomiting blood disease. I felt like the lone voice of reason. 'What about Frankie? Would you really leave him?'

'I'll ask him to come too.' Felix sat up straight, his eyes glinting blue in the light. 'What reason is there for him to stay? It's a miserable life as a Barren.'

'Better than no life!'

'I'm going to ask him. Will you come with us?'

Of course I was tempted by the idea of escape. *I wouldn't have to see Macon again. Why didn't he stand up for me like he promised?* But before I could spiral into self-destruction, sanity reasserted itself. *I can't leave the children—everyone and everything I know. And I'd probably die in the attempt.*

I sighed. 'I'm sorry, but I'm not going to get drawn into one of your schemes again. We're not children anymore! We need to calm down and be practical.'

Felix sulked. 'What ideas do *you* have?'

I looked him in the eye. It felt like I was seeing my oldest friend for the first time, all his courage and vulnerability. I put my hand on his knee. 'Let's register our partnership.'

CHAPTER 5

Like many others born shortly after the Catastrophe, the Registrar had weak bones and bowed legs. People called him Bent Bran, and his predicament had led Lionel to develop his famous Lights. One look at Bent Bran was enough to convince anyone of the need to attend sessions.

Bran sat in a small dingy room off Selwyn Common, not far from the Strikeforce Common Room. It still housed the remains of obsolete machinery, although most of it had been cleared out to make room for Bran and his registers. Someone had scavenged a swivelling stool so he could turn and access the shelves behind him without having to stand. Bran also sent out the bell ringers and measured the days, weeks, and years since the Catastrophe.

Bran looked at my tattoos and then Felix's, checking the records to make sure we weren't related. Then he took out his big Register book and wrote our names in it, with a record of our progenitors' tattoos. I couldn't resist looking at the list of names under the date of the latest Month Party. About ten lines down, I saw Macon and Pia's names, and directly below that, Conor and Rilla's. I shuddered involuntarily.

The stacks of books behind Bran recorded every relationship from the beginning. The lower books were thin, but the recent books were thicker. Once Bran had returned the current Register to the stack, he swivelled back and looked at Felix candidly.

'Felix, it's been a while since you've registered a partnership, hasn't it? You don't want to end up like me, and I've got a *good* life for a Barren.'

Felix chewed his thumbnail. 'No, I don't ... No offence, Bran—'

I winked. 'I'm sure he'll get lucky with me! I fall pregnant even when I'm not supposed to!'

Bran laughed. 'Yes, your record in the Register is quite *unusual.*' Then he frowned. 'At least you were unpartnered and on duty with the babies with your third child. Worse if you'd been fooling around when in a partnership with someone else, of course. We wouldn't have known *what* to do with the progeny!'

'Has that ever happened?'

'Not in my time. Anyway, may your partnership be fruitful!'

As we walked back to the partnered dormitories on the Upper Level, the tunnels seemed darker and more claustrophobic than they had before. I started to wonder whether Felix was right, and it was time for us to escape. I hoped our partnership would be fruitful as well: it would take the pressure off us both. But was that possible in the time we had?

At the evening meal, Seana sat next to me and began to chat, as if she had not ignored me for months. This was a relief because Seana and Paul would be in the couples' cubicle next to us for the duration of their partnership.

Suze approached us to ask whether it was really true that we'd entered into a partnership. I confirmed that we had. Suze grinned, and said loudly that she was looking forward to something coming of it. I agreed. 'I know Felix will sire beautiful children.'

Afterwards, when we were getting ready for bed in our curtained cubicle, Felix muttered, 'I hope something comes of it too: a way out of here ...'

I didn't respond. Instead I placed my few belongings in the

box under our bed. I had hidden them before I was sequestered, and retrieved them as soon as I could: a forbidden coppery lock of Lilah's hair, a disintegrating picture of the supraterran world I'd torn from an old book, and an interesting rock Macon had collected for me on a Strikeforce run. I touched the curled snail shell hidden in the rock, shiny and different from the surrounding rock.

Felix lay on the other side of the bed, his back to me.

I ground my teeth. 'Partners usually touch each other ...'

He rolled onto his back, and I snuggled up to him, ignoring the tension in his body. 'This is nice.'

Eventually he relaxed, and we chatted quietly about nothing. Seana popped her head in to say goodnight, her eyes sharp, but her face softened as she saw that I was snuggled up to Felix. I hoped Felix realised she was reporting on our progress.

We established a pleasant bedtime routine. Felix read to me each night, and we talked. I hadn't realised how lonely I'd been in the last few months. Having a warm body to hold made me feel better.

Felix started to steal dried food and water bottles and stash them in our cave. I had forgotten to return my torch, so he added it too. I left him to it. Stealing from communal stores is harshly punished, and I didn't want to encourage him.

'We need to discuss my *plan*, Marri,' he whispered as we lay in bed, a week after we'd registered our partnership.

I yawned. 'This is the plan. We stick to the rules, keep our heads down.'

'I need to be ready, in case they come for me.'

I stretched and yawned again. 'What have you done so far—?'

Felix frowned. 'I've collected some food. Not enough, but a start.'

I snorted, still on the verge of sleep. 'What about a map?'

Felix's face went still, and he looked away. 'Not yet.'

I roused myself and looked more closely at Felix. 'Did you ask—?' I silently mouthed Frankie's name, a secret.

Felix stared at the wall silently.

I raised my eyebrows. 'He agrees with me?'

Felix chewed his fingernails, still refusing to look at me. 'He's thinking about it. They exiled his birth mother—Above. They told him she died up there.'

I could see he was affected by Frankie's reluctance. I raised myself up onto my left elbow, and smiled down at him. 'I have a better plan.'

'What are you talking about?'

I leaned over and kissed Felix on the lips. His shocked look made me laugh, but I moved closer, pressing my body to his.

Then I reached for his trousers.

Felix wriggled back, frowning. '*Marri*! Are you ... *seducing* me?'

I blushed. 'I'd like to have another child—if it's with you. It's the best way to protect us both.'

His brows came down and he pulled away from me.

I tried to cajole him. 'Let's just try it, see what happens—!'

'I remember how sick and tired you were in your other pregnancies. We can't escape if you're feeling like that ...'

I stared at him. *He never listens!* 'Felix!' I tried to calm my anger. 'If I'm pregnant, nobody needs to escape. We'll have done our duty. That's more important than anything to them.'

Felix gave me a look that was almost pitying. '*Power* is more important to them. If they can use me to shift the balance in the Council, it won't matter if I sire a hundred children.'

'A hundred!' I said. 'I thought *I* was being optimistic!' But Felix didn't smile, and I looked down. 'I never said I was coming. Why can't you go by yourself?'

'It was always us—together,' he said. 'You were the only reason we got as far as we did. You were the one who knew where to go. Don't you remember?'

Standing at a crossroad. I remembered Felix forging ahead, hardly hesitating. But—then he'd stopped at every fork in the tunnel, waiting for me. Had he actually been following me? My memories looked totally different as the realisation came to me.

It was like he could see me remembering. 'Why don't you want to go?' he asked.

'I can't leave the children,' I said. 'What if they're punished for what I did? Or even neglected—disgraced.'

'*A parent to one is parent to all*,' Felix said. I couldn't tell whether he was trying to reassure me or point out my own transgressions. I turned away, cried a little, and then fell asleep.

The next day, Felix and I didn't speak.

Worse, while I was eating dinner, Macon came late to the dining room, and had to sit at my table because it was the only one with a free seat. I hadn't seen him since the Month Party. I sneaked a glance at him, only to catch him doing the same to me. We both looked at our meals abruptly. I gritted my teeth with frustration and rage. I wasn't sure if I was angrier at Macon or at myself.

I'd told Felix I couldn't leave the children, but I knew that was only half the truth.

In the morning, unusually, Felix was up before me. He stood by our bed. 'I'm sorry,' he said. 'I don't want to pressure you. Are you still angry with me?'

My heart softened. 'Not any more. But I'm sorry—I'm late for the babies.' I hugged him. 'Talk tonight?'

I hurried down the corridor to the babies' room. I gazed at

Tomas. Jenn came up behind me and spoke softly in my ear, her short curly hair tickling my neck. 'Have a cuddle before I feed him.' I buried my face against his neck and inhaled his milky sweet scent, then rubbed my cheek on his soft, downy head. He started to cry and I handed him to Jenn, feeling an unbearable wrench in my chest.

Another baby wailed. She was hungry, but the breastfeeding women were busy. I sang to her, soothing her. 'Shh, shh, shh. I'd feed you if I could, lovely girl. Someone will feed you soon.' I rocked her, and put my cheek on her head until she stopped crying.

Someone said, 'See—' I looked up and found that Seana and Jessie were watching me. The two women moved to the other side of the room.

I turned to Jenn and shrugged. 'What was *that* about?'

Jenn patted Tomas's head. 'Rilla's been saying that you and Felix are just a partnership of convenience. Seana told Jessie that it's rubbish.'

I raised my eyebrows. 'Why did she say that?'

Jenn smiled. 'Look at you with that baby. Anyone can see you want this partnership to be productive.'

'I … I do.' I was on the verge of tears.

Jenn's face was gentle. 'I hope it is.'

That night, I told Felix about the rumours Rilla was spreading.

Felix's face drew in with distress. 'I told you you're better off staying away from me …'

'Oh Felix!' I hugged him. 'No, I'm sorry—'

I went to kiss his cheek, but at the same time Felix went to kiss me. We met in the middle, and laughed.

Then he leaned forward and kissed me on the lips, tenderly. When he pulled away, his eyes were shining with tears. 'You're my best friend. I couldn't have survived without you.'

My eyes filled with tears too. I wasn't sure how to respond. We stood for a while, not speaking or looking at each other.

Eventually, Felix lay on the bed, and I lay facing him, but not touching him.

I lay still when Felix leaned over and kissed me again. He had never initiated this kind of contact before.

Then his hands went to the strings on my shirt and fumbled with them. *Oh.* He undid my shirt, and I took his hand and guided it to my breast. He didn't know what to do, and I had to show him what I wanted. I felt acutely aware of the ridiculousness of sexual interactions.

We continued kissing, and my self-consciousness was slowly replaced by desire. As I pressed my body against his, I realised that I wasn't the only one who was aroused. *Interesting! Although it won't be like—*

I broke off that thought and concentrated on the moment.

He lay on his back. I straddled him and grabbed the drawstring on his trousers. *I've missed this.* I tugged at his trousers, but they resisted—hadn't I undone them properly? *I must be out of practice!*

Suddenly I heard someone speak. 'I think it's down here. Seana?'

That sounds like Rilla! I turned around halfway. Felix half-raised himself on his elbows.

Rilla, Jessie, and Neena had pushed through our curtains and were gaping at me. Without thinking I rolled off Felix, pulled my top together with my right hand, and sat heavily on my bottom facing the women. It was soon obvious that I had in fact succeeded in opening his trousers. *Very* obvious.

The women stared, looking surprised and—I thought— perhaps a little impressed. Felix blushed a deep scarlet. *'No!'* He grabbed my pillow and pulled it over himself, closing his eyes.

'Get out! *Now!*' I flapped my hand at the three staring women, furious.

'Earth Above!' Neena's hand flew to her mouth. 'I'm *so sorry*, guys!'

I got off the bed and walked towards the women, my teeth clenched. 'Just ... *get out!*'

Seana and Paul poked their heads through the curtains at the kerfuffle. They stared at me too, and I realised that my own trousers were falling down. I yanked them up before I could expose more of myself. Everyone backed out hurriedly.

I sat on the bed with a thump. Felix rolled onto his front and buried his face in his pillow. 'Great.'

I tied up my trousers and paused before I tied up the strings of my top. 'I don't suppose you're in the mood to continue?'

He rolled back over and tied his trousers closed. He was still very flushed. 'Sorry.'

Suddenly, I began to laugh, so hard that I could barely breathe. Tears ran down my face in streams, until I coughed and choked.

Felix sat up and clapped me on the back. 'Are you okay?'

I gasped, 'They can't say it's a partnership of convenience any more, can they? You might even get a few more offers at the next Month Party. Even Paul looked interested—!'

Felix gave a small smile as we lay back down. Neena's shocked face came into my mind's eye, and I giggled again. I was pretty sure that Seana would report the incident tomorrow, but for once I was glad of her scrutiny.

'Do you think that Rilla was really looking for Seana's cubicle?' Felix whispered after a time.

'She knew exactly where she was going!' I laughed again. 'She got more than she bargained for.'

'Serves her right.'

The next day, Allie, the woman opposite us at the breakfast table, grinned as we sat down. 'Late for breakfast today, why could that be—?'

Felix blushed, and I nudged him. 'Don't be so modest.'

Paul clapped Felix on the shoulder as he passed us. 'Hey Felix, Marri, I hope you have a *better* night tonight.'

He continued to the porridge bowls, smiling to himself.

I smiled too. *Rilla, you've been bitten by the rat you tried to catch.* I felt we'd bought ourselves some time. But I knew we wouldn't be safe for long—unless we could produce a child.

Over the next week Felix refused to do his duty, and then I started bleeding. So I was already grumpy when he started telling me much food he'd collected for our escape.

I rolled over in bed and put my back to him. 'I don't want to talk about this!'

Felix persisted. 'Marri, you always used to leap at a daring plan! It can't just be the children they forced you to have. What's changed?'

I gritted my teeth. I didn't want to talk about what had happened to me in sequestration. *The footsteps, crack of light through the door.* I didn't even want to think about it. *Will I ever heal?* I knew I couldn't face that again.

'Nothing's happened.' I closed my eyes. 'I just ... don't ... want ... to ... go!'

I heard Felix roll over, and we went to sleep in silence.

I woke during the night. I discovered that Felix was weeping bitterly into his pillow, burying the sound as much as he could.

I put my hand on his back and whispered, 'What's wrong?' Guilt flooded through me. 'I'm sorry I was grumpy—'

Felix's voice was so muffled I could barely understand him, but I eventually worked out that he was saying, 'It's not you—'

'What is it then?'

There were more muffled sobs. I waited until Felix said, 'Frankie doesn't want to come either. He … won't.'

'*Oh!* I'm sorry.' I sighed. I didn't want to tell him I understood Frankie's point of view.

'We're not going to meet any more. I told him yesterday.'

'I didn't realise you were still, uh, meeting.' I was annoyed, though I knew I had no right to be.

'If he's not coming with me—if I keep seeing him, I'll never leave.'

I could hear how much it pained him. I sighed again. 'Well, it's probably for the best. Less risky this way.'

Felix's sobs had slowed. 'Sorry. Sorry I woke you.'

'That's okay.' I kissed his cheek. 'Let's get back to sleep.'

Soon I heard Felix snoring, but I didn't sleep for some time.

Despite Felix's sadness, I began to feel more optimistic. I finished bleeding, and I was looking forward to the next opportunity to do my duty when I became fertile again. There were still many weeks until this partnership ended.

One morning I was allocated mushroom duty, and I made the long trek down to the damp, dirty Lower Levels. I hummed as I descended the metal stairs, even though I had to walk past the sequestration tunnel on my way to the mushroom beds.

The mushroom beds were spread over the tracks in a deep rail tunnel. It was officially called Rowley Street One, but we all called it 'Mushroom Platform'. I greeted Mack, the old Barren in charge. He smelled like rotten rat-meat, underarm sweat, and something indefinable but rank. He was tolerated because he had a rare talent for growing mushrooms, an essential part of our diet. I breathed shallowly through my mouth as I got nearer to him. He scratched at his matted yellow-white hair, and muttered something. No one could ever understand him.

I picked up a battered metal bowl and looked around. It was just Mack, me, and the mushrooms today. People often tried to get out of mushroom duty, probably because of Mack's unpleasant smell and the constant drip, drip of the water. The mushrooms thrived in the damp, growing on scraps of wood and paper and dirt.

I didn't mind being alone. Since I had been sequestered, I had come to look forward to time by myself. I became lost in daydreams as I picked the mushrooms, brushed dirt from them and placed them in my bowl. I imagined the child Felix and I might produce in the next few weeks. I hoped it had dark hair like Felix and light eyes like me, an unusual and attractive combination. *And surely our child would be clever?*

Heavy footsteps broke my reverie. I looked up and saw booted feet striding across the platform. *Councillor Conor.* I froze, and pulled myself into a crouching position. My throat tightened with panic, and I felt dizzy, almost as if I couldn't feel my body.

Conor's lips stretched over his teeth in a parody of a smile. 'Look who we have here!' His tone was without surprise.

My heart stopped. *Did Conor make sure I was the only person here today?* He managed the Barrens, so he had access to the Duty Master's list.

Conor cupped his hands to his mouth. 'Mack! You filthy, stinking shit, get over here!'

Mack shambled over, climbing the ladder up to the platform and scratching his head. He stopped a short way from Conor, his posture servile.

Conor pointed at Mack. 'Get my pen from my office. *Now.*'

I tried to calculate whether I could outrun him. I mouthed *Help!* to Mack, trying to keep my face turned away from Conor. *Help me!*

Mack mumbled at the roof, scratched under his shirt, and loped away. I didn't think he'd even seen me, and if he had, he hadn't understood me. *I'm in trouble.*

As Mack walked away, I inched sideways, hoping to get a head start. Conor pinned me with his gaze.

'Don't even think of running. We've got unfinished business. I was teaching you a lesson last time we met—'

I half-stood. 'I need to go to the toilet.'

I ran, but Conor jumped down onto the tracks, lunged and grabbed my arm.

'No. You *don't.*' His grip hurt, and I tried to twist away. He was too strong. He steered me towards the wall and pinned me there, holding me by my upper arms. I felt his hot breath on my face, and I could see the pores in his reddish skin. I turned my face away, nauseated.

'I'm doing you a favour, Marri. Not every girl attracts the interest of a Councillor. I've got your best interests at heart. You need to learn how to share, and I can help you.'

I squirmed in his grip. 'I know how to share. I'm with Felix now—we're doing our duty. A *lot.*'

Conor laughed so widely that I could see his back teeth. '*Felix*? That's going to be a short partnership, that's all I can say.'

I froze. 'What do you mean?' I had a terrible flash of Felix hanging from a noose, like poor Petra. Then I returned to my senses, and tried to pull away.

'You're wrong—!' My voice rang false and shrill in my ears.

Conor grinned. 'Let's continue our lesson. Why don't I show you what Felix likes to have done to him?'

He pushed my face against the wall, and pressed his body to me. His sweaty hands shifted on my arms. *No, not again, no, no, no—!*

I fought with blind panic, unlike the last time, when I had been so shocked and so weakened by sequestration that I had failed to react. I bit, I scratched, I screamed, I kicked. I got in at least one kick, although my overshoe went spinning into the air. *Yes!*

I managed to run a little way down the track, and to get to the ladder. He pulled me off the ladder, and picked me up bodily. I struggled again, but he pinned me against the wall by the throat. He was so much stronger than me.

I struggled to breathe. Meanwhile, Conor ripped my top, then took hold of the waistband of my trousers. I closed my eyes.

Suddenly, I heard quick footsteps and a loud female voice. 'What's going on here?'

Conor stopped, and I dropped to the dirt-covered ground. I held my ripped shirt over my breasts. Three frayed ties lay on the ground, like worms.

Conor's jaw jutted as he turned to the platform. 'Get out, or I'll kill you, Barren!'

To my astonishment, Ramala stood on the edge of the platform, puffing and coughing, brandishing a large spoon like a weapon. It was a long trek from the kitchen to the Lower Levels. She must have run fast. I hoped she wasn't about to hit Conor; she'd be hanged too.

Before I could say anything, Pam came leaping off the metal stairs and appeared behind Ramala. When she saw me, she gave a cry and leapt down onto the track. She put her arm around me protectively.

Conor's eyes narrowed. A non-Barren witness made his situation more difficult. His face reddened. 'Where's that smelly arsehole gone?'

Ramala cringed as Conor strode towards the platform and climbed up to loom over her. Pam cried out.

From the metal stair tube, a male voice said, 'Down here?'

Someone else muttered an answer which echoed in the tube.

Macon and a young Striker whom I didn't know walked onto the platform. Mack cowered behind them. Macon scanned the scene.

'What's going on?' His eyes widened. 'What *under the Earth* has happened here?'

Conor scowled. 'None of your business, Macon.'

'Have you been threatening women again? I'll report you.'

Conor guffawed. 'Who's going to believe anything *you* say?' An unpleasant smile slid across his face. 'Rilla's told me some things about you, Macon. She says your heart wasn't in it.' He looked over at me and then back at Macon. 'Your sire can't save you every time.'

The young Striker looked at Macon uncertainly. Mack plucked at Macon's sleeve and gestured in my direction.

Before anyone could move, Conor lashed out, smashing the frail old man to the concrete platform. I screamed, and blood dribbled from Mack's head and his mouth. A tooth lay on the ground beside him, red and yellow.

Macon fisted his hands. 'You can't hit a Barren without provocation. Three, no *four*, non-Barren witnesses can testify against you.'

Conor glared around the space. 'You'll be laughing on the other side of your faces soon enough.' Then he spat at me. The warm spittle ran down my wrist.

Macon advanced on Conor. 'I think you'd better get out of here.'

Conor paused. Strictly, the Strikeforces are commanded by the Council, but individual Councillors aren't supposed to be above the law. I could see Conor weighing his options. I flinched when he turned and stamped up the metal stairs.

I collapsed, sobbing uncontrollably. Once I recovered a little, I pulled from Pam's grasp and crawled up the ladder to

Mack, who was now sitting up and poking at the bloody gap where his tooth had been.

'Thank you, thank you,' I cried to the old man. 'I couldn't bear it to happen again. I'm sorry you got hurt because of me—'

My face was coated with tears and snot, and my knees, shins and hands were grimed with dirt and rubbish from the mushroom bed. My torn top had fallen open again. Mack picked up my missing overshoe and dropped it beside me with a mutter. Pam came up and wiped my face and arm with the apron, saying 'shh, shh,' just as we do to the babies.

Ramala joined her, and clasped me to her warm bosom. Mack inspected his dislodged tooth ruefully, holding it between forefinger and thumb. The young Striker stood awkwardly to the side. I couldn't see Macon.

'Girl, we need to get you to bed. You're in shock,' said Ramala. She helped me up, and Pam supported my other arm. Meanwhile Macon returned down the stairs, holding a wet cloth. He handed it to Mack, who pressed it against his swelling jaw and dabbed at his eye.

'Wait,' said Macon. He didn't look at me directly. 'Is ... Marri okay?'

'We're trying to take care of her.' Ramala dragged me off, muttering about the stupidity of men both young and old.

Pam and Ramala took me up several flights of stairs, down the Marsham Branch and into the kitchen. Ramala gave me moss tea while Pam wrapped me in two aprons. Peter, Suze's current partner, stood by the stew, scratching his head. No one explained anything to him. I was glad. I didn't want to talk about it.

Ramala directed Peter to stir various pots and then turned to me again. 'Do you have a partner, Marri?'

'Yes, it's Felix. I think ... he's on duty ... teaching the

ten-year-old boys … today.' *If they haven't come for him already.* I began to sob quietly. Who had seen him and told Conor? Who else knew?

Pam ran off to look for Felix. My teeth started to chatter again. *I'm filthy and selfish. I deserved it. I needed to be taught a lesson.*

I realised I'd spoken aloud when Ramala stopped cutting the mushrooms and stared at me. 'No! No! If anyone deserves to be called that, it's Conor.' She rubbed her arms and shuddered. 'All the Barrens know that he just takes what he wants.'

I stared at her, bile rising in my throat.

Ramala's face twisted. 'You poor sweet pea, it's not your fault. It's *not*. Have some more tea.'

When Pam returned with Felix, my teeth had stopped chattering, but I was still shivering. I sighed with relief as Felix rushed over. '*Marri*! What happened?'

Ramala put her hands on her hips. 'Conor had a go at her. Stopped him just in time.'

Felix gaped. 'What?'

Ramala nodded. 'Not the first time, neither. Get her to bed and wrap her up warm. I'll fetch some medicine from Talla.'

Felix helped me to our cot. Ramala arrived with a cup of steaming liquid. She handed it to Felix, and then kissed my head.

'At the last Month Party, I tried to steal some fruit for you,' I whispered to her, tears welling and clinging to my lower eyelashes. 'I'll do it next time. You were *so* brave—'

She patted my hair back from my forehead. 'I'm not worth getting hung for.' Then she wagged her finger at Felix as she drew the partitioning curtain with her other hand. 'Mind she drinks that medicine! Talla said it would help her sleep.'

'I will,' said Felix. Ramala left, satisfied.

Felix pulled the woollen blanket to my chin, and put the

drink on the ground. Then he lay down beside me, stroked my head and whispered, 'It's okay, it's okay.'

It isn't, no matter how many times you say it. Everything's terrible. I wish I didn't exist.

Finally, he said, 'Conor's done this to you before.'

I nodded.

'When you were sequestered?'

I nodded again, and started to wail. My whole body shook, and I wanted to curl into a ball so tight I'd disappear.

'Shh.' Felix held me tighter until the wailing stopped. 'Does the Chief Councillor know?'

'He caught him in the act. I think Marvin told him what was happening. He's the overseer—'

Felix said nothing.

I continued speaking to fill the terrible silence. 'At least nothing came of it. I suppose it was too soon after I had Tomas. And Conor didn't get to ... finish ...'

Felix blanched. 'How is he still a Councillor? This is *outrageous!*'

I drew in a shuddering breath. 'That's not all. Conor ... he *knows* about you. He made it sound like you don't have much time.'

Felix took a terrible intake of breath and then closed his eyes as if I'd punched him in the gut. 'I need to go back to the old plan.' Then he stroked my hair. 'Marri, I know you don't want me to ask any more, so I won't. But I'm going to escape, and I hope you'll come with me.'

I started to cry again. 'I don't want to escape. I want to *die*! If I could have killed myself in sequestration, I would have. That limping Barren took away everything sharp, so I couldn't.'

Felix's eyes filled with tears. 'Drink that medicine. Sleep will help.'

The medicine was now lukewarm, and so bitter that I

gagged as I tried to swallow it.

Felix patted my head, and kept up a steady stream of conversation. 'Once you're asleep, I'll find Frankie. When I tell him about this, he'll help me get the maps—he might even come with me. I'm going to make it okay.'

I wished that I could go back to when Felix and I were fourteen, before I met Macon. Back then, everything seemed easy. I might have believed that Felix *could* make things better, but now I was wiser—now ...

Before I could complete the thought, I fell asleep.

CHAPTER 6

When I woke the next day, the pain in my throat made it difficult to swallow. I reached out an arm, and touched a warm, empty depression next to me. My breath came quickly. Had Felix been caught? *Don't tell me they've hanged him overnight.*

I closed my eyes and tried to slow my breathing. Executions were usually public affairs, used to teach us a lesson. *He's probably just gone to the toilet.* I was finding it hard to think straight.

My upper arms and throat felt bruised, but in the dim pre-breakfast light I couldn't see the damage. I got up, even though the morning bell hadn't rung.

I slipped on my overshoes and padded down the semi-lit corridor to the partnered female showers. I sighed with pleasure as the warm water ran over me, and put my head back into the generous stream. *So much nicer than the sputtery ones in the non-partnered women's area.*

I was scratched, and I had bruises on my upper arms and neck. A vision of Conor's hand around my neck flashed into my mind, and I closed my eyes and shook my head. I scrubbed, trying to remove all traces of Conor's fingers.

Then I put on my clothes and inspected myself in the dim mirror. I undid the top set of ties on my shirt, and tried to rearrange the neckline to cover the red and purple bruising on my neck, but it didn't work very well.

Someone touched my left shoulder, and I jumped. It was Pia. We hadn't spoken since she'd partnered with Macon. When I turned, she stared at my throat, her eyes wide.

'Oh *Marri!* Macon told me about yesterday. He asked ... I

wanted to check … if you were all right.'

How can I answer that? 'It could have been worse. You're here early?'

She broke eye-contact. 'Yeah.'

'Everything okay?'

She peered from beneath long, black eyelashes, her eyes wet. 'I wasn't sure if you were angry with me—?'

'*No.*' I hugged her. 'I wanted to give you space, and I can't talk to … anyway …'

'Thanks. He said you'd be upset for a day, but then you'd think about it logically.' She pulled away with a bitter laugh. '*Quick-burn temper*, he said.'

My heart fluttered in my chest. 'How are you going? Is he … okay?'

She looked down at the tiled floor, her eyes brimming with tears. 'Fine.'

I tried to squash the concern rising in my breast. It was none of my business. But I was sorry Pia wasn't happy. *She deserves better.*

She looked up again, blinking away her tears. 'We heard *your* partnership was going well. If anyone was going to get Felix out of his shell, it was you. Has anything come of it?'

'Not yet. I just finished bleeding. But I hope … as we all do—'

Pia chewed her lip and nodded. 'Yeah.'

During her only successful pregnancy, she had almost died. I wondered what her real hopes were, but of course I couldn't ask.

The morning bell rang, the lights turned on, and other women entered the bathroom. I couldn't bear the stares at my neck. As I left, Pia ran after me, her feet pattering along the corridor. 'Marri, can … can we have breakfast together?'

I swallowed. 'I'd love that. I've missed you.'

At breakfast, Pia and I reminisced about how we'd misbehaved in Motherhood Studies, a subject we'd both loathed. We laughed until we cried.

But my mood became grim as I finished my breakfast and looked around the meals area. Felix still wasn't there. I tried to hide my disquiet from Pia.

She beamed when I said I was on laundry duty. 'I'm on too!'

As we went arm-in-arm down to the laundry, the Chief Councillor came walking down West Pinford Alley from the other direction. I was surprised; he didn't usually come to the lower levels. We dropped our eyes to the ground.

'Ah, Marri,' he said affably. His green eyes were disturbingly like Macon's. 'I've been looking for you. Pia, would you mind if Marri and I had a *private* chat?'

Pia stared at me, astonishment laced with concern, and my stomach clenched. She melted away down the corridor, and I tried not to panic. *Is he going to tell me he's had Felix hanged? Has he discovered Felix's plans? Did someone tell him I cuddled Tomas the other day?*

The Chief Councillor stood in the pose he used for his weekly lecture, his face grave. 'I've been informed about Conor's behaviour yesterday. The Council has been notified and he has been censured. I will take firm action if he approaches you again.'

The tension left my body as I realised neither Felix nor I were in trouble. Then I processed what he'd said about Conor's punishment. *Censured? Is that all?*

Out loud, I said, 'Thank you, Chief Councillor.' I kept my eyes low.

The Chief Councillor frowned at my throat, his eyes narrowing. 'Do you need a day off from your duties?'

I blinked with surprise. 'Thank you, Chief Councillor! I appreciate it, but, ah, I'd prefer to keep busy—'

As I looked up, I saw a cut on his chin. It looked like he had nicked himself while shaving. *He's human. Just like me.*

He smiled, but his eyes didn't match the smile. 'Your dedication to your duties is admirable—at least in *this* regard.' He steepled his fingers. 'I was pleased to see you've partnered with Felix. I do hope something comes of it. We're keeping an eye on you both.'

He smiled again, but this time without any kindness.

My gut roiled. *Is this a threat? A warning? Both?* I waited to see whether he had anything else to say, but he simply looked at me, as if I was an insect of particular interest, or perhaps a troublesome cog in a machine.

I forced my stiff lips to smile. 'Thank you, Chief Councillor. I'll tell Felix what you said.'

'Good girl, Marri, off you go.'

My first instinct was to run, but I forced myself to walk sedately. I looked back. The Chief Councillor was still watching me, his jaw set.

As I opened the laundry door, a cloud of steam escaped. Pia stood behind the door, chewing at her lower lip again. I patted her arm to let her know that I was all right.

The laundry room had once housed machinery, but we had cleared it out and filled it with metal tubs of hot water. There were two large boilers which supplied the water, with wooden junk and other flammable material burning underneath. The room always smelled of smoke and scavenged soap, mixed with the steamy scent of wet cloth.

I wrung out the wet clothes with Jack, a tall, silent man with dark brown skin, as unusual as my own colouring. His height and strength gave him extra leverage as he twisted the mangle. I fed the wet clothes in and took them out. We must have looked an odd pair, but we were efficient. As we worked,

I thought furiously, sweat running down my face and arms.

I'd never questioned the Chief Councillor's principles before. I thought about what Felix had said last night. *If the Chief Councillor doesn't even sequester Conor … what does that mean?* I gulped and picked up another shirt, feeding it through the twisting mangle. *What does it mean for the new fair and just society he talks about?*

At the end of the shift my hands were wrinkled, red and raw, and my neck and arms ached. Jack and I gave each other a high five and went to lunch together.

As we walked back down West Pinford Alley, Jack looked around. There was no one nearby. He turned to me.

'It wasn't fair,' he said in a low, fast voice. 'I don't see why you got sequestered and Macon didn't.'

I sighed. 'What's done is done.'

'Yeah, but what if things changed?'

I blinked. 'What do you mean?'

'Nothing.' Jack's face closed. He nudged me with his shoulder as a bunch of Strikers came the other way down the corridor, and I took the hint.

At the meals area, I was relieved to see Felix, until I saw that he was talking to Frankie. They stood out like a rat in a food sack because Frankie wouldn't eat until we had finished. *Foolish men. Do they want to be hanged?* I walked up to Felix and put my arm around his waist.

'Hi, Frankie,' I said. An amused glint flickered in Frankie's eyes, but he turned solemn as he saw the bruising on my throat.

'I heard what happened. Ramala asked me to give you a present. I was asking Felix if I could come by later—'

'Tell Ramala I'm okay. See you soon.'

'See you then!' Frankie walked off without a backwards glance.

That evening, Felix and I sat on the edge of the bed. I put my arms around him, with my mouth next to his ear.

'The Chief Councillor bumped into me in the corridor for a private chat. They've reprimanded Conor. But … he knows about you too. It was a warning, I think.' I shook Felix a little. 'I can't believe you were talking to Frankie in the meals area!'

'Rat crap and cockroach dung!' Felix swore. He dug his fingers into my arm and whispered. 'Frankie hasn't been able to get the key to the Commander's room. They've clamped down on access to rooms and Strikers are patrolling more often. But he's found *something*, I think.'

Someone coughed outside, and we froze. Relief filled me when Frankie poked his head through the curtains, and then came in. 'Here, Marri! It fell off a load today—a little bruised, but one side's fine.'

He pulled a hydroponically-grown apricot from his sleeve. It was a beautiful orange, dappled with red. I stroked the soft, downy surface, and picked off the bruise as best I could. My fingernails were soft from the laundry work I'd done earlier.

'Do you want to sit down?' I asked Frankie, my mouth full of juicy apricot. 'Will they let you?'

'Not for long.' He sat next to Felix.

Felix sighed, and I realised that Frankie was silently wiping tears from his cheeks. Felix reached over and took his hand.

Then, to my interest and shock, Frankie caught Felix in a fierce embrace. The passion and tenderness between them was obvious. Felix had never kissed me like that, no matter how much we had practised. Tears welled in my eyes. *No one's going to kiss me like that again …*

Felix pulled away and held Frankie at arm's length. 'Don't.'

Frankie wiped his eyes carefully, and shoved something under the pillows. He stood, and tried to make himself look normal again.

'I'm glad you're doing better, Marri. I'll let Ramala know.' He squared his shoulders and left.

Felix and I sat in silence.

'Sorry you had to see that,' he said eventually.

'Sorry that I saw how much you were loved?'

Felix looked away. 'Not enough. He'd rather stick with the tunnel he knows. He's terrified of the supraterran world: the disease, the radioactive poison, the unexploded bombs, the lack of clean water.'

'You told him what Conor said?'

'That's why he's helping now.'

Later, I found two pieces of paper underneath the pillows. I slipped them into the waistband of my trousers, and went into the toilet to study them in private. The first showed a plan of some tunnels and a set of stairs leading above. The second showed supraterran thoroughfares, as well as station exits. Most exciting of all, it seemed to show another supraterran settlement or town some distance away. I stuffed them back in my waistband, went back to our room and wrote M-A-P-S on the back of Felix's hand with my finger. Felix's eyes glinted with excitement.

We went to our secret hiding place briefly before breakfast the next day. To my horror, a Strikeforce patrol almost caught Felix outside the entrance. I could hear him speaking to them as I crouched in the blue glow of the pool, waiting until he evaded them and joined me.

He studied the maps, his face avid. 'This one shows another settlement! I *knew* it!'

'Does it show the way?'

'I have to follow the Black Line. It's easy! We're already partly on that line. There's an abandoned station with stairs leading up Above. They must come out at this exit on the supraterran map.'

Felix guessed that he had a day of walking underground, followed by one or two days of walking aboveground. 'I can do this, Marri.'

I was still anxious. That evening, I whispered 'Felix, what if you're injured? What if the settlement doesn't exist? Or if it does—what if they send you home? Or kill you?'

Felix tightened his arm around me. 'I've stolen some medical supplies. I can scavenge more. If it's terrible up there, I'll return. I'll be sequestered, but maybe I can pass it off as a prank?'

'They'll *hang* you! You must have noticed that they're watching us!'

'If I'm dead either way, I'd rather be dead up there.'

'I hope this isn't an elaborate way to kill yourself.' I shivered.

The earliest Felix could escape was the afternoon before the next Month Party. Everyone would be getting ready and we hoped it might take them a while to work out he was missing. We'd used this tactic in our childhood tunnel explorations. But that meant we still had nine days before he could leave.

Our tunnels were an ants' nest poked by a stick. The Strikeforces patrolled the corridors constantly, and Councillors rushed from place to place. We could no longer meet in our secret cave.

As I left Parental Duties one afternoon, Rich and Leo emerged from a storeroom, talking softly, their faces grim.

I heard a snatch of Leo's conversation: '... can't see straight any more ... emotional attachment ... you have to agree that a firmer hand ... Jack is on board with us ...'

They jumped when I approached, but relaxed when they saw it was only me. Leo's lips curled and Rich looked away. I watched them leave, and wondered who they'd been talking about. The Strikeforce Commander? Surely not the Chief Councillor?

Felix and I spent every day tense and sick with the thought that he might be arrested. He had recurring headaches, and I felt constantly ill. I had overcome my qualms about stealing. We took enough food to last Felix four or five days. He also planned to shoot, kill, and eat animals with his slingshot; I wished he could steal a crossbow from the Strikeforces, but neither of us knew how to use one. I also stole him some old sheets and pillow-cases from the laundry, and at night I sewed a bag for him to carry on his back. At least I knew how to sew: the one useful thing I'd learned in women's classes. But I hadn't made a bag before, and the first one wasn't great. The second one was much better.

As it happened, Felix wasn't the one we should have been worried about. Two days before the Month Party, Councillor Adam, the man responsible for maintaining the food supply, was arrested and put in sequestration. I remembered that Felix had met his unnamed Councillor on the walkway above the hydroponic gardens. When the arrest was announced at the evening meal, I didn't dare look over at Felix. I ate my meal and tried to talk as if nothing had happened.

When I got back to our room, Felix wasn't there. I sat on the bed and waited for a long time, chewing my lip where I had bitten it earlier in the week, tasting salty blood. My mind immediately leapt to the most terrible conclusion.

But Felix finally returned, and I sighed with relief. I looked more closely at him. It looked as if he had been crying. He slumped next to me.

'I was worried you'd been caught too.'

Felix blushed and looked away. 'No.'

I looked at him sidelong, and saw a love-bite on his neck. 'Oh! Passionate goodbyes?' I grinned. 'I hope you gave him something to remember you by.'

Felix's face went redder, and he put his hand over his neck. 'You're *so* embarrassing, Marri.'

'No, I'm teasing you. I'm *jealous*.'

'If the Council hadn't banned you from going anywhere near Macon, do you think you'd want to ...?'

It was my turn to blush. 'Absolutely *not*.'

Felix slept the sleep of the emotionally exhausted, but I tossed and turned. First, I worried that he hadn't packed everything, and ran through lists in my mind. Then I hoped he'd be able to get away tomorrow. Finally, I wondered if I'd be blamed for his escape. I'd protest innocence, but I wasn't very good at lying. My stomach churned, and I had to go to the toilet several times.

In the bathroom, my hands shook as I rinsed them. I washed my face in the basin.

When I emerged from the women's toilets, Macon was entering the men's toilets next door. Our eyes met as I pushed open the door. We stared at each other, caught off guard.

'Hi,' he said in a low voice. His eyes were hollow and empty.

There were so many things I wanted to say, but I knew I shouldn't speak to him. Not ever.

Instead, I simply said, 'Take care.' My heart burned as I walked away, and tears filled my eyes. I'd lost him already, and now I was about to lose my best friend too.

CHAPTER 7

On the night of the Month Party, Felix and I lingered in Colwell Road tunnel, on the way to the Laundry. I pretended I had a problem with my overshoe.

Suze and Peter turned the corner. They stopped when they saw us.

'How are you both?' Suze asked, touching my shoulder. She looked younger, and her eyes were shining.

'Looking forward to tonight,' I said. 'Just got to fix my shoe.'

Peter glanced at Suze. 'Sure everything's okay, Marri?' *I forgot, he saw me after Conor and the mushrooms.*

'Fine. Thanks, Peter.'

Suze's mouth twisted. 'I hate to say ill of anybody, but—' she looked up and down the corridor, and lowered her voice '—some people get away with *too much*.'

I blinked with surprise. *Does she mean Conor? Macon? The Chief Councillor?*

Suze switched on a smile. 'Let's not talk about miserable things. Let's go and have a great time at the Month Party!'

I smiled back. 'I need to get a new overshoe from the storeroom first.' Then I frowned and put my hand to my head. 'All the way back up again? Why do my shoes *always* have to break on the Lower Level?'

Felix was eyeing me sidelong. I suspected I'd been slightly too melodramatic, but Suze and Peter didn't seem to see anything unusual.

When they walked off, Suze put her arm around Peter's waist and he kissed the top of her head. *An unusual display of affection! She'll be sad when this partnership is over.* I thought back to her kind words after my first partnership had ended. *It will be my turn to comfort her this time ...*

We watched them round the corner. Then Felix scratched his head. 'Do you think she was talking about what happened at the mushroom beds?'

'I don't know. She's more complicated than you'd think.'

We ducked into the passage to our cave, just near the Laundry. We'd stashed spare lanterns, oil lamps and flints, and a large kitchen knife stolen from the rubbish heap. Felix's bag was rolled up and ready. The first bag I'd made—the less successful one—held random stuff that I planned to return to the stores later.

We squeezed back out into Colwell Road tunnel. We were heading for a disused maintenance tunnel at the rear of the laundry, and so he carried his bundle in front of him, like laundry. The lantern and other things were pressed to his chest and hidden by the cloth.

As we walked, someone called, 'What are you doing?'

I swung around and saw Jack poised in a doorway, his head at a questioning angle.

A rictus grin spread across my face. 'Just dropping these dirty clothes at the laundry before we go to the Month Party.'

Jack frowned, one eyebrow raised. 'Ri-i-i-ight.'

I kept my smile going, although my lips were stiff. 'What are *you* doing here? Broadway's the other way.'

Jack's face set, and his eyes darted to the side. 'Took a wrong turn. May your night be fruitful.' He walked off in the other direction, and I sagged with relief.

'I knew we'd need brains as well as beauty on this mission!' Felix struck a pose and fluttered his eyelashes. 'I'm the beauty, of course!'

I laughed and stuck out my tongue. Then I wrinkled my

nose. 'What was Jack up to, I wonder? I hope he's not going to report us.'

'I'd better get going, just in case.'

A rusted iron bar sealed the door at the rear of the laundry, but we managed to lubricate it with stolen lamp oil. We hugged and kissed goodbye.

Felix turned to me. 'Last chance to come with me.'

I shook my head, tears running down my face. 'You know I can't …'

Felix bowed his head. Then he ducked into the passage. 'Wish me luck!'

'With all my heart, Felix.'

I closed the door and sealed it behind him.

After Felix left, I squeezed behind the boiler and sobbed. I planned to wash my face afterwards, and then go to the Month Party. Hopefully in the drunken turmoil, no one would notice Felix wasn't with me.

But I had to stifle my sobs when I heard footsteps, followed by a braying laugh.

'Where are they?' Leo said. 'You wouldn't think it'd be so hard to arrest someone down here—'

I hunkered down as much as I could. My heart began to pound. I was barely breathing, barely in my body at all. As Leo approached the boilers, I could smell whiskey on his breath.

Then Rich spoke. 'The door's still barred! They can't have gotten out that way.' There was a pause and a metallic rattling sound. 'Although it looks like someone's oiled it recently—'

Leo snorted. 'That way's blocked, anyway. Let's check the tunnel behind the mushroom beds—'

Rich grumbled. 'Can't believe we're missing the Month Party for this shit, I'll hang them myself if I find them—'

The men searched the laundry room, but they didn't check

the small narrow space behind the boiler.

Rich sighed. 'Let's try their cubicle *again*—'

I closed my eyes and tried to keep calm, although my blood was pounding in my head. They could only have been looking for Felix and me—Felix for who he was and what he'd done with the Councillor, and me? For helping Felix, embarrassing Conor, everything I'd done with Macon and any number of last straws.

They were after him, and they were after me. I remembered what Felix had said about our tunnel explorations all those years ago. He wouldn't survive without me. We wouldn't survive unless we were together.

Suddenly everything was simple.

I waited until the footsteps faded into the distance, and then dashed to our cave. My first attempt at a bag was still there, along with the spare torch I'd taken and a spare slingshot. I shoved the torch and the slingshot into the bag, put it on my back, and ran back to the laundry boiler room. I passed some Barrens, who called out, but I ignored them and kept running, and they didn't follow. I got to the maintenance tunnel and unlocked the door, then ran as fast as I could.

The soft click of the door behind me was ominous and final, and my breath caught. The tunnel was narrow and unlit, with an earthen damp smell, and rock and rubble littered the floor. Puddles of water penetrated my overshoes and wet the undershoes beneath. *I hope it doesn't flood.* I walked as fast as I could. I could hear someone further running ahead of me. I presumed it was Felix, but I didn't dare call out to him, in case they were following me. I had to keep stopping because I had a stitch.

Eventually I rounded a corner and found Felix standing with his back to a heap of rubble that reached the tunnel roof. He had a rock in his hand and a murderous look in his eye.

He saw me and lowered his hand. 'Marri! What are *you* doing here?'

I bent over, and my breath rasped in my chest. 'They're … after … you! … And … me …!'

'*Who?*'

'Rich … and … Leo …' I coughed and looked at the rockfall behind him. 'You *are* stuck. Leo said the tunnel was blocked.'

Felix smiled. 'That's why the Strikeforces don't guard this exit,' he said, peering at the rubble. 'But there's a gap. I think I can squeeze through.' Then he looked back at me, saw what I was carrying. 'You're coming too?'

'I think … they were going to … sequester me again. Maybe even hang me.' I shuddered. 'But honestly? I can't face another Month Party alone.'

His smile was a wonderful thing. 'Help me move some of this rubble then.'

Before long, my hands were scratched and bleeding from the rubble. I pressed the small of my back and stretched. I'd had a backache ever since I birthed offspring. *Lilah, Cady, Tomas—No, don't think about them.* I bent and shone my torch at the narrow triangular gap under the block. It was not much wider than me, and as high as the distance between my fingertips and my elbow.

Felix squatted to inspect the hole as well. 'We can crawl on our stomachs, there's just enough room. I'll go first, and call you if it's okay.'

We took off our overshoes and put them in our packs, as we were worried that they would come off in the narrow space. Felix wriggled into the gap on his belly, his torch in his teeth. He had tied the rope around himself, and his pack dangled behind him. He crawled forward, the pack scraping after him. I hoped that the rope wouldn't break.

After a long wait, I heard a whistle and a low echoing call:

'It goes through. It's tight, but you can do it.'

I roped my pack firmly around my middle, and then switched off my torch and put it in my pack—I didn't feel safe holding in in my teeth. I lowered myself to the ground and wriggled into the gap on my elbows, moving by feel.

It was soon pitch black, and the pack dragged. Suddenly, I found myself stuck; I'd put on weight after having Tomas, and I was wedged in.

'Felix!' I called. 'I'm stuck! I can't mo-o-o-o-o-ove—!' I put my face onto the damp, rocky ground and whimpered.

Felix called to me. 'You can do it, Marri. You're the bravest person I know. And the most stubborn! You're nearly there!'

I strained and unwedged myself, scraping my hip and knee badly. Felix continued to call encouragement. Just as I thought I was going to scream again, I saw torchlight. I scrabbled towards it, and felt hands grip mine. Felix pulled me through, and I clung to him, panting and half-sobbing. Then we dragged my pack out, careful not to break the rope. The flickering lamplight showed blood on my knee and a large hole in my trousers.

'That was worse than the time with the ventilator shafts,' I remarked. My voice echoed in the dripping corridor and I wished I hadn't spoken so loudly.

Felix rubbed his elbows and nodded agreement. Then he looked at the gap behind us. 'Jack could tell them the direction we were going in when he saw us.'

I sat on a rock. 'How do we stop them?'

Felix pointed upwards. 'If we can shift that stone, the whole lot will fall.' The large block had partly cracked. We put our lanterns and packs some distance away, and then tried to pull it down. My hands bled again, but it didn't move. Felix tied the rope around it and we pulled, our hands burning. Suddenly the smaller part shifted and there was a rumble.

'*Run!*' said Felix. We backed away as quickly as we could. The block fell with a crash, dust and stones flying. I coughed, tears running down my face. Felix also doubled over, coughing.

'Well, we can't go back *that* way!' I spat up more dust and phlegm, and wiped the tears away. 'Lucky we didn't kill ourselves!'

Felix extracted the rope. He picked up the lantern and pointed in the other direction. 'That's the Black Line there. We were in a maintenance tunnel, but this is a main tunnel. It should be easier, no more crouching or crawling.'

I patted my head, and dust came off in clouds, lit by the orange lantern. '... As far as *you* know.'

Felix was right: it was easier, but it still wasn't pleasant. The only sounds were the constant drip of water, and the echoing clip-clop of our feet on the rubble. We had to wade through water as deep as our waists. The only good thing was that, as far as we could work out, no one was following us.

It was easy to track our progress, because each platform had a name, and the names of each platform were prominently displayed on the walls: 'Botanic Gardens', 'Chippingforth', 'Sixsmith Avenue' and 'Pritchard Gate'. They sounded more exotic than the names we were used to, and I was glad we could mark off our progress.

After we had passed the fifth platform, I realised that my overshoes, made from scavenged materials, weren't designed for walking long distances so quickly. Blisters were forming where the black rubber straps went around my heels. The dampness of my undershoes didn't help.

'My feet are sore. I wish I'd stolen some Strikeforce boots.'

Felix had outpaced me again, and stood waiting, his silhouette outlined in the glow of his lantern. 'We have to move faster. I planned to do this underground part in a day.' His shoulders dropped. 'They store those boots in the lockers off the Strikeforce Common room. There's always someone there, patrolling or watching.'

Because we were tired and in a hurry, we took a wrong turn and ended up on 'Horses and Hounds', a platform that wasn't on the map. We kept going but the tunnel seemed to be going in the wrong direction. We dithered in the corridor, trying to work out where we'd gone wrong.

'The problem is, it's a black coloured line too,' muttered Felix.

I sat on the ground and tried to keep my voice steady. 'I'm sore all over—'

Felix helped me up. 'Let's get to the next platform. We'll sleep there and work out where we need to go next. I got a few bandages off Talla—I told her I was restocking the school cupboard.'

The next platform was a jumble of rubble and iron girders. An acrid smell filled the tunnel and made my eyes sting, and squeaking noises filled the air. As Felix held up the lantern, I stifled a scream—the roof was moving!

After a few dark patches flapped away, I realised it was a colony of bats, their eyes glinting orange in the lantern light as they shuffled uneasily.

We searched for somewhere else to sleep, and Felix found a drier room off the tunnel. It had housed rusting machinery of some sort; now all that remained were colourful wires. A rusted yellow triangular sign warned of 'DANGER' and showed a person being hit by a zigzagging arrow.

We ate quickly, and tried to sleep. The cold rose off the floor, and a ridge of concrete dug into my hip. We put our blankets down, lay side by side to keep warm, and turned off the lantern.

Blackness.

Skitter. Skitter. I sat up as something small dropped onto me and crawled over my face. And another. I screamed.

'What is it?' Felix turned on his torch, exposing cockroaches everywhere.

I danced around, brushing myself and shivering. 'No, yuk, *YUK!*' The cockroaches scattered as Felix's torch lit on them.

This calmed me. 'They don't like light! Keep the light on.'

'We can't! We don't know where we'll find more batteries—or oil.'

I lay back down, still shivering. 'I can't sleep. You *have* to leave the light on.'

We argued for a while. Eventually, Felix crawled around, removing all traces of food, squashing any stray cockroaches and flicking them away. Then we turned out the lights. I whimpered, and Felix held my hand.

We fell into an uneasy drowse. When we woke, we had no idea of the time. Time had always been kept by the lights, the changing of the shifts, the ringing of bells, the calling of the weeks and the days, and the rhythm of everyone else's movements. The loss of this structure was both liberating and terrifying.

We chewed on dried rat jerky and drank a little water. When we stood, I realised how sore and tired I was. Walking was agony, but sleep had helped. We studied the map but we weren't sure where we were.

'Which way?' Felix asked me.

I stood quietly, feeling the shifts in the air and the echoes through the tunnels. I really had nothing to go on but an instinct, but Felix was right: my instincts had been good before. 'That way—I think,' I said, and we turned around and headed in a new direction.

My brow crinkled when I heard a sudden rushing rumble, moving closer by the moment. 'Felix, is that—?'

'Flash flood!' shouted Felix. We scrambled away from the

sound until we found a small side niche to shelter in. We held onto the old wires on the wall as tightly as we could as the water rushed past, brown and filthy in the light of our torches, filled with sticks and rubbish. I sighed with relief when it finally slowed and dropped to our ankles. We began again.

A glistening rectangular structure loomed out of the darkness, and I had to stifle a scream. It was just an empty transport vehicle from before the Catastrophe. We levered opened the door to one of the carriages and peered inside. Mud, plastic refuse and sticks covered the floor. The vehicle was filled with chairs wrapped in coloured fabric—tomato red, lettuce green, and a blue colour I'd never seen before—but there were no bodies. I studied the posters on the walls. Who was Wi-Fi and why did they need to be freed? We left the vehicle and started walking again.

Eventually, to my immense relief, we reached the abandoned platform on the map. The wall was not finished with bricks or tiles like the others. A number of signs proclaimed 'Authorised Access Only', and black and yellow striped tape was still tied across several entranceways.

After some searching, we found a door with a green sign on it reading 'EMERGENCY EXIT ONLY'.

'Good thing this is an emergency,' said Felix.

We pushed open the door and shone my torch around. Dusty, mud-caked stairs spiralled upwards into blackness.

'Let's try this one,' Felix said. 'At least it goes *up*.'

After a few turns of the staircase, my thighs burned with pain and my hair was slick with sweat. 'Felix ... stop ... need ... to rest!'

Felix stood on the step above me while I got my breath back. To my amazement my torchlight picked out a message, written in bright yellow letters on the wall: *'You've still got a way to go.*'

I showed it to Felix and he laughed. 'We're not the first ones to come up here.'

After six more rounds of stairs, I was worried. 'Maybe we should go back down.'

'It must come out,' said Felix. 'It said it was an exit.'

We passed another message on the wall in the same writing as before: '*Almost there!*'

'I hope they knew what they were talking about.' I shone my torch down the stairs, and regretted it. I had a terrible sense of vertigo as I saw the looping downward spiral of the stairs, and the hole in the middle which went all the way to the bottom.

The top of the stairs reached a small walkway. The door had another note in the same promising yellow writing: '*You made it!*' I didn't have the breath to cheer, but we pulled at the door. Then we pushed. It didn't move, or even rattle. It felt as if several tonnes of rubble were blocking it.

Felix showed the map to me: 'It says, "Exit here!" I wasn't making it up!'

I began to cry. 'We're stuck. Again!'

Felix chewed his nails. 'We have to keep trying. There must be another way.'

Dejectedly, we headed all the way back down the stairs, our legs cramping. It was almost as hard as it had been coming up. We trudged through the abandoned station again. We passed a series of metal doors with metal circles beside them, arrows pointing up. But nothing happened when we pushed at the arrows. Felix found a door which said, 'Heath Station Plaza—No Exit to Ground.' We took it anyway. The staircase within had only four turns, but ended in another door which led onto a wide thoroughfare.

The thoroughfare was reasonably intact, although wires and panels from the ceiling had fallen on the floor. Like some of the areas at home, it was lined with decrepit rooms and structures.

We cleared an area next to a half-collapsed structure. I shone my torch over it and saw the words 'Donut Fiend' written on it in red letters. *What does that mean?* A grinning red O-shaped creature with pointed red ears, a tail, and a fork in his hand stood next to the words. I hoped it didn't live in the structure, though it looked cheerful enough, for a fiend.

I switched off my torch and lay down, the muscles in my legs still twitching. I removed my shoes, and Felix peered at the maps with his torch while he ate a dried mushroom. Suddenly I heard something. I sat up.

'Who's that?' I whispered. I thought I saw a glint of light— or two?—in the distance, coming closer. I rubbed my eyes. Then I heard a scuttling sound, and grabbed my slingshot. Something large was running towards us. *Not the Donut Fiend?* Felix shone his torch, and I screamed.

The rat was the size of a large cat, scarred and misshapen, the living incarnation of my childhood nightmares. It was hard to say who was more startled by my scream—Felix or the Monster Rat. The Monster Rat flinched, but kept coming towards us. I couldn't think, didn't even use my slingshot. I pelted away down the causeway, my heart beating and my palms covered with sweat. Felix followed me, calling 'Stop!' The rubble and debris hurt my bare feet, but I didn't notice. I was lucky I didn't cut my feet to shreds.

Felix's sweeping torch showed little open-sided rooms filled with collapsed shelving. One had belonged to 'Fast Mart', like the three in our complex at home. He'd clearly travelled far.

The stuff on the shelves had rotted or been scavenged long ago. I ran into Fast Mart's room and crouched behind a ruined shelf, trembling. Felix pulled a metal strut from the shelf and brandished it like a spear. We waited.

Then we heard the other sound—human footsteps and voices. Felix crouched behind the shelf with me, and switched off his torch. My breathing was horribly loud, and my heart thudded in my ears. Cautious footsteps echoed through the thoroughfare. The other people had torches too—the beams caught sparkling dust motes as they lanced across the thoroughfare. At least they had scared the Monster Rat away.

A male voice spoke, only faintly audible. 'I *knew* they'd try those stairs. Here's their stuff. Check the abandoned shops.'

A second voice said, 'Yes, Sir.'

I bit back a gasp. *We pulled that tunnel down. How did they know?* I gripped Felix's arm. *We're rats in a trap!*

Someone entered the small room and torchlight wavered down each aisle. We stayed as still as possible. I cowered as the torch shone onto me, and covered my eyes with my hands.

'I found 'em!' called the younger man, his voice squeaking and echoing.

Running footsteps approached and another torch shone on us. Just as I had feared, the two silhouetted figures held Strike-force crossbows, and wore helmets with torches on them.

The taller man pointed his crossbow at us. 'Felix and Marri, come out with your hands up. We're taking you in.'

His voice was a crossbow bolt to my stomach.

'Macon,' muttered Felix into my ear. '*Of course.*'

I stood up and spread my arms. A surge of panic and anger went through my body. 'I'd rather *die* than be sequestered again! Shoot me and be done with it, Macon!'

The boy beside Macon raised his crossbow in a jerky, nervous motion, and fiddled with the safety catch. I couldn't remember his name. *Something starting with V.* He'd only recently graduated from the children's rooms.

Macon shook his head. 'Don't be stupid, Marri. You're coming home.'

'How dare you call me—?'

Felix grabbed my wrist and squeezed it. 'Leave it.' Then he turned to Macon. 'But she's right. We're not going home.'

Both men stared at Felix, and Macon scowled. 'For the Earth's sake! Felix, I thought *you* had more sense. That's enough from both of you!'

He moved towards me with his hand outstretched. I swung my fist, and Macon dodged and levelled the crossbow. I readied my slingshot and narrowed my eyes. *Why did* you *have to find me?*

Macon's face was hard and pitiless. 'I'd rather not shoot you, Marri, but I will if I have to.'

After a tense pause, Felix nodded at me, and I tucked my slingshot back into my pocket while he put the metal strut into his pack. Then we put our hands up.

Macon gestured to the younger man. 'Vin, take them to their gear. You patrol the area and I'll interrogate them.'

They made us put our hands behind our heads and escorted us out. We sat down with our gear while they stood over us.

'I'm hungry,' Vin announced.

Macon sat opposite us and closed his eyes for a few heartbeats, massaging his temples. 'All you think about is your stomach.'

Vin pouted. 'So?'

Macon snapped at him. 'I've told you not to answer back! Patrol the perimeter *twice*, and then do twenty push-ups!'

'Sir, yes, sir!' Vin started to walk away, and then turned back. 'All right if I, um, relieve myself while I'm patrolling?'

'Just do it where we can't see you.'

Vin trotted off. Macon removed his helmet and put it on the ground, the torch still providing light. 'You'll both be sequestered or ostracised, but that's better than being shot or hanged. If you can convince them that it was just one of your stupid pranks—'

I blinked. 'Do they know we've gone?'

Macon stared into the darkness, his jaw set. 'They've been watching you for weeks, suspecting that you'd try to escape—' He glanced at me, and then looked away. 'I won't *accidentally* shoot you for resisting capture, but Leo would have shot you in a flash.'

Felix's eyebrows quirked up. 'You've had your eye on us too.'

Macon turned to Felix. 'I saw the door in the laundry had been oiled—only you two would be crazy enough to squeeze through that gap. You know some Barrens died that way? We had to pull their bodies out after the rock fall—'

I shuddered.

'Vin and I have been waiting here for three hours.' Macon rubbed his hand over his chin. 'You tried the stairs, didn't you? The exit has collapsed. I knew you'd have to come here.'

I crossed my arms. 'We're not going back with you.'

'We can't let anyone else leave,' Macon said. 'There are too many stories already, people get ideas. Our society is at risk. We have to bring you home—or bring back a body to show them.'

'You may as well kill us.'

'Well. If you're not going to give me a choice.' Macon lifted his crossbow and pointed it at my head. He squinted his eyes, and took a deep breath.

My heart stopped.

'No!' Felix shouted, and threw himself in front of me.

CHAPTER 8

Felix knelt in front of me, his arms out and his chin up, shielding me. His whole body was trembling. I could see the tendons in his neck straining and could only imagine his eyes staring at Macon, daring him. 'Don't hurt her!'

I grabbed Felix from behind, held him close and braced myself. He'd have to shoot both of us.

Macon's hands shook. He jerked the crossbow, and a bolt zipped to the side, skidding across the floor into rubble.

The crossbow fell from his hands. I only just heard his whisper. '*I can't.*'

I let go of Felix, and he sank to the ground.

We sat in silence for a time. Then Macon spoke. 'You would have let me shoot you, Felix.'

Felix's answering look was venomous. 'And you would have shot Marri. Not that I'm surprised—!'

I had forgotten how much the two men disliked each other. I put my hand on Felix's knee. *Don't make Macon lose his temper. He could knock us out and carry us home. There's only two of them, but they're Strikers ...*

Macon's eyes dropped to my hand on Felix's knee. Then he stretched, his eyes following Vin's bobbing torch beam. 'Please come back with me. It's the only solution—for all of us.'

I crossed my arms. 'Send Vin home, and help us escape. You owe me that much—for Tomas. You said you'd help me but I was *sequestered*. Not again.' My voice shook with rage, unleashed and deepened by fear. I was now shivering all over.

Macon flinched. I could see that I'd wounded him. *At*

last. 'It's my *duty* to bring you back,' he said. 'I'm ... so ...' He couldn't meet my eyes. 'What reason would I have to send Vin home?'

I stared at him and shrugged. 'You're *supposed* to be so clever—'

Felix stopped chewing on his fingernail. 'We're on a secret mission for the Chief Councillor and you're helping us. Vin has to go back to tell him the mission is on track.'

I laughed. 'That's ridiculous.'

Felix turned to me. 'That's why it'll work. We were chosen because no one would suspect us.' He turned to Macon. 'He can't tell anyone else on the Council. Because of the factions.'

Macon gave Felix a look of surprise and—perhaps—respect. He stood up. 'Well, Vin's not the brightest light globe. He's only been a Striker for a month, that's why I chose him for this search.' He looked down, still holding the crossbow. 'Get up, both of you.'

I glanced at Felix as we stood. *What now?* Felix narrowed his eyes with suspicion.

Vin trotted back. He had evidently relieved himself and patrolled the area twice.

Macon was stern. 'Did you do the push-ups, Vin?'

Vin was crestfallen. 'Shit ... I mean, shit, Sir.' He dropped to the ground.

Macon waved his hand. 'Get up! Felix and Marri are on a mission for the Chief Councillor. I've seen their authorisation. I need to help them.'

I only *just* managed to stop my jaw from dropping. I had to bite my cheek. Felix's face was carefully expressionless.

Vin scratched his head. 'Are you sure, sir?'

'I think I know the Chief Councillor's signature.'

Vin nodded. 'What do they have to do?'

'That's classified, but I can tell you it's to do with the future of our society. Tell the Commander I'll be back in a day. *Do not tell anyone else*—if you have to say anything, just say you lost me and came home. This is your first secret mission.'

Vin's eyes grew wide, and he looked at Felix and me with awe. I bit the inside of my cheeks again to stop myself from laughing hysterically. Felix stomped on my toe, *hard*.

Vin saluted Macon. 'Sir, yes, sir. Return to the Commander! Top secret mission! You can trust me!' His face fell. 'I'm *really* hungry. Can I eat before I go?'

'Good idea.' Macon turned to us, his face opaque. 'Are you hungry?'

'Yes,' I admitted, still shocked that Felix's plan had worked—and that Macon had agreed to it.

As Vin set up a small fire, Macon criticised his technique and I listened carefully, trying to remember his instructions for later. The smoke shifted in my direction, and I waved it away from my face.

'I've got dried rat meat if you want some?' Felix offered.

We shared our food. Even though I was unsure whether Macon was on our side, and even if Vin would have shot us, it was unthinkable not to share.

'Mmm, Strikeforce biscuits are *nice*,' I said. 'Why can't the rest of us have them?'

Vin's mouth was stuffed with biscuits. 'Yep, they're goob. I luff 'em.'

Macon grimaced. 'Too many, Vin. You'll choke—'

I bit my tongue. I had just been about to say the same thing.

'He's a growing boy,' said Felix.

I patted Felix's shoulder. 'You ate three bowls of stew at that age, back when there was enough for more than one helping.'

Vin watched us, his eyes bright. 'So, are you two, like—*partners*?'

'Yes,' Macon and I said, but Felix said, 'No.' Then he clapped his hand over his mouth.

Macon said, 'Huh?'

I pinched Felix's arm, and he amended his answer. 'Yes. Sorry. I forgot. We registered this month.'

Vin laughed nervously. 'Is that normal? To forget who your partner is?' His cheeks turned pink. 'No one's accepted my offer yet.'

'No,' said Macon, his arms crossed. 'It's not normal. But at the same time, it's typical. I don't know why my sire picked *you two* for the mission?'

Felix smiled beatifically. 'I *told you*, Macon! No one would suspect us of a mission this complex and difficult. It's genius!'

I bit into my biscuit forcefully. '*You* shouldn't criticise anyone's partnerships, registered or not, Macon—' Then I stopped, pinned by Felix's warning glare.

No one spoke for the rest of the meal. My appetite was gone, but I knew I should eat when I could.

Suddenly, Vin leapt up, crossbow in hand. 'I heard something!'

Macon sprang up in turn. 'Rich and Leo? They came this way too—'

I crouched, ready to grab our bags and run. *Please, not them.* Felix was shoving food into our packs. We hadn't unpacked much. I wondered if I could snatch Macon's pack when we ran. My gear was seriously deficient.

Two red glowing points glinted in the gloom, reflecting the firelight like small lanterns. I almost laughed with relief.

I joined the two Strikeforce men. 'Watch—!' I whispered.

I took some rat jerky from my pocket and threw it. Macon and Vin jumped as it hit the ground, and Vin fired a bolt into the dark.

'Don't shoot,' I whispered.

The red lights approached—nearer, nearer.

Our old friend, the Monster Rat, crept into the circle of light. It looked around, its whiskers and nose twitching. In a horrible act of cannibalism, it scuttled up and ate its preserved comrade. *Yuk.*

'The *size* of it!' breathed Vin. 'Think how much jerky we could make!' He reloaded, and made to shoot again.

I grabbed Vin's arm. 'Don't! ... Let it go. We've got enough food.'

'No one thinks about what *I* need,' grumbled Vin, but he lowered his crossbow. The Monster Rat vanished into the darkness.

'It wouldn't have hurt us, would it?' asked Felix, behind me.

Macon turned to Felix. 'Older Strikers say there used to be huge packs of rats in the tunnels. They had to fight them off when they were desperate for food or trapped in a dead end.'

After that observation, we packed our bags quickly. Macon stamped out the fire, and the two Strikeforce men picked up their helmets. Macon stared at the helmet for a moment, thinking.

Then Macon looked up at Felix and me. 'Vin—remember what I said about the secret mission—?' My heart beat faster, and Felix seemed poised to run.

'Yeah?' said Vin.

'Yes, *Sir*,' sighed Macon. I held my breath. He shook his head infinitesimally. 'Never mind. I'll explain when I get back. Oh ... before you go, can I borrow one of your spare masks?'

Vin fumbled in his pack and pulled out a yellow mask. 'Here, Sir!'

'Do you know your way back?'

Vin saluted. 'Yes, Sir!'

'Tell the other men you lost me in the tunnels. Remember, do *not* tell anyone other than the Commander that we found

Marri and Felix.'

Vin saluted again, even more smartly. 'Yes, *Sir*!'

'Excellent work, Strikeforce man.'

Poor Vin puffed out his chest. He picked up his pack and loped down the thoroughfare towards home, his torch flickering through the gloom. Macon's face was rueful as he tried to shove the mask in his pack.

'Don't back out now!' I pleaded. 'You have to help us—'

Macon frowned. 'I know things have been bad, but they'll get better—'

'How do you know? You have *no* idea, none at all! I have no control over anything that happens to me.'

Macon's eyes moved as if to judge the distance between us. I backed off so that he couldn't grab me. Felix picked up his pack, and pulled his slingshot out of his pocket.

As Macon neared, I bared my teeth and hissed at him. 'Don't touch me! I'll bite you!'

He clenched his jaw, and then breathed deeply. 'Marri. The rules are harsh. But my sire—I mean, the Chief Councillor, told me that the Council is considering relaxing the rules, gradually. The Council has our best interests at heart.'

He sounds like Conor. I picked up my pack. 'Does *Councillor Conor* have my best interests at heart, Macon? We're going! You can help us, or you can go home to your sire.'

I shouldered my pack and marched into darkness, my torch on. Its light was dimming. Felix followed.

After a short distance, I turned. Macon held his pack in one hand and his crossbow in the other. He appeared to be considering whether to shoot me or to follow. I squared my shoulders and kept walking, despite the prickling between my shoulder blades.

Eventually, with a sour look on his face, Macon jogged up. 'You're going the wrong way, Marri.'

He shouldered past me, and walked in a different direction.

I stopped. 'How do I know you're not leading us back home?'

He smiled. 'You know this isn't the way home.'

I stopped and looked around. I could almost hear the Monster Rat scuttling far in the distance, Vin stumbling back through the tunnels. There was the faintest movement of air in the direction Macon was heading, and a smell I'd never known before.

Felix was looking after Macon with distaste. 'Arrogant arse-hole of a rat! I never understood why you accepted his offer in the first place. You know it was all because of a bet with Rich and Leo? They were sure you'd reject him.'

I blinked, stung. 'No—!' *Although that does explain why all those Strikers turned up with bottles of alcohol the day after we began our partnership! I thought it was some kind of Strikeforce tradition ...*

Felix sidled closer and whispered. 'We could wait until he's asleep, and steal his gear? His shoes? He must take them off to sleep ...'

'*If* he double-crosses us, sure. He can't stay awake the whole time. There's two of us and one of him.'

Macon stalked back. 'Can you two *hurry up*?' As I tried to walk faster on my lacerated feet, I glowered at Macon's back. *Yes, I'll take his shoes.*

The route wound down metal stairs, onto and across the platforms and then up other sets of stairs. Macon stopped to update his map when we encountered a rockfall. Felix eyed the map with a covetous gleam in his eye.

I was worried. 'What's going to happen to Vin? Isn't it going to cause huge trouble when he tells the Commander?'

Macon shrugged. 'It'll buy you more time while they're

sorting it out. I'll take the fall for it when I get back.'

'But you might be sequestered—'

Macon shrugged again, and moved away.

Further down the platform, skeletons sprawled in postures suggesting an agonised death. I choked with horror: we cremate our dead and put the remains in urns.

'*Don't* go near the bodies,' said Macon. 'We don't know how these people died—'

Felix grabbed Macon's sleeve. 'Do you hear something?' Macon cocked his head. Then he gestured for us both to kneel behind a broken screen. Felix turned off his torch. Mine was already off. Macon put his finger to his lips, took off his helmet and turned off its torch. The sudden blackness made me wonder if I had been struck blind. My hands shook, and I clamped them between my knees. Our breathing sounded unbearably loud.

A faint glow appeared in a doorway. I doubt I would have noticed it had we not been in darkness for so long. Men spoke in the distance. One of them brayed with laughter. *Leo.* Eventually the voices and their light retreated. We sat silent in the darkness.

When Macon eventually switched his helmet-lamp back on, my eyes watered and stung, and I had to scrunch them closed. Felix said, 'Thanks, Macon.'

Macon stood. 'If anyone brings you home, it's going to be *me.*' I wondered again if he were really helping us or whether he was leading us back to face our fates.

A few hours later, we stopped for our evening meal. It was indescribably blissful to stop walking.

After we had eaten in stolid silence, Macon said, 'I'll watch; you sleep.' He sat at the fire he had laid earlier, his back to us.

I was desperate to sleep, but my legs twitched and cramped,

and the pain from the blisters made it impossible. When Felix began to snore in my ear, I gave up and looked through Felix's pack for his bandages.

I glanced at the flickering fire as I scrabbled through the pack. A pot of liquid stood on the fire, sending steam wafting up into the circle of ruddy light.

I jumped when Macon spoke in a low voice, without turning around. 'Want some tea?'

I was tempted to ignore him ... but I *did* want tea. 'Okay.'

I sat opposite Macon, and threw my wrecked undershoes onto the fire. *Flash!* They went up in an orange flare. Then I bandaged my feet. When I had finished, Macon handed me a tin cup identical to the one he held.

We sipped, watching one another over the rims of our cups without speaking.

Suddenly Macon stood. 'Look at your feet! This is suicide, Marri.' He held out his free hand. 'Come back with me. I'll do what I can to help.'

I snarled at him. 'You said that before, and look how it turned out—!'

'Don't kill yourself just to punish me. Come home.'

'No. Felix found a map showing another settlement. We're making for it.'

He shook his head slowly. 'Come home, love.'

'Don't call me that *ever* again!' I swallowed and closed my eyes. 'I'd rather die than go anywhere near them—the Council, Conor, all of them!'

He looked at me closely. 'What was he doing—when we found you in the gardens?'

I opened my eyes. 'He was *trying* to do what he did before. When I was sequestered.'

Macon drew a sharp breath. 'What did he do?' I turned my cup in my hands, staring into it. I couldn't look at him.

A metallic crumpling noise made me flinch and look up. Macon had crushed his cup in his fist, and the tea had spilled over his hand.

He stared at the cup as if he wasn't sure what it was, and dropped it with a clatter.

'I'll kill him.' His voice was disturbingly matter-of-fact. His knife made a metallic rasping whisper as he drew it from his belt. It was one of those large scavenged hunting blades that the Strikeforces carry.

I stood and put out my hand. 'They'll execute you!'

'Worth it.'

'No, no, *no*. I wish I hadn't told you! Please don't. It's not helping. *Please—*'

He sheathed the knife, but his expression made me step back.

'Who knows about this?'

'Felix, obviously. Um, the Council—'

'*The Council?* Does Fa—the Chief Councillor know?'

I stared at the small fire, watching the flames writhe.

Macon stepped towards me. 'Marri, *does he know*?'

I drew back further. 'Yes. He—'

Macon strode to the fire and kicked the tea pot, and I jumped. It spiralled to the other side of the tunnel, and the boiling water hissed as the pot clanked across the floor. Felix snorted and rolled over, but didn't wake. *He can sleep through anything.*

I fetched the pot, and placed it next to the fire. It still had a little tea in it. Macon sat and tried to straighten out the crushed cup. I sat down on the other side of the fire.

Eventually, he put the mangled cup down. 'He should have been executed.'

'I think your sire thought I deserved it ... because I got you into all that trouble ... I'm a bad influence ...' I looked down at my hands. 'He was right—'

Macon choked. 'No!' He clenched his fists. 'I'm so sorry, Marri—'

I grimaced. 'Didn't you wonder why I've been avoiding you—why I can't forgive you?'

To my surprise, he recoiled, as if I'd fired the slingshot at him. *Felix is right, he is too self-satisfied.*

We sat in silence again for a time, but I began to feel bad.

'Conor's not your fault—he's responsible for what he did. And I freely accepted your offer. But—you have to take responsibility for what *you've* done. And what you didn't do.'

He still looked lost, and I didn't know how to explain it any better to him. I didn't have the words for what I wanted. Even if I did, would he have understood them?

His face was carved in grim lines as he stood and made a few circuits of the fire. Then he rummaged in his bag, pulled out a folded piece of paper and sat next to me.

He dropped the paper into my lap. 'Felix will be able to read this. The dangerous areas are red. Don't go there. The yellow zones are less radioactive, and the green zones are better still—'

I unfolded it and inspected the map in the flickering firelight, holding it close to my eyes. It was the one he'd been carrying earlier, painstakingly hand-drawn and coloured by different men. There was an underground map on one side and an aboveground map on the other. I decided not to tell him that I could read a lot of it myself. To my relief, a place called 'Farm Settlement' was marked on it, outside the green zone.

I refolded the map. 'Won't you get in trouble?'

'If you follow my directions and the map, you might make it.' He looked away.

'What's going to happen to *you*?'

'I'll deal with Conor. That will distract them.'

I grabbed his arm and shook it. 'Please, *please*—don't do anything stupid.'

'I have to do something, Marri. I'll talk to my sire—'

The flames shifted blurrily before my eyes: orange, yellow, pale blue. *I'm so tired of everything. Sometimes I wish I didn't exist anymore.* 'I just want Conor to fall into a pit and disappear—'

'I'll call for Conor to be executed.' He looked at me sidelong. 'If he's gone, will you come back—?'

'It's hard to explain. Felix—' I bit my lip.

Macon looked away and frowned. 'What if the supraterran settlement doesn't accept you? What if they try to kill you?'

I twisted my fingers together. 'Then we'll feel right at home, I guess—! But if you know anything that can help us ...'

'Nobody knows much about the settlement, even the Strikeforces. But ... my sire told me ... that we trade with them. He's made deals with them.'

'What kind of deals?'

'They give us blankets and wood, and at least half of our meat and vegetables. We give them scavenged technology and medicine. And mushrooms, of course.'

I chuckled. 'Mushrooms! Lucky them.'

One side of his mouth quirked up. 'Sometimes I think we get the better side of the deal.'

'Sounds like you know some ... useful things ... about the settlement.'

Tiny fires reflected in his eyes, as well as my own dark silhouette, twice over. He was so close we were almost touching. I could have kissed him. I was suddenly reminded of when we'd met, when I was fourteen. He'd asked me to dance, but we'd ended up sitting on uncomfortable plastic chairs instead. *Did he* really *ask me because of a bet?*

I'd told him to leave me alone. I had wanted to hold off

birthing babies for as long as I could. I had been worried that I'd lose the little freedom I had. And then ... he'd said that he understood why I didn't want a partnership; and that I was free to go. My breath caught. *I wish I'd walked away then, like I meant to. Why did I kiss him instead?*

I drew away, folding my arms. 'Come with us. Help us.'

After a long pause, he folded his arms too. 'Fine. You win. You should sleep. You've got shadows under your eyes; I can see that even in this light. Felix can take the next watch.'

CHAPTER 9

The next morning, after we had eaten breakfast, Macon began to pull gear out of his pack.

'We need to get changed. It's a yellow zone. Not the most dangerous, but not the safest either.' He frowned. 'Neither of you have proper gear.'

He drew two yellow plastic masks with white filters from his pack, and handed one to me. 'This one's my spare, Marri—you wear it. Felix, have Vin's spare. And you'll have to take some of my medication.'

Felix's brow creased. 'What is it?'

'It stops us getting sick—' He held out some little tablets. I refused to swallow mine until I'd seen him swallow his.

Then he put on more complex gear—first a strange belt with a box hanging off it, and then a cover-all yellow suit. I laughed when he stepped into the belt, adjusted it low around his waist and then adjusted the box over his groin.

Felix's eyes bulged. 'What is *that* for?'

Macon glowered. 'Lined with thin sheets of lead. Supposed to stop us Strikers from becoming infertile ...'

Felix glanced at me, and waggled his eyebrows at Macon. 'Seems to be working so far!'

Macon turned bright red and turned away. 'Guess so.'

Felix chewed his nails. 'Should I wear one?'

'You won't be exposed for too long. And I don't have a spare.'

Macon zipped up his yellow suit, and put on his mask. While he was busy dressing, I stuck my tongue out at Felix, and Felix winked.

I put on my mask. My breathing sounded loud in my ears, and it was difficult to see through the transparent plastic eye-holes.

We set out towards the surface. The yellow zone didn't seem too different from the place we'd come from: more tunnels and platforms, small stations. I noticed we were slowly heading upwards, but we hadn't gone far when Macon had to stop to look at the map again.

I shifted my weight to relieve the pressure on each foot. Then I looked down and screamed. 'Argh! Look at that—!'

A grotesque creature lay on the ground: it looked like a rat, but it had two heads with long yellow teeth.

Macon shrugged. 'You get that, close to the surface—strange plants and animals. They seem to grow wrong. Just don't touch it.'

I turned away, but my eyes stung and watered as the light streaming down the nearby stairs hit them. I turned away.

'Why's the light so bright?' I asked Macon.

'It's sunlight. The sun's a giant blazing ball of gas. You'll see it in the sky during the day. Don't look at it directly, okay? Sunlight powers our solar generators.'

'What happens to it during the night?'

'The earth turns away from the sun and it gets dark.'

'Oh, so the lights go off, just like at home!'

Macon's eyes met mine and I could tell he was smiling under the mask. 'We turn the lights off at home because we're copying what happens above.' Then he broke eye contact and walked ahead.

His eyes had looked ... almost *fond*, for an instant. *Did I imagine that?* I adjusted my bandages to give myself time to think. They had bunched uncomfortably under the arches of my feet.

Felix came up behind me and muttered, 'He's trying to get you to go back with him, you realise. That's why he's being charming all of a sudden.'

'He's helping us, Felix. I wasn't sure either, but he convinced me—last night.'

Felix stared at me through his mask. 'You *didn't*, did you—?'

'It's none of your business, but no, of course not—!'

'I'm your registered partner!'

Macon turned and came back. 'What's wrong?'

Felix and I looked at each other. 'My feet are sore,' I said eventually.

'You should borrow my boots.'

The boots were far too large, so I removed the bandages and stuffed them in the front. I tried to walk. *Clump, clump, clump, clump.* The stiff leather dug into my ankles, hurting them.

Macon was disappointed. 'You can barely walk.' He turned to Felix. 'Want to try them?'

Felix put his feet next to mine. His feet were like his hands: slender and fine. 'I'd have the same problem.'

I replaced the bloodstained, frayed bandages and stepped into my overshoes.

Macon pointed to what had once been a stairway, but was now a heap of twisted metal and rubble. 'We've got to go up there.'

The stairs were choked with skeletal remains, coiled over one another. A horrible vision of people rushing to reach cover flashed through my mind. The sunlight picked out the vacant eye sockets, the grasping hands.

I quailed. 'I don't want to go near them!'

Macon sighed. 'Look, their bones are blackened. Any trace of disease was burnt away.'

I put my hand to my mouth. 'Why hasn't anyone cleared the exit?'

'I haven't been this way for years. This isn't the best route.'

'We could only work with what we had.'

'What *did* you have? Where did you get your information?'

Felix glared, and I could tell he was trying not to think about Frankie. 'As if we'd tell *you*.' His glare softened. 'At least they won't expect us to go this way.'

We stepped over the skeletons and emerged into sunlight.

We had made it to the surface.

I couldn't see. I held my hands to my mask and squinted eyes as tears ran down my face. The plastic eyeholes fogged up. *So bright. Is this normal?*

I groped my way to Felix, and grabbed his arm. I gasped as I became aware of the world around me. *Colours. Sounds.* A wave of dizziness passed over me.

Structures loomed on either side of us, green trees growing through them. We sat down in the doorway of a gorgeous stone building, with a collapsed burgundy-coloured building nearby. I tipped my head up. Above the structures was a strip of pale blue.

'What's that *blue* up there? It's amazing!'

Macon smiled. He'd removed his helmet, and his hair was sticking up crazily. 'That's the sky. Remember, don't look at the sun.'

The black surface we were sitting on was cracked, but I suspected it had once been smooth. The buildings stood in a circle around a central area, and thoroughfares branched off in all directions.

The roads were crammed with abandoned vehicles of a kind I'd never seen before. The most extraordinary were the tall two-storey vehicles that stood leaning and abandoned, skeletons sprawling from their windows. I gaped. 'They're so tall!'

Macon frowned. 'Lots of bodies, but not much of use, apart from the batteries. We scavenged them last time.'

I inspected the circle of surrounding buildings. The lowest floors had large glass windows, most of them smashed. A body lay in one of the windows, in remarkable condition, but dressed in ragged clothes.

I pointed. 'A dead person!' Then I saw more bodies and put my hand up to my mask.

Macon put his hand up. 'A real body would have decayed long ago. They used to put full-sized plastic or wooden models of people in these windows.'

'Why?'

Macon shrugged. 'No idea.'

We started moving through the ruined landscape. The buildings loomed, and the colours and smells were overwhelming. Some distant buildings looked burned or smashed. Others sagged as if they had been hit with a huge hammer. Some were slowly melting into the ground, with trees, plants and flowers growing on top of them, or inside them. Other buildings were almost fully intact, and beautiful in a faded way. Quite a few buildings had life-sized model people in the shattered windows. Others displayed objects whose use or purpose I couldn't guess. I would have loved to explore. I gave up trying to decipher the strange signs everywhere.

Felix didn't seem interested. He crouched over, and then suddenly stopped. His voice was squeaky with panic. 'There's nothing above us. It's just *space* up there.' He ripped off his mask, walked two steps, and vomited.

I put my hand on Felix's shoulder. He was paler than usual, and sweat ran down his face like tears. He muttered: '*No roof, no roof, no Earth above.*'

I looked up at Macon, alarmed. 'What's wrong with him?'

'It happens sometimes. They feel exposed, or like they'll

float away.'

'Does it get better?'

'Usually.' He crouched by Felix's other side and spoke soothingly. 'The sky is a roof. It's just a different colour, that's all.'

Eventually, we convinced Felix to hobble along. He had kept the metal strut he'd scavenged from the Fast Mart, and he used it as a walking stick. The ground was littered with chunks of concrete, rusted metal, plastic and old wheels from vehicles. The plants pushing through the black surface made it difficult to walk, particularly with bulky overshoes on. I kicked them off, but Macon made me put them back on in case I stepped on something sharp.

We were forced to halt by a wide crevasse which cut across the thoroughfare. Water rushed down it in a torrent of froth and spray.

Macon frowned. 'Another reason we don't go this way. A lot of the old sewers or subways have collapsed on this side of the city.'

Felix peered downwards. 'I suppose the underground water had to go somewhere.'

'Exactly.'

I ran my hands through my sweaty hair. 'How do we get across?'

'We'll find somewhere narrower.'

We followed the crevasse as it sliced through streets and buildings. Finally, we came to a place where a building had collapsed, and tumbled pieces of concrete lay in the water.

Macon took a rope from his pack and we tied it to our waists, forming a chain. 'I wish you'd brought proper boots,' he grumbled. 'I'll go first—less likely to slip.'

He slowly lowered himself down. He moved his feet into a secure position and then reached up. 'Come on, Marri.'

I sat, my legs dangling over the rush of water, then grasped Macon's hands. I dropped onto the rock, teetered in my wretched overshoes, and pulled him off balance. My leg sank into the water and my overshoe started to float away. Macon's foot slipped and he swore.

We grabbed one another, and clambered back onto the rock. I hooked my overshoe up from the water before it disappeared forever.

My heart pounded as the water rushed past. We could have pulled Felix in too if we'd gone into the water. Then I realised Macon and I were still holding each other. 'Let go!' I gasped, taking my hand off his elbow. I've hated being held by the upper arms since Conor.

He let go. Felix dropped down lightly. We moved cautiously across the chunks of fallen building, helping each other as we went.

The sheer side of the crevasse was hard to scale. Eventually, Macon boosted Felix, and then Felix helped each of us up.

I looked back at the ravine. 'How are you going to get back without us, Macon?'

He turned away. 'Don't worry about me.'

We traced our way back to the thoroughfare we'd started on, and kept going. Spray had drenched our clothes, but now the sun dried us. It was much more efficient than the drying rooms at home.

We had to weave through vehicles crammed along the way. They had once been painted in bright colours, but were now marred with rusty streaks. The large black ones intrigued me.

Macon peered at a white vehicle. 'This one has petrol! They were mostly obsolete by the time of the Catastrophe, so it's useful if you can find one.'

He prised at a small door at one end of the vehicle. I looked through the glass panel at the other end. Through the grime, a face stared out; desiccated brown skin stretched over yellow-white bones. The eyes had shrivelled in their sockets and the lips had shrunk over the teeth. The shreds of bright, cheerful clothing were grotesque. I backed away. *Will I spend the rest of my life scavenging from the dead?* I recalled the tangle of skeletons at the place where we'd emerged above ground, and my breath came quickly. *I wish I was home.*

Macon became aware of my panic. He turned, his voice hollow and muffled behind the mask. 'Rookie mistake—you looked at the body. I freaked out on my first Strikeforce run too.' He shrugged. 'Other guys didn't care. Leo'd be checking that corpse for jewellery—'

I wrapped my arms around myself. 'Scavenging means taking from the dead. I knew that, but it's different when you see it for yourself—'

'Don't think too hard about it. No point getting sentimental when it's a matter of survival.'

I nodded. 'Are you going to check the body?'

'She doesn't have anything we need.' Macon paused. 'Rilla got angry if I didn't come back with any scavenged suprater-ran jewellery.'

Sudden dismay filled me. 'My snail rock—the one you gave me—I left it under my bed!'

He paused. 'You kept that fossil?'

Then he turned back to the vehicle. After some banging and under-the-breath swearing, he levered open the small door. A hiss sounded as he loosened the lid. He lifted his mask slightly and sniffed. His nose wrinkled.

'Air must have gotten into it.' He lowered his mask, screwed the lid on, and closed the door.

'Why don't we make our own petrol?'

'Petrol was distilled from crude oil, which was made from

tiny sea creatures and plants, squashed under pressure in the earth. There's none where we live.'

I was reminded of when we had first registered as partners, when we didn't know each other well. He had shyly shown me the books he was reading, the inventions he had made, and when I'd shown interest, his eyes had sparkled. I felt a pang of sadness.

We helped Felix get up and started again.

'Don't leave this road,' Macon warned. 'The north-east is a red zone, and full of unexploded bombs and mines. Oh, and watch out for dogs.'

'What are *dogs*?'

'Meat-eating animals, with sharp teeth. Usually about so high ...' He indicated the height with his hand. 'They run in packs.'

'I hope we don't see any—'

With a whirring noise, something fell slowly out of the sky and settled on a rusted piece of metal. It was white and grey with an orange pointed nose.

Felix cried out, and slumped to the ground.

I backed away. 'Is it a dog?' I fumbled in my pocket for my slingshot. The beast inspected me with a beady black eye and cocked its head. Then it made an *aaarrrk* noise. I jumped.

Macon's shoulders were relaxed, and his crossbow remained at his side. 'A bird. It won't hurt you.'

The bird followed us, but flew off once it realised that we weren't going to feed it. Its wings were covered in strange material, but it wouldn't let me look at it closely.

Suddenly, Macon stopped and peered around. Felix crouched on the ground again, and stared at the space between his knees. He seemed to find it more difficult when we weren't moving.

'Are we going the right way?' I said.

'I don't think anyone's scavenged from that shop down this side street.' He glanced at me. 'You need new batteries, and there might be medical supplies and food. I'll give you a quick lesson. You'll need to know what to do if you stay here.'

I scanned the blue and yellow sign on the building he'd indicated, sounding out letters under my breath. '*Kwi-kk-a-Mart.* Was he related to Fast Mart? They must have been rivals!'

Macon laughed. 'I don't know.' Then he stared. 'Did you *read* that?'

I tried to avoid Macon's eye. Eventually, I said, 'Yeah.'

'*How?*'

'Um, I just ... I kind of ... picked it up. Some of the older women can read, the ones who knew people who lived before the Catastrophe.'

I avoided looking at Felix, but Macon looked straight at him.

Felix muttered at the ground, 'She hassled me until I taught her. *You* know what she's like.'

Macon folded his arms, his eyes glittering. 'You didn't trust me?'

My face was hot with shame under the mask. 'I trusted you when it came to *me*. Too much. But ... you'd guess who taught me ...'

Macon glared. 'For the Earth's sake, Marri! I don't like Felix, but I wouldn't have—!'

'Well, now you know.' I pulled at my hair. 'I can write a bit too.'

Macon turned his back on me. 'Whatever.'

'The feeling's mutual,' Felix muttered behind me. 'By the way.'

Tears burned in my eyes and my heart beat erratically and twinged in my chest. To distract myself, I strode to the

Kwik-A-Mart and pressed my hands against the filthy glass.

'How do you get into these places?'

Macon handed a brick to me, his face still angry. He was wearing his helmet again. 'Take your hands off there! We'll smash our way in.'

The glass was very tough, but I felt better after smashing at it repeatedly. Eventually Macon shot the crossbow at the window, making a spiderweb of cracks around the bolt. We went for the cracks and the glass began to yield. Macon pushed, and the glass fell inwards with a splintering crash, disintegrating into square bluish chunks. I went to enter, but Macon flung an arm out. 'The building might be unstable.'

We shone our torches into the room, and waited until everything had settled. Despite the different name, this place was laid out like a Fast Mart. The shelves were mostly intact, but signs and other material dangled from the walls. I wrinkled my nose at the rank smell. Creatures had managed to get into the room, and long-dried animal poop covered the floor.

We cautiously inspected the shelves. Macon directed me to find tins of food. I knew from my time in the kitchen to discard the damaged and puffed-up tins, and filled my pack and my arms with cans.

Macon methodically emptied a medicine shelf. Then he gathered different sized batteries, and some tools, and placed them on top of my armful of cans. 'You'll need these.' I could barely carry them all.

Finally, he looked at the roof with longing. I wondered if he'd gone mad.

'Light bulbs,' he said, after he'd noticed me staring. 'Usually we carry a portable ladder. These shelves are too unstable. I'll tell them to come back here when I get home.'

'This stuff's heavy! Can we go back now?'

Felix still sat where we'd left him. I put my supplies on the ground, and caught Macon looking at the sun.

'What's up?'

'I need to be back before dark.'

I nodded. 'I can look after Felix.' I tried to get Felix to stand and strained at his elbow. We managed to get upright but then I fell onto all fours because my heavy pack pulled me off balance. Felix flopped back down. He tried to haul himself up but his legs buckled underneath him.

Macon ran his hand over his hair. 'Earth's sake! This is hopeless.' He shook his head. 'I'll turn around tomorrow. You need a bit more training.'

A treacherous feeling of relief washed over me. I mentally stomped on it as hard as I could.

We packed the scavenged stuff into our bags, and then pulled Felix up and steered him along. More trees grew in and around the buildings the further we went: amazing shades of green, more luscious than hydroponic plants. Some had riotous flowers of purple and yellow, with astounding, heady scents. Fruit dangled from some trees, but I didn't recognise it. Macon explained that the Strikeforces generally didn't eat fruit or drink water from the city. Also, some plants were poisonous, so I was better off avoiding anything I didn't recognise.

A brindled four-legged shape slunk behind a broken-down building. Another brownish beast followed. Both had long, predatory snouts.

I pointed. 'Over there—?'

Macon turned his head sharply. 'Shit! Wild dogs.'

I took out my slingshot and loaded my pockets with rubble. Macon fired his crossbow towards the lurking shadows, and they retreated. We recovered the bolts and kept an eye out, but no more appeared.

The sun moved across the sky, and the shadows lengthened.

The sky began to change colour, from blue to pink to orange. At first, I wondered if I was imagining it, but as we went on it was unmistakeable. The edge of the world was burning.

'Look!' I pointed at the orange glow. 'Fire!'

'It always looks like this when the sun goes down. It's not dangerous; it's sometimes beautiful. Anyway, let's find somewhere to sleep tonight.'

We sheltered in a square, dark grey stone building with large round pillars. The stern sign on the front read 'Western Bank'.

The front door led into a large open room with high, ornate ceilings and intricate hanging lights, glinting in the darkness. At the dark end of the room there was a row of booths. Wooden and metal panelling hung off the walls, and wires protruded, making the room look indecent somehow, as if it was unclothed, or violated.

We shuffled across the dusty stone floor, and small rectangular bits of paper flew up in the draught from our passage. Macon led us to the massive metal door at the back, hanging off its hinges. We squeezed our way into the stairs beyond and underground. Felix heaved a sigh of relief. I was also secretly relieved to have some respite from the exhausting assault of supraterran colours, sounds and smells.

Macon gave a small smile. 'I thought we'd all be happier here.'

We found a room with a relatively clear floor. Banks of metal drawers had been set into the wall, but the drawers sagged out, weighed down by paper, and many had fallen out of their sockets.

Felix and I dumped our packs and sank to the floor. Macon cleared a large open space, and then smashed a wooden chair. He built a fire with chair pieces and paper, and made us watch how he did it. I removed my bandages and looked at my oozing feet. *Ugh.* I put some fresh bandages on.

My lower arms and parts of my face felt hot and sore. I hadn't noticed earlier because I'd been distracted by the dogs and the pain in my feet. Felix's arms were a little reddish too, as were the parts of his face which hadn't been covered by the mask. I was sure it wasn't just the orange light of the fire. I looked at Macon and saw his face was red as well.

'What's happened to our faces? Is it the disease? The poison?'

'It's just sunburn. It's annoying; Felix is lucky to have browner skin.'

Macon taught us how to open cans with an implement he'd collected from the Kwik-A-Mart, and gave us some of his gear. He explained that sometimes water fell from the sky, and we should collect it in old cans.

I fell asleep without realising it, despite my aching muscles and the hard floor.

The next morning, after a hurried breakfast, we stood on the broad steps outside the Western Bank. The sun peeped above the buildings, bathing the ruined city in a glowing light. Macon turned to Felix and me, and held out his map. 'Keep going down this road. *Don't* get too far off it. You're almost in the green zone now. Remember where I told you to shelter tonight.'

I took the map, my fingers touching his briefly.

'Thank you for helping us. Look after the children—I mean the ones from my body, okay?' I swallowed, unable to continue, and tears escaped down my cheeks inside my mask.

'Get to the settlement safely. Maybe ... maybe ... one day I can visit you? I'll keep an eye on the children, Marri, if they let me. Goodbye.'

Macon hesitated, but then walked away without looking

back. I watched him, and then became aware Felix was staring at me.

'What?' I said to Felix.

'Nothing.'

We started walking again. Felix still struggled with the open terrain, but I didn't mind as much, although the changing light, temperature, and breeze were disconcerting.

The tins were very heavy, and the straps of my homemade pack cut into my shoulders. With a sudden *rip*, the bottom of my pack tore apart, and tins, medicine and batteries rolled into a deep crack in the road. We couldn't reach them, even after we'd snapped off branches from the trees. I tied a knot in the bottom of my bag, but we had to transfer most of the important and heavy stuff to Felix's. I wished I'd checked for needles and thread in the Kwik-A-Mart.

We didn't get to the place Macon had planned for us to reach because we'd wasted too much time trying to retrieve the tins. Instead, we stayed in a strange building full of broken-down machinery. We buttressed the doors with junk to hold them closed. The floor was too cluttered to safely light a fire. We ate cold food out of tins, and then huddled together on the broken floor. Eventually we slept.

Something woke me. I thought of Monster Rats and rolled over in panic. Felix was huddled in his blankets. *Snuffle*. The sound had come from him.

'Everything okay?' I mumbled.

'Mmph,' said Felix.

I sat up and switched on the torch. 'Are you sure?'

His face was tearstained. 'I just—I wish I hadn't needed to run away. I wish I hadn't dragged you with me. I wish I never had—*those feelings*.'

I put my arm around him. 'I'm here.'

After a time, he said, 'I had this idea that they'd go away

when we escaped. Those feelings.'

I took a deep breath of the cold night air. 'My experience is that those feelings don't go away.'

Felix put his chin on his knees, his face half-lit by my torch. 'I knew it,' he said into the echoing darkness. 'You still like him—'

'I was talking about general preferences, not a specific preference. And I don't like him.'

After a long pause, I said, 'I was sad when he left. Never tell him, okay?'

Felix stared into the night. 'I was scared that you'd go home with him. After all, you never meant to come—!'

I jerked my head back. 'And leave you here? No way!'

'I ... still ... want *him*. Frankie. I've taken you up here for nothing.' I sensed that Felix was wiping his eyes. 'It's not how I thought it would be ... up here. The death and destruction, the openness, the wind, the smells. Maybe we should go home.'

'We *can't*, Felix. You're being irrational. We have to keep going.'

Felix looked away. 'What if we told them that I'd changed? We ran away together, but we regretted it and came home?'

'They wouldn't believe it.'

'They might if ...' Felix looked sidelong at me. 'Are ... are you fertile right now?'

I recoiled. '*Felix!*'

'Remember what they told us?' Felix adopted a didactic tone. 'Intercourse is not about emotional attachment. Emotional attachment led to the Catastrophe. It's our duty to create a diverse population, to repopulate the earth and put aside emotional attachments.'

I shook my head. 'That's *enough*, Felix. Everything will be better in the morning.' I lay down and closed my eyes, but it took me a long time to go back to sleep.

We had put out tins to catch water, but to our dismay they were empty, for reasons we did not understand. We had hardly any left. My feet were bleeding and weeping through the bandages. Every step was like walking on knives.

I found a foetid pond, but it looked undrinkable, even if we boiled it. Using my slingshot, I killed a reddish-furred animal with a large fluffy white-tipped tail. It was larger than a cat, with pointed ears and snout. We skinned and roasted it. The meat was stringy and awful, but we picked it to the bone anyway. Then we opened two tins and cooked them over the fire. We only had a few tins left, and I wished again that my bag hadn't broken.

Unfortunately, reddish fluffy creature didn't agree with me. Cramps racked my gut after lunch, and I threw up. Felix insisted that I should drink the last of the water.

We couldn't find anywhere to scavenge. This area was strange and barren, full of wire fences and tumbled-down buildings, no Mart houses of any kind. I checked the map and the compass again, as Macon had shown me. 'We're still nowhere near the Strikeforce wayhouse Macon told us to get to last night. We're too slow.'

We kept walking, one foot in front of another, barely thinking. My whole body was in pain, and my stomach muscles ached. The sky darkened, and a pink light began to rise where the buildings met the sky. Great white puffy things hung in the sky, like the clouds of steam or dust in our tunnels, and their undersides began to glow orange. I couldn't appreciate the beauty of it.

As night fell, keening howls sounded. Hair rose on the back of my neck as I wondered what creatures made those noises.

We couldn't shelter in nearby buildings because they had collapsed or crumbled, so we lit a small fire on a flat part of the thoroughfare, and opened the last cans I'd taken from the Kwik-A-Mart. I raised ideas for scavenging more food and water.

Felix said, 'I should have made you go home with Macon.'

'I'm not giving up.'

We slept on the thoroughfare, one watching while the other slept: neither of us trusted that the howls would stay distant. Felix woke me when water fell from the sky, and we collected it in our tins. It barely reached from the tip of my thumb to my first thumb-knuckle. We shared it, even though it tasted metallic.

Felix yawned. 'Two good things! A bit of water, and the howling's stopped. I'd feel safer if I had Macon's crossbow, but I guess he had to return it.'

While Felix slept, I kept watch. I was used to the closed darkness of the tunnels, not the expansive darkness of aboveground. Strange noises filled the air: creaks and chirrups and occasional howls. In my imagination, terrible creatures lurked in the darkness, but none appeared. A big, almost-round, white circle floated in the sky, emerging from behind cloud cover. *I'll have to ask Macon what that is.* Then I remembered that I was never going to see him or anyone from home again. I put my head on my knees and tried not to cry.

We had no way of measuring time, so I had to guess when Felix had had enough sleep. I'd nodded off a few times already.

I put my head on my lumpy, depleted pack. 'My neck hurts.'

Felix sat next to me. 'Put your head on my lap.'

'Thanks.' Felix stroked my hair absently. I slept, and dreamed I was running down endless corridors. I never came to the room at the end: every time I opened a door, another tunnel opened.

Something woke me. It felt as if I'd been kissed on the cheek. *It must be a dream.* Then Felix leaned over and kissed me again.

'What are you doing?' I sat and glared at him blearily. 'Did you *kiss* me?'

I couldn't read his expression in the dim firelight, but I felt him shrug. 'Maybe it's possible to love people in different ways. I'm ... confused. I love you.'

'Not like you love Frankie—'

'And you don't love me like you love Macon.' I flinched. *I don't love him. I don't* want *to love him.*

As if Felix had heard my thoughts, he said, 'You *do* love him. But you came on this journey, and you've stayed with me, that's love too. An amazing love—'

The tears I'd suppressed earlier rose. 'I've been so lonely and scared ...'

'I know, and I'm sorry! I don't know how to thank you—' Felix reached for me and we embraced.

Then he kissed me. It was nice. I felt guilty and conflicted, but also, almost against my will, somewhat aroused. *What now?*

Again, it was as if Felix read my mind. He pushed my matted hair away from my face. 'Share with me.' He looked embarrassed. 'If I do my duty, I won't feel so bad. And ... I'd want you to be the mother of my child.'

'Wouldn't Frankie be upset?'

'He *wanted* you to have my child. We fought about it.'

'*He what*—?' I shook my head. 'That's just odd.'

'Frankie would have loved to sire children, if he wasn't Barren. It's just that he might not have enjoyed the process as much as ...' Felix looked away. 'Also, we, um, sometimes met with other people, by agreement ...'

I counted on my fingers. 'I might not be fertile anymore.'

'Come here. You're cold.' He opened his arms.

I went to him.

CHAPTER 10

When I woke, Felix was still asleep. I watched the sun move above the shattered buildings, accompanied by twittering and tootling noises as it rose. I wasn't sure what creatures made those noises, but it felt like they were singing the sun upwards. A dusky haze on the ground lifted, and the sky changed from red to yellow to bluish white. There were so many things that I didn't understand here.

Felix woke, and we ate our paltry breakfast in silence. My stomach still ached. I caught Felix looking at me, and pulled my eyes away. I fiddled with bits of black paving as I ate.

Last night, to get things started, I'd described all the things I found attractive about Frankie. We both liked his arms *a lot*, and apparently his bare chest was even better. The discussion had become explicit. We'd giggled, but it worked, and it made things less tense.

I ate the rat jerky slowly, drawing out each mouthful so I'd feel like I'd eaten more. As I chewed, I felt guilty relief that last night hadn't been my first sexual experience. It hadn't been terrible: we both cared about each other. I'd felt comforted afterwards, as if our partnership had been completed. But at one point, my mind had wandered before I remembered what we were supposed to be doing. And I discovered it was much harder to ignore a stone sticking into your back when you were not entirely consumed with passion. I felt a moment of frustration that Felix hadn't agreed to my plan back when we had a comfortable bed.

As we finished eating, Felix said, 'No regrets?'

I looked up. 'We've done our duty. For a change!'

He fiddled with a ragged nail. 'It's a relief for me, too. It was okay?'

I played with my hair. 'Yes, fine ... Was it okay for you? Given that you don't really ...?'

Felix flushed. 'Fine. Better than I thought it would be.'

'That's all we can expect.' I laughed.

Felix became solemn. 'I'm taking you home to your children. You're not going to die up here because of me.'

When I opened my mouth to protest, he said, 'No. No more arguments.'

In fact, we had a tremendous argument. Eventually, I got out the map and showed him that we were closer to the settlement than home. We needed water and real food. Reluctantly, almost sulkily, Felix agreed to keep going, muttering that if I killed us out of stubbornness it would be all my fault.

Something about the argument felt familiar, and I thought back to when we were children, exploring the tunnels, getting into trouble. Felix always came up with these plans, but he was the first to tire of them, and I was the one who saw them through. Maybe I was always waiting for him to give voice to my secret desires. Maybe I needed someone to blame.

I adjusted my bandages before we started. They were crusted and stained, but wearing overshoes without them was excruciating. The blisters had burst, and the skin below was bright red and weeping gunk. I couldn't peel the bandages off in some places.

We searched for water or for places suitable for scavenging, in case we had missed any, but we saw nothing.

'Do you think anyone lived here?' I asked Felix as we passed another collapsed wire fence, overgrown with climbing plants.

'They can't have done? But these buildings must have been

used for something.'

After the sun had risen a hand's breadth above the buildings, a lean black shadow passed between two houses. And then another.

I pointed. 'Felix—!'

'Dogs,' said Felix. We got our slingshots and loaded our pockets with rubble.

We tried to walk faster. I had to walk almost on the sides of my feet, otherwise the pressure on my blisters was unbearable. I tripped and grazed my knee on an uneven part of the road.

'Stop,' Felix said. 'Don't hurt yourself—'

Blood ran down my knee: the same knee I'd injured in our escape down the maintenance corridor. 'Too late.'

The sun beat on my aching head. It was hotter than the day before. My mouth was dry, my tongue thick. My head started to spin. I wanted to swallow, to stop myself from feeling so ill, but I couldn't.

I began to panic. Was this the supraterran disease? I'd probably given it to Felix too, especially after last night.

Eventually, I had to tell him. 'I'm not feeling well.'

'You're pale and sweaty. Let's stop.'

'We can't—the dogs! What if they realise I'm so weak?'

Felix watched the shadows. 'They're definitely waiting to attack. Look how they sniff! But if we run, they'll chase us.'

He gave me the metal strut he'd scavenged from the Fast Mart and I used it as a walking stick.

Whenever we saw shadows, we shot at them with rubble. This kept the dogs out of slingshot range, but I was sure more were following now.

I stopped to check the map, and gave the strut to Felix. Felix grabbed my arm and shook it.

'There,' he said, pointing, and I followed his finger.

A pack of five wild dogs had emerged from the plants on

either side onto the path. They were small and stunted, apart from the lead dog, which was much larger. It had black fur dotted with ugly white patches and scars, and something had chewed off its left ear, leaving it ragged. It was covered in lumpy pink and black tumours. Slobbery foam dripped from its jaws, and a low rumbling noise came from its throat. One of the other dogs had milky eyes and was surely blind, and I wondered how it seemed to know where we were standing. A third dog had strangely short legs and a large head compared to the others.

I was rigid with fear for a moment, but I recovered and loaded my slingshot. *Thwap, thwap!* I hit the big dog twice on the shoulder. It flinched, but moved forward. Felix raised the strut. The dog made the deep grumbling noise again and the fur on its neck rose. Its lips curled back, showing ugly, pointed teeth and black-spotted gums. It crouched as if it was about to spring. I wondered how far and how fast it could jump. The other dogs were right behind. *We're dead.*

'Oh crap,' said Felix. 'Oh shit, oh *fuck*.'

I screamed, 'Help, help!' I don't know who I was screaming for in the dead, empty city.

Four grey and white birds flapped up from the buildings around, *whup whup whup*, but there was no other response. The other dogs were unmoved, although the big dog paused when the birds flew past.

We used the big dog's hesitation to back away. Felix held out the strut, angling it across both of us, ready to spear the dogs. I only had my slingshot. I fired it again, hitting the big dog in the eye. It yelped, and I think I stopped it from spring-ing at us, but the other dogs advanced on either side. My heart sank. *We don't want them to surround us.*

I didn't have a suitable weapon. *Maybe I can strangle them.* I looked at the girth of the big dog's neck. *I don't think my grip is wide or strong enough. Our cooking knife? I'd have to get close, and it's still at the bottom of Felix's pack.* Then I had an idea. I removed my pack, and hooked the straps over my left arm so it became a shield. Felix glanced at me and did the same.

The big dog pawed at its injured eye. I had a moment of hope, but then it crouched and leaped. I screamed.

Felix stepped in front of me and hit the dog in the chest with his strut, holding it away with his pack. It howled in a way that made my teeth hurt, and tried to snap at him. The strut broke, and Felix was left with a shorter, jagged spear. He danced back, pushed his pack in the dog's face, and held it off. Then he kicked it in the side of the head, stunning it. Meanwhile I kicked its scarred, tumour-covered flank. *Yelp!* It looked back at me in confusion. I kicked again. *Yelp!*

The other dogs surrounded us. I crouched, growled, and bared my teeth, just like the big dog, and then ran at them. The dog with the oversized head tore at my pack-shield, and the empty tins fell out. I picked up a tin and threw it as hard as I could at the dog's huge head. It backed off as the tin clattered to the ground. I pelted tins at the dogs until they retreated, then looked back to see how Felix was doing.

The big dog was trying to bite him. Felix shoved his pack in its mouth, stabbed it with his stick and kicked at it. It was bleeding in several places. I dropped my pack, picked up a rock from the road and smashed it, two-handed, on the dog's back. The dog howled. I hit it again with all my might, and it rolled on its side, whining. Felix stuck the strut through the big dog's eye. He twisted the strut and shoved it downwards. *Crunch.* It shuddered and went still, its foam-covered tongue lolling out.

I grabbed Felix. 'Were you bitten?'

Felix was shaking. 'No. But it almost got my arm.' He showed me a rip in his sleeve. 'Let's chase away the others;

they're not as brave without the big one.'

I picked up my pack again. 'They don't like it when you act like the big dog.' I growled at the dogs again, showing my teeth.

'You're right!' Felix ran at the other dogs with his new spear, also growling. They retreated to nearby buildings.

I heard a noise like running feet behind me and turned. I couldn't see anyone. If my reckoning was right, the settlement was still at least a day's walk away. *I'm imagining things. Not feeling so good. Not. So. Good.*

I shrieked when something sprang from between two buildings and knocked me over. At first I thought it was an even bigger dog, but then I realised it was a human wearing a yellow mask. I had a horrible flashback to Conor, and scrambled away. *No! I won't be caught again!*

The person brought up a crossbow and fired two bolts; two dogs thumped to the ground, one shot through the eye, and the other through the head. They yelped and died. The last of the dogs melted into the shadows.

I laughed and dropped my shredded pack on the ground. 'Bit late, whoever you are! We've done it ourselves.' Sweat ran down my face.

The person on the ground had clothing like mine. I blinked, and rubbed my eyes.

'Rat shit on a stick! *Macon?* Is that you?' My heart was beating fast. *It's a flapping bird, trying to get out of my chest.*

Felix sat, shaking, on the broken ground. 'That was close.'

The person removed his mask. It *was* Macon. He got up, breathing heavily, doubled over, his shirt covered in small rocks and dirt from the road. 'Are you okay? Were you bitten?' I still wasn't sure if I was imagining him.

'No,' we said.

'My stupid pack is ruined,' I added.

Macon prodded the big dog's corpse with his toe. '*Earth Above!* It's huge! Nice work.'

We stood catching our breath, and I wiped sweat off my face. Felix wanted to know if we should eat the dog, and Macon said we shouldn't touch it.

As the excitement of the dog attack wore off, I was sure I had dreamed it. Everything was unreal and distant. I was in the sky.

Cloudlike, I floated to Felix and sat by him. Then I smiled up at Macon. 'How nice to see you again, my love. I'm dreaming, right? You're a dream—'

Macon stared at me, his expression odd. 'I tracked you here. Are you *sure* you're okay?'

'I feel weird.' I leaned my head on Felix's shoulder, and closed my eyes, tears of exhaustion squeezing from beneath my eyelids. There wasn't much moisture to form them.

'She's not well,' said Felix, his arm around my shoulder.

'Shit,' said Macon.

I opened my eyes to see what the dream of Macon was upset about. The world seemed depthless, as if everything was cut out of paper, like the puppet shows they used to hold when we were young. The Chief Councillor puppet had always saved the day.

Macon crouched and inspected me. 'When did you last drink water, Marri?'

'Yesterday? And that bit of rain last night?' My eyes widened. 'We forgot to boil it, Felix! Maybe it wasn't the fluffy orange animal!'

Macon felt my skin. 'You haven't had enough for a hot day. I stopped at a Strikeforce way station last night, and got water from the tanks.' He handed me a bottle of water.

The metal bottle felt real. The first few sips were wonderful.

'Thank you.'

Macon sat opposite us. 'You haven't got very far.'

Felix sighed. 'Can you take us home? I don't want her to die because of me.'

Macon frowned. 'They'll hang you both.' He looked at me. 'You were right to refuse to come home. It was … selfish … of me to ask.'

I smiled, but I was still floating with the clouds above.

Felix chewed his nail. 'You're putting yourself in terrible danger.'

'I'll be sequestered either way, so I may as well get you to the settlement first.'

Felix's eyes widened. 'Won't they hang *you*?'

'They've invested too much in my training. They'll sequester me, but I deserve it.'

I had another question. 'Is that how you shot those dogs in the eye after running like that? That was *amazing*! *Wham*! Into the eye!'

Macon turned pink. 'I slowed my breathing, then lay down on the ground to shoot. You have to adjust for your heartbeat—' He stopped. 'You don't look well, Marri—'

'We're in trouble, aren't we?' said Felix.

'Let's get Marri out of here and to the settlement. This area's no good for scavenging; it's industrial. Forget the stinking masks! We're almost out of the yellow area—'

Macon and Felix helped me up and guided me. There was no shade on the road, and the sun burned like the flames from a laundry boiler. Nausea gripped me, and I dripped sweat. *Keep going. Get to the safe place.* I closed my eyes as I walked. Sparkles of white light floated before me. I wasn't sure whether this was a good or a bad sign.

'Try to keep awake, Marri,' said Macon. 'Open your eyes.

Talk to me.'

I opened my eyes and looked at the black, cracked thoroughfare beneath my feet.

'Don't know what to say.'

Macon cleared his throat. 'You were asking where oil comes from? We could talk about that—?'

On the other side of me, Felix laughed, on the brink of hysteria. '*Please*, don't tell me this your pillow talk, Macon—!'

'Shut up, Felix,' I said, too tired and dizzy to look at him. I stared at my plodding feet and racked my fuzzy brain, but all topics were problematic: offspring, partners, Councillors ...

'I've got a question,' said Felix in a mollifying tone. 'Why did you come back for us?'

It took a long time for Macon to answer. 'That night in the way station—I couldn't sleep. I knew it hadn't rained enough, and there were more dogs than I remembered. Plus the two of you are basically hopeless—'

I opened my mouth to object to being called hopeless, but the cold sweat dripping from my face intensified.

'Not ... well...'

I needed to lie down. Before I could do anything, my vision narrowed to a pinprick of light. The pinprick disappeared, as if I was heading into a tunnel, and everything went dark.

When I roused, I was slumped on the ground. Macon and Felix were crouched on either side of me. Macon's hand was on my shoulder.

'Oh,' I said, sitting up and leaning over. 'Gonna be sick.' Tears stung my eyes as I retched, bringing up everything that had been in my stomach. I vomited on Macon's trouser leg.

I grabbed at him, gulping to try to stop the retching. There was nothing left but my gut was still heaving. 'I hate this. Sorry, sorry!'

'It's okay. We'll get you into the shade,' said Macon. The men hoisted me under the arms and moved me under a tree.

'Sorry, love, I got your trousers,' I said to Macon as he lowered me down.

He put his hand on my forehead. 'You're burning up.'

I closed my eyes, my wrecked bundle still on my back. I wanted to take it off, but I couldn't move. 'Can't get up.'

'It's not the supraterran disease, is it?' Felix's voice quavered.

'If it was the disease, we'd see blood in her vomit. Have you tasted blood, Marri?'

I opened my eyes to find Macon staring at my face. 'No.' Everything wobbled, so I closed my eyes again.

Someone patted my cheek. 'Open your mouth.' I didn't understand the command. They said again, more insistently, 'Marri, come on, love, open your mouth …'

I opened my mouth wide, hoping that they would go away.

Breath tickled my face. 'No blood,' said the voice. Someone else nearby let out a great shuddering breath.

'Face dirty,' I complained. 'Yuk.'

The other voice said, 'I'll wipe your face.' I felt a damp cloth on my face.

The first voice said, 'Felix … there's another possibility. Is she pregnant?'

The cloth stopped wiping my face. 'Would she get sick *that* quickly?'

There was a silence. *Whump, whump, whump.* Blood pounded in my ears.

I opened my eyes for a moment. 'Wouldn't. *Shut up.*'

'It wouldn't explain the fever, either.'

Opening my eyes was a mistake. A tree floated above, along with Felix and Macon's concerned faces. Then the world spun further away from me, or perhaps I was spinning away from it. I wasn't sure. I closed my eyes to stop the spinning.

I felt a cool hand on my forehead. 'She needs water.' The voice sounded as if it was coming from a great distance.

Someone lifted my upper body and propped me against his own body. Cold sweat sprung from my forehead again. I moaned and struggled.

'Let me down! Down!'

The person who held me patted my hair and let me lie mostly back down. 'Here's the bottle! Try to drink some water—Marri? *Marri!*'

The world faded, leaving me behind.

Images danced behind my eyelids. Myriads of spinning white birds swirled past in a geometrical formation, like the tiles on the dormitory roof at home. Their orange beaks flashed as they whirled. The birds called, '*Wake up! You need to drink some water or you'll die.*' Then they started pleading: '*I need you to wake up! Please don't die.*' The birds sounded upset, but I couldn't help them; try as I might, I couldn't open my eyes. I waited to hear what the birds said next, but they didn't speak again.

Instead, they turned into trees, then the trees shrank to mushrooms. The mushrooms became yellow snarling dogs. The dogs twirled and snarled for a while, showing spotted gums, then turned into desiccated skeleton faces. The withered eyes of the skeleton faces winked at me. Finally, the faces turned into giant rats. The giant rats squeaked and fled into darkness.

I don't know what happened then. I must have blacked out or slept. When I woke, the shadows were longer. Someone had pushed up my sleeves and my clothes were damp. Felix was fanning me with a flat piece of discarded plastic.

When he realised I was looking at him, he let out his breath. 'Thank the Earth, thank the Earth!' He looked like he had been crying. I wondered why.

I sat up slightly, although I couldn't get up any further as my head was spinning. Macon wasn't there. *He was a dream, just as I thought.*

A thick line of reddish-black ants climbed up the tree next to me. They were quite different to the small black ones we had at home.

Suddenly an enormous ant the size of a cat emerged from the tree trunk. Its pincers snapped, and its antennae twitched at me. As I jolted back, the ant disappeared, as quickly as it had come. *Good.*

'How are you feeling, Marri?' said Felix, holding me, his face creased with worry.

'The giant ant is back in the tree, so I'm feeling much better,' I said truthfully.

'The *what*—? I don't understand what you're saying.'

I clicked my tongue in irritation. 'The giant ant! It poked its head out of that tree and looked at us. I'm glad it went back into the tree.' I waved my hand in front of my eyes to illustrate. '*Whoosh!* It disappeared!'

Felix stared and wrinkled his nose. 'This isn't good.'

I shrugged. I didn't understand how he had missed seeing the ant. Then I looked around again.

'Did Macon go into the tree too? With the ant?' Somehow this seemed the logical destination for all dreams.

'He's running to the supraterran settlement for help.' I waited for him to say something sarcastic about Macon and his motivations, but he didn't. Instead he stroked my hair and muttered to himself. 'Not quite so hot now, good.'

The birds were worried I was hot. They turned into trees! Wake up, they said. Hello rats. Not going to die. The giant ant is helping me.

From the look on Felix's face, I'd spoken my thoughts aloud. But when he saw that I was looking at him, he pasted a bright smile onto his face.

'Macon said you had to drink some water if you woke up. We'll fix you up.'

I drank a little water and managed to keep it down. I realised then that someone had put a pack under my legs. I drank some more, then said, 'Feel sick again.'

Felix helped me lie back down. There was a bundle of clothes under my head. I wondered how that had happened. Before I could ask, darkness claimed me again, and I knew no more.

CHAPTER 11

When I opened my eyes, I was lying on hard wood looking up at four strangers, the fluffy white clouds moving in the blue sky behind them. The surface I was lying on was jolting up and down. I was unsure whether this was part of another bad dream. My nostrils flared as I smelled a strange animal scent; I later learned it was from the beast that pulled the cart that carried us all. I tried to get up and run.

'No, lie down and rest,' said a female voice, and a hand pushed me back down. Her accent was strange, like she was speaking around a mouthful of porridge. I was so weak that I couldn't move.

Felix spoke from nearby. 'It's okay, Marri, they're here to help.' I smiled at him. His hand gripped mine.

Then I passed out again.

When I next woke, I was in a dark building, lying on the floor. A herbal scent filled the air. A strange woman stood over me, removing my clothing. Her hair was an unusual yellow-ish colour, and her face was leathery-brown and lined with wrinkles. I struggled and cried out. 'Where's Felix? Where's Macon? Where am I?'

'Other people are looking after yon fellas,' she said. 'They're okay. You're in our village. Hush, now, I'm just going to put you in a bath. It'll make you feel better.' Her hands were cool and slightly rough. She removed my clothes and helped me lower myself into a shallow tin bath filled with cool water.

'Honey, you got heat exhaustion, stay there,' she said.

I couldn't relax. 'Where are my friends?'

'Don't fret. They're resting elsewhere.'

I stared at the shadows on the roof as they shifted. The building appeared to be made from wood, bricks, and mud. On one side of the hut, near the largest window, was a bench covered in jars. Leaves hung from the roof in bundles. Curtains partitioned other parts of the hut. I wondered how many people lived here. *This must be the other settlement. We made it.*

The woman's blue dress was beautiful. *Like wrapping yourself in a piece of the sky.* We don't wear coloured clothing, except sometimes for Month Parties.

She made me drink water slowly, and then gave me a strange white liquid. It smelled thick and fatty and unfamiliar. I turned my head away.

'Sorry, I don't want it.'

'Are you right to get out? I'll dry you down. I'm Lily Frederick, the medicine woman here.'

'Hi, Lily Frederick. I'm Marri.'

'That's what yon fellas told me.'

She helped me get out of the bath and patted me down with a blanket.

'You gotta sleep, honey.' She gave me a soft, loose dress, and then helped me to a curtained alcove with a sleeping mat. Beside it stood a bucket, like the one they gave me as a toilet in sequestration. I stopped, suspicious.

'You're not going to sequester me?' She looked at me uncomprehendingly. 'You know, lock me up?'

She was shocked. 'That wouldn't be hospitable. You're our *guest.*'

As I lay down, still wary, three blonde children peeped into the hut. When Lily gestured to them, they entered. They appeared to be aged about nine, six and four, but it was hard to tell because they looked bigger and sturdier than our children. They stared at me, their eyes wide and their mouths hanging open. I stared back, wondering what they were doing here.

Lily put her hands on her hips. 'This here's Marri, from Below. She's been sick and I'm looking after her. She's having a kip now. You kids have to be very quiet and very nice to her, all right?'

'Yes, Mama,' chorused the children. Lily pulled the curtain, enclosing the bed, giving me privacy.

I wondered what 'Mama' meant. I reminded myself to ask later.

The children talked quietly nearby. The youngest one got over-excited and the others shushed it. Despite this, I quickly I fell asleep.

I woke early the next day. I studied the wall: mud bricks, scavenged red bricks, straw and wood, but no giant ants. *Thank the Earth for that.* Eventually, I sat up. When I didn't collapse, I stood. *Yowch, forgot about the blisters.*

I peeked from behind the curtain. Five people were seated around a wooden table in the centre of the building: Lily, the three blonde children and a man. The man had brown, thinning hair and like the others, he was tall, tanned and well-built. They were eating a gloopy white food.

Lily saw me. 'Marri! You're up!'

I was filled with questions. Why were the children with these adults? This was too small to be a communal eating area. Were these the *only* people in the settlement? But I was sure I remembered seeing other people. And Felix and Macon must be nearby, unless Macon had already left.

Lily helped me to the table. Then she gestured to the man. 'This here's my husband, Jon. And these are our children, Elize, Willem and Freya.'

'Hello, Myuzband Jon,' I said to the man. The children giggled, and Lily gave them a stern look.

'Just Jon.' The man's voice was deep and resonant. He held out his hand, and seemed to expect a response. Tentatively, I held out my own hand and he grasped it and shook it. After he'd let go, I waved to the children. Fortunately, this seemed to be a shared gesture. They waved back, smiling.

Lily had described them as '*our* children.' Did she mean they were hers and Jon's? *Surely no one would confess* that *kind of thing over breakfast!*

The food was called 'porridge', but it wasn't grey and slimy like ours. Lily poured first white liquid and then golden liquid into it. It reminded me of the time we found a stash of treacle. Lily watched me demolish the porridge with pleasure.

'We use our home-grown milk and honey. You all don't look like you get enough to eat.'

Home-grown milk? The only milk I knew of was breast-milk. I almost choked on my mouthful.

'Where does this milk come from, Lily Frederick?' I asked, trying not to look at Lily's breasts.

'The *cows*, silly!' said little Freya.

I didn't know who or what the cows might be. 'Is that where this orange sweet milk comes from too?'

Everyone stared at me. 'Ain't you never had honey afore?' said Willem.

I shook my head. 'It's delicious! Could I have more?'

'If you ain't used to it, it might upset your stomach,' said Lily.

I followed Lily's advice. I seemed to remember I had already vomited on Macon recently. I hoped it had been a dream.

Lily, Jon and the children cleared the table. I tried to help, but they made me sit down.

Jon stood and kissed Lily's cheek, and I looked away with embarrassment.

'I'd better get the cows milked and pastured,' Jon said then.

'They don't milk themselves. Elize and Willem, you don't have to help today on account of our guest.'

To my surprise, before he left, he kissed each child on the head and they said in unison, 'Bye, Papa!' I wondered what this ritual signified.

The children started playing a noisy game, and soon tried to draw me in.

'You kids leave poor Marri alone,' said Lily. 'Go collect the eggs, then you can play *somewhere else* if you want to be noisy. How about you find your cousins? Remember, school this afternoon. You can come back and talk to Marri later.'

Little of what Lily said to the children made sense to me, but the children understood and scattered out the door.

Lily stacked the clean bowls on a shelf. 'That dark haired boy—Felix?—came by this morning.'

I smiled. 'He's my best friend.'

'He was so pleased you were recovering—he was blaming himself for your illness.'

'It wasn't his fault.'

Lily took out a wooden board, and began to chop leaves on it.

'Can I help, Lily Frederick?' I asked, fidgeting.

Lily waved her hand. 'You rest. And just call me Lily, honey.'

I admired her neat cutting actions. *Chop, chop, chop!* The knife sliced through leaves and stalks, leaving even pieces behind. Her fingers were long and slender, and her hands were tanned and strong. I breathed in the aromatic smell of the leaves.

'What are you making?'

'Well, I'm the medical woman. This herb is one my gramma said is good for reducing fever, specially mixed with yarrow. Do you use herbs down Below?'

I shook my head. 'We use scavenged medicine. There was a man who used to be a doctor before the Catastrophe, and he knew a lot, but he's dead. We have Strikeforce medics, and the Barren midwives help with birthing.'

'Barren midwives? Who are they?'

'Older women who've finished producing offspring. They help us with births. One of the best jobs for Barrens.'

Lily frowned. 'Okay.' After some rhythmic chopping, she said, 'Never heard of "Barrens" afore.'

'Oh.' *Maybe they have a different word for it?*

Lily scraped the herbs into a scavenged jar with a metal lid. After she had put the jar on the shelf, she asked, 'Do you have any children yet, Marri?'

I looked at my hands. 'Yes. They're at home.' My eyes filled, and I blinked, trying to stifle inappropriate emotions. I hoped the three-year-olds weren't too sad that I wasn't on duty.

Lily's face fell. 'It must be hard, being away from them. Who's looking after them while you're up here? Their father?'

I was taken aback. '*Everyone* looks after the children, not just sires.'

'Right.' She looked me up and down. 'You look too young. You can't be more than fifteen.'

I pulled myself up. 'Actually, I'm *almost* nineteen. I've produced three live offspring. Two girls, one boy.'

'Just like me. So how old were you when you had your first?'

'Fifteen.'

She whistled. 'Usually we leave it a tad later here. Seventeen or eighteen at least. I was twenty-four when I had Elize.'

'It's our duty to repopulate the earth. And I was glad I wasn't Barren.'

'That means when you can't have kids, right? Or you don't? That happens up here too, sometimes. It's sad if they wanted them, but not everyone does.'

I stared at her. 'You're not a useful member of society if you're Barren.' I pushed my sleeve up to reveal the tattoo on my left inner elbow: three interlinked circles. 'This shows I've produced live offspring. My children bear that tattoo on their left wrists.'

Lily stared at my tattooed arms. 'What're the other marks for? I saw them last night.'

I looked at her in surprise. 'The left wrist shows which woman birthed me and the right shows which man sired me.'

I held up each arm as I spoke, then looked at her arms. 'You don't have any tattoos!' I paused. 'How do you know your parentage? How do you ensure that you don't—ah—partner with a half-sibling?'

Lily's mouth gaped in a comical round shape. 'We know who our parents are, who our brothers and sisters are. Do you not know down Below?'

I hastened to fix her misunderstanding. 'Of course we do— from the tattoos.' I paused. 'Full siblings are rare, apart from twins, but—anyway, I've got twenty-three half-siblings still living. Maybe twenty-four?'

She whistled. 'Were your mother and father married to other people afore they had you? Or after?'

Married? It sounded like my name, but I didn't know what it meant. 'Maybe, I don't know. They're dead.'

Lily opened her mouth to ask another question, but a hesitant sound outside interrupted us. Someone pushed the hut door open and peeked in.

'Come in,' said Lily.

Felix's strained face appeared around the door frame, but as soon as he saw me, a smile replaced the frown. He hugged me so hard that my ribs creaked. His eyes were wet. 'I would never have forgiven myself if you'd died.'

I pulled away, embarrassed. 'Felix, I'm tougher than that.

Anyway, I hear I have to thank you and Macon for saving me.'

Felix turned red. 'Macon did the running. I just sat with you—'

'You got her to drink water and cooled her down; that was important too,' commented Lily. She cleared the table. 'Why don't you have a cup of tea?'

The tea was bitter and strong; nothing like moss tea. I took very small sips. Felix asked me how my feet were; his were still sore. Lily found something to put on the blisters which she said might heal them. We couldn't thank her enough.

Then Lily asked to see Felix's tattoos. I explained to Felix that they didn't have tattoos here. Felix was as surprised as I had been, but he readily showed his wrists, and I held up mine.

'See, his are different, that means we have different progenitors.'

'Do you have one on your elbow, like Marri?' Lily asked Felix.

Felix and I gaped. This question raised the possibility that Felix was or could become Barren, but I realised that Lily had no idea that she'd been rude.

'Not yet—' I stopped. *I'll find out in a week or two whether anything's come of our partnership.*

Felix glanced at me, blushed, and chewed his nails.

Lily realised from our mutual discomfort that she'd asked something inappropriate, and her face filled with worry.

I tried to think of something to take the conversation in a different direction, and blurted out the first thing on my mind. 'Has Macon gone home yet?'

Felix looked at Lily, and she frowned.

'What's happened?' A horrible thought hit me, like a crossbow through my heart.

Lily stood and patted my shoulder. 'Your friend's scarce in

a better state than you right now, that's all. He's staying with my sister Kayla across the way. He'll recover in a few days.'

'He has to go home! He *should've* gone home already. They'll think he's with us.'

My heart hammered in my chest. *If they find him here, they'll hang him! It's my fault!*

Lily patted my back. 'Hush, chick. I'll get you a drink to calm you down.'

I sat rigidly while Lily boiled some leaves in a pot. Her stove was made of blackened metal, and had a compartment underneath for putting in fuel, as well as a metal pipe taking the smoke out through the roof. Ramala would have loved it.

Felix leaned back and chewed his thumbnail. 'Macon never told us why he didn't go home that night—when he had the chance.'

'He did, he thought we were too hopeless to survive.'

'Don't get me wrong, I'm grateful. But we both know he wouldn't have come back if it wasn't for you.'

'He wanted to be the hero, as usual.'

'For you—because he loves you. And you still love him.'

I crossed my arms, my face burning. 'I don't care what happens to him.'

Felix rolled his eyes. 'Don't be stupid! You almost collapsed just then—!'

I was prepared to admit to myself that perhaps my statement wasn't the most convincing I'd ever made, but I glowered anyway.

Lily returned with a cup. 'Marri should drink this and go back to bed.'

I drank the bitter medicine. Felix stared at the table as if something fascinating was written within the grain of the wood. A lassitude filled me and my breathing calmed.

Lily flapped her hands at Felix. 'Shoo—come back this

afternoon and check on her.'

Felix hugged me again. 'Glad to see you're looking better. Sleep well.' He left.

Lily tucked me into bed, and looked at me with her head on one side. 'You went pale as a sheet then. Is Macon your sweetheart?'

'Sweet ... heart? Not if that means what I think it means.' I turned my face to the wall. 'Maybe once. It's—messy. Everything's a mess.'

'I got that sense. Anyway, go to sleep, or I'll spank you like one of my kids.'

The threat was made in jest, but I settled my head on the pillow anyway.

As I drifted into sleep, I worried that I'd dream of times past, but thankfully, the herbal drink gifted me a deep and dreamless sleep.

CHAPTER 12

On my second day in the settlement, I asked where the communal eating area was. I was worried that my illness had kept Lily and Jon from joining everyone else. They were confused, until I explained that everyone ate together at home. They explained in turn that people in their settlement ate meals in separate huts. Everyone only ate together during celebrations. I wasn't sure how the hut groups were chosen, and it sounded lonely.

Lily said, 'No, honey, there's always people about.'

That morning, Lily turned the cows' milk into a thick yellow paste by attacking it with a wooden paddle, and I watched with silent fascination. The children asked about my life Below and about the children of my body. To my shame, I couldn't answer all their questions, although I did my best.

In the mid-morning, Lily's sibling Kayla visited. She was a smaller, brown-haired version of Lily, with a ready smile. Her three offspring were the mysterious 'cousins' that Lily's offspring often played with. The eldest two were blonde-haired and blue-eyed, but the third child was dark-haired and dark-eyed with brown skin. The children rushed outside.

Lily put the kettle on the black stove, and Kayla sat opposite me. Lily laid out tea cups and poured the tea, and the siblings chatted about people in the settlement.

Then Kayla turned to me. 'Lily said you got upset yesterday, honey, but don't worry, he's recovering well. You're always welcome to visit. Don't be shy!'

I gave into temptation. 'Okay. I'll see him.'

Lily made me slip on her old shoes they were far too large. My eyes watered as I emerged from the hut. I shaded my eyes with my hands and looked quickly around. The settlement was on a long straight road with huts on either side. They were built of mud brick and wood, but they had used scavenged material here and there. The air smelled of wood smoke and dung, quite different to Lily's herb-scented house.

They led me to a hut across the road. Kayla held the door open. The hut was full of balls of thread, fluff and wooden frames filled with half-finished cloth. There was a wooden wheel in the corner of the room.

Kayla followed my gaze. 'I'm a weaver.'

I inspected a wooden frame, admiring the interwoven threads. I stroked it gently with my finger. 'I never knew blankets were made like this?'

Meanwhile, Kayla checked behind a curtain. 'Want me to wake him?'

'No, please don't! I'll just check he's okay.'

Kayla pulled back the curtain and fetched a three-legged wooden stool for me.

Macon looked vulnerable while he was sleeping. I had a sudden desire to kiss his cheek, but instead I patted his knee through the blankets. He stirred. I stood and drew the curtain before he could wake and see me. I wanted to work out what to say before we spoke again.

'I should get back to Lily's place.' Shamefully, my voice quavered.

Kayla's face was sympathetic when we returned to Lily's house. 'Is he your brother then?'

'Is he what?'

'You know, are you brother and sister?'

I'd heard Lily call Kayla her *sister*, but I wasn't sure what it meant.

Lily intervened. 'She calls it *sibling*, from what she's said afore. I don't think he is.'

My jaw dropped. '*No!* Didn't you notice that his wrist tattoos are different to mine?'

Kayla looked distressed. 'Sorry.' Then she paused. 'So, he's your husband, then—?'

'Shh!' Lily shook her head at Kayla.

I ran my hand through my hair, and looked at both women. I'd thought that Jon's name was *Myuzband*, and I realised that this *yeruzband* was probably a similar idea. But I had to confess: 'I don't know what an *uzband* is.'

'You know what marriage is, right—?' said Kayla, slowly.

I gave them a helpless look. Kayla and Lily stared at one another.

Then Kayla began to explain. 'You know, where two people agree they'll live together as a family? They might have kids, too. *Husband*'s the word for a man, *wife*'s the word for a woman, at least that's what we call it here—'

'*Oh*, like an offer at a Month Party? No, I'm not registered with Macon at the moment, although we were once—' I trailed off as I realised that the women were looking at me with incomprehension.

'What's a Month Party?' asked Kayla.

'Registered?' asked Lily, at the same time.

It was my turn to struggle. 'Well, Month Parties are for people who aren't partnered or Barren—'

Lily's brow creased. 'And what do you do at these parties?'

'You offer yourself to the person you want to partner with—and if they accept, you register your relationship. Then the woman waits to see what comes of it before entering into the next relationship—'

Kayla pursed her mouth. 'What should come of it?'

'A child, of course.'

'And *the next relationship*?' I could see them both looking uneasily at me, as if they were afraid of what I would say.

'You're supposed to share yourself, to have as many registered partnerships as you can, so you can bear children to different sires. We're creating a diverse new society.'

The siblings stared, disbelief written over their faces. Their gazes were disconcertingly similar. I was unsure what I had said wrong. I bit my lip and silently cursed my careless talk.

'So it's true what they say about orgies and stuff? I thought that was made up.'

Kayla's mouth turned down, but she looked more fascinated than disgusted. 'You sleep with different men at the same time and have babies with them all?'

I corrected Kayla. 'Not at the same time! You *only* share with your partner—but once that partnership is over, you have a duty to form new partnerships, if the woman hasn't borne a child.'

Lily looked disgusted. 'What about sharing diseases—?'

'There's none of that,' I assured her. 'Anyone who's diseased is made Barren, or exiled, or executed.'

Lily composed herself. 'What if there's no one you fancy? Or you don't feel like being pregnant all the time? Even our cows get a rest now and then!'

I chose my words carefully. 'The Chief Councillor knows best. If we don't share ourselves, we're locked up or exiled. At least we can choose whose offers we accept. The men who never get accepted are made Barren, so we don't have to worry about them. It's all quite fair.'

'*Bullshit*,' said Kayla. 'Bull-fuckin'-shit!'

Lily slapped Kayla's arm, then glanced up at a picture of an old woman propped by the jars on her herb shelf. 'Wash your mouth out, sis.'

I watched the siblings. *Don't they share here? Kayla's offspring look to have different sires. What other way is there?*

Eventually Kayla said, 'Why do you have to keep swapping?'

'It's our duty.' I studied the lines on my palm. 'It can be hard. The Council had to force … my first partner and me to end our partnership. They say it gets easier.'

I stopped, suddenly struck by sadness. I had cried bitterly for days afterwards and had been consoled by Suze, then heavily pregnant with her eighth child. *I hope she's all right.*

'Well, that's a funny kind of marriage,' said Lily, still looking unsettled. 'Though there's plenty of marriages are kind of funny, I suppose.'

Kayla held up her empty cup. 'More tea!'

'Good idea,' said Lily. She filled the kettle with water from the big barrel outside the hut.

After Lily had come back inside, and put the kettle on the stove, Kayla turned to me. 'You offer yourself to people at this here party for a time, right? And then you swap?'

I nodded. 'The maximum is twenty-six weeks. Then you have to end the partnership, unless something's come of it already.'

'Well, with marriage, you're partners with someone for good, no swapping.'

It was my turn to be astonished. 'But … what if you offer yourself to someone and later you don't want to be with them anymore?'

'Hah!' said Kayla. 'I wish I thought of that when I was your age!'

Lily sighed. 'Our Ma let Kayla marry a man from the other town. Oh, he was devilish handsome and charming, but he was no good.'

Kayla shrugged. 'Yeah, Bert's the father of my oldest two. He went back to his town in the hills, but he sees them twice a year when he comes trading. Course, he's got lots of other wives back home.'

I blinked, trying to process what I'd just heard. 'There's *another* settlement? This man was from there?' *This could be important. If things don't work out for Felix and me here ...*

'The hill town,' said Kayla impatiently.

'That kettle's boiled,' said Lily, and poured more tea. I hadn't finished the first cup, but Lily refilled my cup to the brim.

I held the warm cup with both hands and stared into it. 'Kayla, how come this man went away?'

'We *divorced.*'

I frowned. 'What's that?'

'Ended the marriage. Wouldn't've been allowed to divorce in the hill town. But he married me here, so bad luck for him. At least the Council had the sense to insist on that—'

I narrowed my eyes. 'You didn't stay together for good. That's like what we do—'

Kayla laughed. 'I hadn't thought of it like that! 'Cept it's not the same, cos we ain't *forced* to end it. We end it if we decide we want to. Or one of us does.'

'Oh, okay.' I paused. 'Why did you end it? If you don't mind me asking—'

Kayla scrunched her eyes closed. 'He hit me, and he carried on with other women.'

I winced. 'If someone's violent at home, you can end the partnership after eight weeks. And men who are like that find it difficult to get women to accept their offers—'

'Well that's something, I suppose—'

'But why was it wrong for that man to do his duty with other women if he'd already sired children with you?'

The two women stared as if I'd sprouted rat's whiskers.

Lily frowned. 'He'd agreed to stay with *Kayla*. Part of the problem was, in *his* town, fellas can have as many wives as they want. Ma should never have let you marry him.'

Kayla shook her head, her eyes suspiciously shiny. 'I thought I loved him—'

I cocked my head as I recalled something Lily had said. 'So men can have many women in the other town?'

Lily wrinkled her nose for reasons that I didn't understand. 'Yeah.'

'Then ... can the women have as many men as they like too—?'

Both women burst out laughing, as if I'd said the funniest thing in the whole world.

'Now that'd be interesting!' said Kayla, when she could breathe again.

'One's more than enough for me, thanks,' said Lily, slapping Kayla's back.

I didn't understand why they had laughed. 'Why doesn't it work that way? My home isn't perfect, but at least we share. We're *all* supposed to swap, regardless of who we are.'

The two women looked thoughtful.

'You're right, it ain't fair,' said Kayla. 'The big fellows benefit, but I bet it's the same Below.'

I sipped my tea then grimaced; it was cold. I pushed the cup away. 'Yeah.'

Lily sipped her tea. 'We're lucky that we have ways of stopping us from having children here.'

I blinked with shock and choked. 'What?'

Such things were outlawed at home. I wondered how to ask more about this in a subtle way, but before I could say anything Kayla spoke again.

'You ain't missing out, anyway. I'm never marrying again.' She looked narrowly at Lily.

'You should marry Alex properly! Ma would've liked it—' Lily pointed at the picture of the woman on the shelf.

Kayla crossed her arms. 'I don't give a bloody cow's arse what Ma would say—!'

Lily crossed her arms. 'What if his parents decide Raf's not gonna get the land?'

Kayla glared at her sibling. 'A kid's enough, and they've said it's fine—'

Lily sighed. Then she saw my confusion. 'Kayla's with a local fellow called Alex—nice man—but they ain't married formal-like.'

'Formal-like?'

'They just had a kid together, but no ceremony. You saw Raf afore, the youngest kid. But what if Alex's parents kick up a fuss—'

Kayla interrupted. 'You're so *stuffy*, Lily. They *won't*, they're fine—'

'It ain't just me being stuffy. Marriage makes you part of someone else's family, and people pass on stuff after they're dead to family. Like ... land that they own.'

Kayla was about to throw her teacup at Lily. I decided to keep the conversation to our subterran customs.

'No one owns anything where I come from, especially not land. We share everything. There's nothing to pass on after you're dead, and you're not supposed to have emotional attachments to the children of your body—or to anyone else.'

'Seems kind of sad?' said Lily.

I shrugged. 'Just the way it is. But Kayla, if everyone knows who the sires of your offspring are, surely there's no need to register?'

Kayla looked triumphant, but Lily subsided with an unhappy expression. I grimaced, worried that I'd offended my host.

After a long pause, while we silently sipped our tea, Kayla raised her eyebrows. 'So, how many partners have you had,

Marri? It must be at least three—?'

I stared at my fingernails and blushed.

Lily frowned. 'Kayla!'

I felt I owed them an answer of sorts. 'Macon was my first partner, when I was fourteen ...'

Lily smiled with triumph. 'Hah! I figured that one out, honey.'

Kayla's brow creased. 'But—but you said you're not partners now—or not *registered*?' Her eyes softened. 'Aw, have you run off with him?'

'You're so bloody romantical,' said Lily. 'Look how it turned out for you—!'

'You're so cold-blooded,' retorted Kayla. 'You just married who Ma told you to marry!'

'*No!*' I yelled over the bickering. 'I did *not* run off with Macon. My present registered partner is Felix—'

Kayla guffawed, almost knocking her teacup over. It teetered but stayed upright. 'No wonder you was asking about women with multiple husbands!'

I bridled. 'No! We don't have two partners at the same time.'

Lily frowned. 'But ... *both* your partners are here, past and present? No wonder they was both fussing over you like broody mama hens.'

'Macon wasn't supposed to come. It was awkward when he joined us.'

Kayla was still laughing. 'No crap! Two husbands together!'

I pushed down irritation with difficulty. 'It's not like that. If we got upset about former partners, we'd tear each other's eyes out. There's sometimes friction, but it's discouraged as inappropriate attachment. It's awkward because—because—'

'Why?' said Kayla.

Lily glared at her sibling. 'Not everyone wants to share their private life with the world, Kayla Weaver.'

'I may as well explain.' I sighed and stared at my teacup. 'Felix and Macon don't like each other. They never have. I don't know where I stand with Felix, because—it's complicated. I'll know more once I find out if anything's come of our partnership.'

The two women glanced at each other, gaped, and then turned back to me, their eyes wide. I wasn't quite sure why they were so shocked.

'You called him your best friend, then your partner—now you're *pregnant* to him?' said Lily. 'Things move fast down Below!'

I reddened. 'We felt obliged to do our duty, even though ...' I wasn't sure how to finish that thought. 'And Macon and I haven't—well, we hadn't—spoken to each other for over a year—'

'Aw! That's sad,' said Kayla, sighing.

I shrugged. 'Like I said, it's complicated—'

But Kayla's mind had gone down another track. 'You know, the first thing he did when he woke was to ask about you?'

I blinked, and my heart turned over in my chest. 'Really?'

'I'm not lying.'

I inspected my thumbnail, trying to pretend that my heart wasn't beating faster. 'Any decent person would do that.'

To my relief, Lily and Kayla's offspring burst into the room, talking about some baby birds they'd found. I made the mistake of wishing that I could see them, and the children tried to drag me out the door.

'Trust me, you don't want to see them. They got no feathers. They're disgusting,' said Kayla.

I looked confused and she took pity on me, like I was a child.

'Feathers are the covering birds have. Underneath they're pink and bald—horrible! And their eyes are big and bulgy.'

I decided I'd pass. Kayla clapped her hands. 'Mama's gotta do some work. No more shilly-shallying!' Her three children stood behind her, giggling and pinching each other.

She bid me farewell, and left. Lily looked me up and down. 'Time for you to have another sleep.'

It took me a while to fall asleep. There was so much information to take in. Everything I'd ever known had been shaken.

I couldn't see how I could return—they'd probably hang me—but the prospect of staying in this strange society was frightening, even though Lily and Jon had been so kind. I didn't know whether they'd allow Felix and me to live here. I hadn't dared raise it with Lily and Jon. I had never fitted into my own society, but this society seemed utterly alien. Maybe we didn't fit anywhere.

Despite the problems with my life back home, I wept silent tears into my pillow. I wished I could see the children again. I wanted a cup of moss tea. I wanted to talk to my friends. Had anything come of Suze's partnership with Peter? She had seemed happy. I hoped Pia wasn't too worried about Macon. What was going to happen with Felix and me?

Then I allowed myself to think about Macon. *Is Kayla right? Does he still care about me?* I stopped that train of thought. *Even if she's right, he has to go home.* I began to cry again.

I screwed my eyes shut and tried not to think about anything. Instead, I concentrated on breathing evenly, in and out, until I fell asleep.

CHAPTER 13

After four days, the settlement was still alien but less scary. A turning point had occurred when I discovered that women could read and write here. Lily wrote down her treatments on a stiff brown paper. She asked me why I was watching her so intently, and I explained that our women didn't learn to read or write, and that Felix had taught me in secret.

Lily was horrified. 'We have to know how to write. How would you keep records? Trading, recipes, all that?'

After that, she let me practise writing and reading. At night Elize and Willem helped me.

It seemed that 'Papa' and 'Mama' were the respective titles for males and females on their Parental Duties. I hadn't seen anyone come to relieve Lily or Jon from their duties, which seemed to place a heavy burden on them, but I was reluctant to ask how duties were assigned in case it was a sore point. I did ask Jon why he kissed the children on the head when he left in the morning.

Jon scratched his head. 'I want to let them know I love them. Do you not do that Below?'

A stab of something between jealousy and surprise went through me. 'No.'

'But what about your own Pa?' When I crinkled my brow, Jon said, 'I mean the man who fathered you?'

'I never spoke to my sire.'

Lily's jaw dropped. '*Never*? In your whole life?'

I shook my head.

Willem piped up. 'Maybe, you could talk to your Papa

when you go home?'

'He's dead. So's the woman who birthed me. She died just after I was born.'

Elize sidled up to me and patted my arm, and Willem frowned. I was unsure why the children were upset. 'Please don't feel bad. I'm fine!'

'Mama, Mama, when can we show Marri the animals?' asked Freya, breaking the miserable mood.

'I won't let you show her at all if you keep hassling me about it, Freya!'

'Awwww!' said the children, and Freya stuck her trembling lower lip out.

Lily sighed. 'Tomorrow. I think she'll be well enough tomorrow.' The children cheered.

The next morning, when I woke, the children were waiting. They had been carefully trying to make enough noise to wake me but not so much that Lily would tell them off.

We visited the cows first, as I'd been keen to meet the providers of my morning milk. They lived in their own hut and made the occasional lowing sounds I'd heard before. The hut smelled like sweaty animal and dung. I was introduced to a cow named 'Buttercup'. She was huge and furry, much larger than the nasty black dog. She had a wet mucus-covered snout and whitish-yellow fur, and her feet were huge and hard. Her eyes were pink-rimmed, fringed by thick lashes, and her horns were the colour of bone. Her colouring was like some of the rats we encountered underground, but I hadn't realised that a similar colouring could be present in other animals. My surprise delighted the children.

'Buttercup has to stay indoors on hot days, otherwise she gets sunburned,' said Willem.

Buttercup stood placidly, swinging her funny tufted tail.

Suddenly the tail lifted and stinking crap spurted out, staining her white fur. I recoiled, and Freya and Willem giggled hysterically. The cow chewed thoughtfully. I looked at the green slobber around her mouth. I was pleased when the children confirmed that cows only ate plants and grass, but I wouldn't be approaching a cow soon. Elize showed off and milked the cow. I decided not to try it myself.

From far off, I thought the next creatures we saw were dogs, and gave a little scream. The children told me they were actually 'goats' and 'sheep' and that they belonged to Lily and Jon's neighbour, who saw us looking and approached us. This confused me: surely the whole community should share in them? The neighbour looked at me oddly.

'These are *my* beasts,' he said. 'Lily and Jon have *their* beasts. We trade stuff: milk and wool and meat. You know, like your village trades with our village? We're a trading village.'

He explained that the fences showed which pieces of land belonged to him. I'd thought the fences were there to keep the animals from wandering off.

'Yeah, that's so, but they also be for showing ownership,' he said.

'What if I want to cross your land?' I asked.

'Well then, you ask me, and I'll probably let you,' he said. I remembered that Macon had once told me that Councillors had private offices that no one entered without invitation. Maybe it was like that? I couldn't imagine having to ask.

But I was glad there was a fence: some of the adult sheep and goats had spikes on their heads. The babies were cute, though. The baby goats were called kids and bounced around like they were on springs. *That's why Lily calls her children 'kids',* I realised with pleasure.

Lily and Jon's neighbour had tame dogs, which he used to round up the sheep and to keep away wild dogs. I stayed away, explaining that I'd come across some unpleasant dogs on my way to the settlement. The dogs frolicked and licked the children—but I didn't know if they might go crazy like that black dog.

I was more comfortable with the chickens. They lived in a small fenced hut next to Lily and Jon's hut. I finally saw 'feathers' for myself: a cross between fur and scales. Willem collected a brownish-red feather for me and I stroked it, enjoying the way its filaments stuck together neatly if you stroked it in the right way. Elize showed me how to feel under the chickens for eggs. I wasn't brave enough to try it; the chicken had pecked her as she slid her hand under it. But I gently patted a chicken and it made a *bok bok bok* noise and bobbed its head. I wished I could show it to the children back home.

A more brightly-coloured chicken strode into the hut. I laughed as an irresistible image of Leo's strutting walk sprang into my head. It made a sudden noise, its throat swelling. *Kooki-roo-ki-koo-rooooo!* I put my hands to my head and grimaced, and the children laughed again.

'What happens when they all do that? It must be deafening!'

'He's the boy, the rooster,' explained Elize. 'The gals don't do that.'

I shook my head at the Leo-chicken, who was still strutting around proudly, and we left the chickens behind.

Our next destination was the lake on the outskirts of the settlement. A growing gang of children followed us at a distance. I waved at them, and they came closer. We found Felix in the centre of the settlement. He looked as if he wanted to hide behind a hut when he saw the gaggle of children approach, but they *adored* him, as the children had back home. I wondered whether they liked his shyness, which made him non-threatening. *Perhaps children are like cats! Maybe they shower attention on people who ignore them!*

As we passed a large round building, an old woman emerged and glared at us. The children scattered, apart from Lily's three offspring—and even they slowly backed away. Felix and I picked up their tension and moved with them.

But the woman followed us. 'When're you going home?'

I gaped, unsure what to say.

Felix stopped. 'We're not sure.'

The old woman narrowed her eyes, and her wrinkled mouth pursed. 'I don't want your perverted ways tainting us. You should go home, sooner rather than later.'

Felix jerked as if he'd been slapped in the face and I gripped his wrist.

A bald toothless man emerged and waved a stick at the woman. 'Oh my *gawd*, Zara, leave the poor things alone.' The old woman retreated, and the old man looked apologetic. 'Zara don't know the meaning of hospitality.'

We asked the children if we could visit the lake another day. Felix pulled his arm from my grip and said that he'd like to go for a walk *alone*.

I tried to reassure him, although I was still shaking from the old woman's words. 'There's another settlement ... there are other places we can go—'

His face twisted. 'You don't know that, Marri! All this could be for *nothing*. I need to think about this.' He stalked away, his shoulders hunched.

The children and I looked at the chickens again. Then they went to school, but I didn't want to go back to Lily and Jon's hut.

Eventually, I lay under a big old tree, and squinted at the sunlight flickering through the leaves. I was anxious about the issue of land ownership, but no one seemed to care that I was lying there.

I worried about the old lady's words. *What will they think of Felix? How do we raise it with them? What will they do to him? Where can we run to next?*

But I couldn't stay worried for long. Each leaf seemed to have its own individual space. Glimmers of sunlight shifted in the green. *Beautiful. Soothing ...*

I fell asleep. When I woke, it was darker, but the sun hadn't set. I yawned and stretched.

'Oops, didn't mean to fall asleep,' I said to myself.

Someone laughed. 'You were snoring! I was going to drop a leaf into your mouth to wake you up. But I didn't want to be vomited on again ...'

I sat up quickly. Macon was sitting beside me.

'I was hoping that that was just a fever dream.' I shoved his shoulder. 'Don't mention it again to anyone, you mean ... *Monster Rat!*'

He grinned. His eyes were green with gold lights, just like the leaves. 'You're so funny when you're annoyed!'

'You're so annoying when you try to be funny.'

The smile left his face, and he paused. 'Seriously, are you feeling all right? You look better.'

'Almost back to normal again, just tired.'

'I was worried—'

I shrugged. 'I was too unwell to be worried.' I remembered the giant ant crawling out of the tree. 'I saw ... some strange things, but they weren't real.'

Macon looked into my eyes. 'You collapsed, and you weren't responding. I've seen someone else in that situation die—on a Strikeforce mission. I was terrified, but that helped me to run faster—'

I broke eye contact. 'I really appreciate it, okay?' I stood, leaning on the tree trunk as I got up, and moved away a little.

'I should get going. It's time for dinner.'

'I guess I should go back too.' Macon winced as he stood.

I stared. 'Are *you* okay, Macon? I don't remember the journey here, but it seemed like a long way on the map.'

Macon turned away. 'When I was running, I kept thinking about all the things I'd stuffed up. There are reasons for what I did, but I'm not proud—'

My jaw dropped.

He took a deep breath and turned to me. 'I should have stood up to him. If you never want to see me again, I'll understand.'

I was distracted by the tears which suddenly rolled down my cheeks, onto the dress I'd borrowed from Lily.

'Don't go.' I reached for him and he embraced me. I buried my face in his shoulder and cried and he patted my hair. We stood like that for a long time, even after I'd stopped crying. I had forgotten how safe I had always felt in his arms. Then my nose tickled, so I put my head up.

I kissed his cheek to show that I appreciated the apology. I loved the scent of his skin. After that, I kissed him on the lips, although I hadn't meant to. *Just like when we first met.* He didn't respond for about five heartbeats, but his eyes widened.

Then he pulled me to him, and we kissed again, passionately, just as we had at that Month Party all those years ago. I remembered why I had accepted his offer of partnership in the first place, despite my reservations. Somehow, it had felt as if we belonged together.

After some moments—I had no idea how long—one of his hands moved to my hip and I pressed myself closer, winding my arm more tightly around his back.

Koo-ki-roo-ki-koo-rooooo! The male Leo-chicken crowed somewhere behind us. We both jumped.

Sense reasserted itself. We let go of one another, and

stepped apart quickly.

The pupils of Macon's eyes were wide and dark and we were both breathing heavily.

We shouldn't have done that.

After a while I spoke. 'Like I was saying, I should get back for dinner.' My voice was unsteady.

'Right,' he said. 'Good idea.'

We walked back to the huts, not touching one another and parting without speaking.

'Ah, good, Jon was just setting the table,' said Lily as I came in. 'We were worried.'

'I was talking to Macon.' Blood rushed into my cheeks.

Lily pretended not to notice. 'Could you put the bread on the table, honey?'

I hurried to get the bread. As we ate, the children told Lily and Jon about our day.

'Marri's really scared of animals,' said Willem. 'She got scared when Mister Rooster crowed, and she jumped so bad when Buttercup pooped—that was real funny—but that's okay cos she's never seen them afore.'

'I'm a little bit scared of cows too,' piped up Freya, sweetly supportive.

I tried to restore my dignity. 'The chickens were good! And Elize did a great job of getting those round egg things out. Maybe I'll try tomorrow.'

The children insisted that I *had* to collect the eggs tomorrow.

Jon, who otherwise spoke as few words as he could, told the children a story at bedtime. I listened, as I had on previous evenings. He was an engaging and inventive storyteller. I couldn't follow the story entirely because of his accent and the unfamiliar words, but a tricky animal got its comeuppance, after twists and turns.

Jon and Lily kissed the children and pulled the curtain on their alcove. I wished I could put my children to bed like that.

Once the children were asleep, Lily boiled the kettle and got out the tea.

'So,' she said in a low voice, 'This morning, Macon told some of the Elders about a man Below, hassling you and trying to force himself on you.'

I felt my throat where Conor had held it and gulped. 'Yes. He's on the Council. The Chief Counsellor knows about it, but—'

Jon's face darkened. 'Sounds like that fellow needs a lesson,' he growled.

'Is that why you came here, honey?'

I sighed. 'It's not just about me. If Felix goes home, they'll kill him. He hasn't hurt anyone, but our society has rules which he's found difficult to follow. He needs to find out whether your society has the same rules. If so … we'll have to work something out.' I twisted my hands.

'Well, yon Macon wants to talk to all the Elders together,' said Jon. 'Any idea why?'

I blinked with shock. 'He didn't say anything about it.' I ground my teeth. *What's he playing at?*

'There's a meeting tomorrow,' said Lily. 'We'll find out what's happening then.'

CHAPTER 14

The Elders met the next morning, in the round building in the middle of the village. Many of the people in the room were women and some were quite old. The informality surprised me too. Everyone sat on benches around the room, talking.

Felix sat slightly apart, chewing his fingernails. I sat beside him. 'Did you know about this?'

'I only found out this morning.'

I spotted the sour woman who had confronted us yesterday. I tugged Felix's sleeve and gestured subtly.

Felix frowned and whispered, 'I saw her too. Not good.'

Macon strode in, nodding to us as he passed. A small lady with brown skin and grey-streaked brown hair stood up after Macon sat. Everyone hushed and looked at her.

'Welcome to our Meeting of the Elders, people from Below,' she said. 'Please speak.'

Macon stood. 'Thank you for your help. You've taken us in, you've healed us, you've shared food with us.'

Felix and I half-rose and nodded our agreement with Macon's words, and then sat again. A pleased murmur went around the room.

I glanced at Felix and raised my eyebrows. *This can't be all, can it?*

The brown-haired lady said, 'We accept your thanks. But you've indicated that you want to ask something further?'

Macon cleared his throat and shuffled his feet. He looked over at Felix and me. I stared back, wondering what he was doing.

'Would it be possible for one or two people from Below to live as part of this settlement—or near this settlement? For example, if a person was in danger or she might be hurt if she returned Below.'

I gaped. There was a stir around the room.

The brown-haired lady leaned forward. 'What kind of danger?'

'She would be locked up and could well be killed.'

'What has she done?'

'All she's done is leave and come here.'

The lady frowned. 'Please, step outside so that the Elders can talk. We'll call you back when we're ready.'

Almost everyone left, but my heart sank when the sour old lady stayed in her seat.

After we went outside, I confronted Macon, my hands on my hips. 'What under the Earth was *that*?'

Macon winced. 'I meant to talk to you about it yesterday, but I was ... um ... distracted ...'

We looked away from each other, and I covered my cheeks so that no one would see they were hot.

Felix frowned. 'You should have spoken with us, Macon.'

I bit my lip. 'An Elder told Felix and me that we should go home yesterday—'

Macon put his hands up. 'I'm sorry! I need to get things sorted before I leave, and wasn't this was your plan? To stay?' I winced, and he paused. 'Don't you want to stay?'

Felix's brow was creased. 'It depends. I need to ask them something.'

Macon turned to me. 'What about you?'

'I didn't plan to leave, or come here—or stay. Now I'm torn. They're happy for me to read and write. I love the trees, and the colours. But—it's so strange. If I stay here, I'll never see anyone from home again—unless they let Felix stay. Not you, not my friends ... not the children—'

I wiped my eyes and studied my fingers. 'I miss the children. *Parent to one, parent to all.* But I miss the three children of my body, Macon. *My* children, as they'd say here. *Our* children. It's terrible to be separated from them.'

Macon looked stricken. He said in a low voice, 'I don't know any of the children I sired. I've hardly ever been on Parental Duties. They never let me see the child you were sequestered for bearing. *Tomas*, you said?'

'Tomas.' I sighed. 'My sire never knew me—'

Macon's face was bleak. 'Sires can know their children here. *Fathers.* I wish—'

I felt grateful that at least I'd been able to develop some connection with my children. I reached out to pat Macon's shoulder, but drew back. *I shouldn't touch him again.*

Suddenly Felix spoke. 'Our society is not loving. It's a lie! They punish people, over and over. You can't love your own children, you can't be with the person you love—' His voice quavered with suppressed passion. 'I'm sick of it. I hate it.' He turned and walked off. I watched and wondered whether to follow him.

Macon's face went still. 'Sounds like you're staying. I hope you'll be happy together.'

I didn't understand the bitterness in his voice. 'What are you talking about?'

He looked confused. 'You can be with each other here. Not just for six months, but forever. Isn't that what you wanted?'

I crossed my arms. 'Is that why you think we left?'

He hesitated. 'I mean—what happened with us, if that happened again with Felix, and you'd got caught—and you *always* got caught ...'

'So I'm a bad influence on him, like I was on you?'

Macon put his arm on mine. 'You have ... strong feelings,

Marri. *Deep* feelings. You always have. It's one of the things I—'

I snatched my arm away. 'I'm sorry I felt too much—so much more than you did. I suppose you kept coming back to *me* just for—what, practice?'

Macon opened his mouth to retort, his brows drawn with anger, but he closed his mouth as Felix strolled back.

'Sorry,' said Felix. Then he noticed our hostile postures. 'Are you two *fighting*?'

'No,' I said, through clenched teeth. Felix raised his eyebrows.

Macon gave an embarrassed smile. 'You're the worst liar I've *ever* seen, Marri.'

Felix laughed loudly, for far too long.

I glared at the men. 'Bull-fucking-shit to both of you. I hope you both get the vomiting blood disease and the Monster Rat eats you!'

Felix sighed at my expression. 'What were you fighting about, anyway?'

I pursed my lips. 'Macon thinks we've run away together because we're desperately in love, Felix—too much for the world Below—'

Felix ran his hands through his hair and scrunched his face up. 'Oh ... I see ...'

'So, close, but no hydroponic strawberry, wouldn't you say?'

'I care about Marri, deeply—' Felix said to Macon. 'But I'm not in love with her, although maybe I thought I was once ... maybe I *wished* I was ...' After a long pause, Felix looked at me. 'I'm sorry—'

'I know—'

Macon stared at Felix. 'I'm confused—'

Felix laughed bitterly. He pointed at Macon. 'Well, what about *you*? If they say we can stay, are you going home?'

I hadn't dared ask.

Macon's face went still again. 'It depends—'

'I thought so,' said Felix.

Someone fetched us before I could ask what Macon meant. As we walked in, the Elders' faces were grim, and my stomach was suddenly full of fluttering bats' wings. We stood together in the middle of the hall.

The small Elder with the brown and grey hair was evidently the leader. She said, 'We've talked. Most of us are inclined to send you on your way, but we've decided to raise our concerns before we vote.'

'What are the concerns?' said Macon, lines of worry on his face.

'The first is Marri's skills. We know that women from Below are unlettered and usually unskilled—'

'Marri can read and write—' said Macon. The lead Elder stared at me.

Felix jumped in. 'She's quick to learn! I teach reading and writing. I taught her—'

I stepped forward, a core of warmth in my chest, touched by my friends' defence. 'I also know some midwifery, and how to grow mushrooms and plants. If I stay, I'd like to learn about medicine. I've enjoyed seeing what Lily does.'

Lily said gruffly, 'I'll teach Marri if she stays.' Jon beamed.

The lead Elder looked at Felix, her eyes narrow. 'You're a teacher, you said?'

Felix nodded. 'And I know a little about engineering and growing hydroponic plants—'

'We've teachers here, boyo,' said one of Elders. 'We don't need you. Engineering might be some use, but I don't what that eye-dro-whatsie is.'

'What are *your* skills, Macon?' said the lead Elder.

Macon put his chin up. 'I haven't decided if I'll stay. However, I've been trained by the Strikeforces. I led numerous expeditions until—anyway, I'm better at scavenging than anyone here—'

The Elders bridled, and I rolled my eyes at the roof. I caught an Elder laughing at me and tried to restore an expressionless face.

Macon continued. 'I'm a very good engineer. Father trained me. I know about solar generators, pumps, electricity, plumbing, and building crossbows—'

The lead Elder's gaze was sharp. 'I've never heard a man from Below call his sire *Father*. Who is he?'

Reluctantly, Macon said, 'The Chief Councillor.'

The lead Elder sat back, looking satisfied. 'You've lighter hair than Willard, but the same eyes.'

My fingers tingled and I swayed where I stood. *She knows the Chief Councillor!*

The sour Elder snapped, 'Does he know you're here?'

'No. It was—' he glanced at Felix and me '—not something I planned.'

'Well, that's our second concern. Surely he's going to be upset that you're all here?' asked the toothless man who'd apologised to us yesterday. 'Sounds like he's put effort into training *you* in particular?'

Macon looked defensive. 'He can't tell me what to do all the time.'

The toothless man snorted. '*Gawd-in-heaven*, teenage rebellion!'

The sour Elder scowled. 'If we take them in, it'll risk our trading deals with Below. We've got to send them back. We rely on trade.'

'Hate to agree with Zara, but she's right,' said another Elder with a narrow face like a rat. 'Those Below fellas with the crossbows might come for them.'

Felix was solemn. 'They won't bother with Marri or me—'

The toothless Elder looked thoughtful. 'But ... they might come after *you*, Macon. Would you want to stay anyway?'

'Only if you accept Marri and Felix—'

The rat-faced Elder snorted. 'Package deal, then?'

Although I wasn't familiar with the expression, the meaning seemed clear. We nodded. The watching audience and the Elders began to talk excitedly.

Macon spoke, and the chatter subsided. 'I'll talk to my sire. I can smooth things over; he wants to reform some of the rules. We don't want to cause difficulties for you—'

A shiver ran down my spine. *What if he can't smooth things over and they sequester him instead?*

Then Macon glanced at me and held out his hand, palm up. 'And I have another request. I'd like to bring three children when I return—'

A welter of emotions filled me, so swiftly I couldn't identify them all. Macon's face softened as he looked at me. I jerked my eyes away, unable to bear it.

An unhappy mutter started among the crowd. '*Three children?*' said the lead Elder. 'You're not supposed to have attachments to your children down Below.'

As the hubbub died, the rat-faced Elder frowned. '*Whose* children are they, anyway? You never know with you lot.'

The sour old Elder stood, shaking with anger. 'Exactly, Terry! Is he gonna bring women here too, to have orgies and corrupt our young? We should send this lot home right now.'

The crowd murmured with agreement, but Kayla called out, 'Don't say that about Marri!'

'Thank you, Kayla, that's enough,' said the lead Elder. Then she turned to us. 'Zara thinks you'll find it difficult to fit in. If you want to carry on like you do Below, the vote *will* go against you—'

The rat-faced Elder said, 'Don't you just sleep with any old person any time—?'

Macon was stiff and uncomfortable. 'We keep ourselves from emotional attachments and share ourselves to repopulate the earth.'

I could tell how it sounded to them. *It's one thing to question your society privately; it's another to hear strangers question it.*

The rat-faced Elder was dubious. 'Really?' There was a long pause.

Felix interrupted, using his teaching voice. 'We're *forced* to bear children with different people, and the Council can sequester, exile or hang us if we don't. We came here because we broke those rules—!'

I put my hand to my forehead, as Macon said, '*Felix*—!' Felix flushed and looked down.

The lead Elder wore the lazy smile of a cat who had trapped a mouse. 'We'd guessed you were in trouble. We were just wondering when you'd get around to being honest with us—'

'How'd you break the rules—?' said the toothless Elder, leaning forward. 'Tell us.'

Eventually, Macon spoke. 'Marri and I undertook an illicit partnership.'

'I also failed to share myself appropriately,' I confessed.

'What's *that* mean, gal?' said the rat-faced man. A few other Elders nodded at the question.

The lead Elder leaned back and crossed her arms, her face grim. 'Explain.'

Macon glanced at me. 'Marri and I were registered partners when she was 14 and I was 15. She had our first child.'

'Lilah,' I said quietly. 'A girl.'

Macon nodded. 'Yes. I registered three other partnerships afterwards, but nothing came of them—'

'Hold your horses, what's *that* mean?' asked the rat-faced Elder.

I took over. 'It means he produced no children with those women. Meanwhile, I was on duty with the babies, but when I was available for partnership again, I may have offered myself to, umm—'

Macon shifted his feet. 'Her second partnership was with me, again. They refused to register it and we got called before the Council.' He looked at Felix. 'We should have listened to you—'

'Earth Above, *that* Month Party ...' muttered Felix. 'I would rather *not* have seen what you two get up to in private—'

My cheeks burned, and I glared at Felix. 'I *tried* to make an offer to someone else beforehand!' The toothless Elder chuckled, but Felix fell silent. He had declined my offer that time.

Macon cleared his throat. 'They allowed that partnership to continue ... very reluctantly ... but they banned us from speaking or meeting once it ended. Marri had a second child.'

'Cady,' I said. 'She's called Cady.'

'But you spoke of *three* children?' asked an Elder with iron-grey hair coiled at her neck. 'Who are the parents of the third child?'

I forced myself to look her in the eye. 'Me and Macon, again. We met secretly, after I had Cady. But we were discovered after—um—I fell pregnant.'

There was a long and stunned silence. I closed my eyes at the shame of it.

The rat-faced Elder said, 'Why did you take that risk?'

'We thought I wouldn't fall pregnant because I was breast-feeding. But it was always risky—'

Macon gave a sheepish, lopsided smile that made my heart turn over. Then he glanced at me again. 'That may have been why we kept doing it. We didn't agree with the rules ...'

I nodded.

'What did they do when you were discovered?' asked the lead Elder.

'I was ostracised, and then sequestered in solitary confinement for three weeks after I had Tomas. They made Macon publicly reject me in front of everyone—'

The lead Elder turned to Macon. 'And you—?'

He sighed and looked down. 'I got off easier than Marri. They stood me down from the Strikeforces for a few months, and I'm no longer allowed to lead expeditions—'

'His punishment would have been worse if—well, if his sire hadn't been who he is—'

The Elder with the bun sat forward. 'So ... let's sum this up ... your crime was continuing your partnership?'

Macon looked at the floor. 'Yes. We were selfish. We're supposed erase personal attachments to create a loving society.'

I looked at my feet. 'I also failed to have other partners—'

'But you've been punished for those crimes—more or less. So why did you have to leave?'

Macon looked at me questioningly. My heart sank, but I nodded.

'She was attacked,' he said. 'Someone in a position of power has tried to force himself on her. Twice.'

I closed my eyes, and swallowed, and the memories overwhelmed me for a moment before I could speak. 'It's true.' *Don't think, don't think.*

Macon muttered, 'He hasn't even been punished. Yet—'

The rat-faced Elder eyed us sharply.

'That explains you two.' The toothless Elder leaned back. 'But Felix, you been quieter than a mouse. What rule did *you* break, boyo?'

Felix's face spasmed. 'What if you don't like my answer? I mean, *really* don't like it. Will you—uh—kill me?'

'We have to know,' said the lead Elder. 'But you're not one of us, you've done nothing against any of us. We wouldn't kill you. We'd just send you home.'

Felix swallowed convulsively, and I worried that he was about to vomit. I whispered, 'Do you want me to tell them?'

He looked at the ground. 'Better to know what our options are.' A tear ran down his face, and he scrubbed it away.

I looked at the Elders squarely. 'He could be executed for—they'd call it wilful failure to share himself for procreation. It's because ... Felix ... ah, generally prefers to offer himself to men.'

The rat-faced Elder stared open-mouthed at Felix and the other Elders looked horrified. Only the lead Elder remained expressionless. I began to feel ill.

A babble of questions arose. I heard one person say, 'Did she say, "generally"?' After what Zara had said about the filthiness of our ways, I hoped I didn't have to go into any more detail.

My apprehension deepened when the lead Elder spoke. 'We have rules here too, and we expect everyone to obey them—even if they disagree with them.'

Felix put his chin up. 'If you let me live here, I'll follow your rules. If I possibly can.'

'Me too. *Please*—our children ...' I twisted my fingers together painfully.

Macon turned to me. 'My sire knows me better than most sires do. Everyone should have the same opportunity.'

Zara spoke again, looking directly at the lead Elder. 'I'm still against them, Rana. You know how they'll struggle to follow our rules. And they don't even know about marriage—'

'What's marr—?' asked Macon. I stepped on his foot. The toothless man chuckled.

I narrowed my eyes at Macon with irritation. 'Lily and

Kayla told me about it the other day. It's like a Month Party offer, but forever.'

Felix gasped. 'Forever? Like ... for *ever*?'

The lead Elder explained. 'Formally, two people agree that they'll stay with each other and have no other partners while the marriage lasts. Or you can marry by having a child together, though that's less formal.' She glanced at Zara. 'You don't *have* to get married if you live here. That's not our way.' Zara scowled.

Macon's eyes widened. 'So it's an *ongoing* partnership—you make an agreement, or you have children together? Is that right?'

'In a nutshell ...' said the toothless Elder. I wondered what a nutshell was.

'If two people from Below have children together—does that mean you'd regard them as—uh, married?'

'Not under our rules,' said the rat-faced Elder. 'You'd all have multiple wives and husbands, and no intention of an ongoing relationship.'

'So, you'd have to make an agreement?' Macon ran his hand through his hair. 'Hypothetically ... if a man from Below made an offer of, ah, an ongoing partnership to someone from Below, and the other person agreed—um, a woman, I should say—would you allow it? Recognise it?'

There was silence while we untangled the question.

Suddenly the Elder with her hair in a bun smiled, her face dissolving in wrinkles. 'If you're asking what I think you're asking, Macon, it's traditional to get on your knees and say, "Will you marry me?"'

Everyone in the room turned to look at me, even Zara. There was an air of expectation and the toothless man grinned like a lunatic. Felix began to laugh silently, tears rolling down his face.

'Are you *serious*—?' I spluttered at Macon.

'I was just asking! I wanted to know what our status was here.'

I glowered. 'Our *status*! You sound like a stinking Strike-force manual!'

'Let's talk about it later,' he said, sensing that he might be heading down an unstable tunnel. He turned back to the Elders. 'I'm pleading with you to let Felix and Marri stay. I'll make sure we don't cause problems for your trading arrangements, and I will return with Marri's children—*our* children. If I can manage all that, I'd like to stay here too—'

I opened my mouth to question Macon's proposal to rescue our children single-handedly, but Felix caught my wrist and shook his head. I closed my mouth with a snap, and swallowed.

The lead Elder's face betrayed nothing of her thoughts. 'Thank you for explaining why you're here. If you could step outside while we cast a vote? There are nine of us, the majority wins.'

CHAPTER 15

Outside the Hall, Felix sat on the ground, his arms around his knees. Macon stood with his hands behind his back, slightly apart, against a scrubby little bush growing by the entrance. I paced back and forth.

'That was a *disaster*,' I said. 'I don't know if they liked us or not, Macon, but they were horrified by Felix. That head Elder's going to report us to your sire. She must be his spy, or something—'

Macon bristled. 'I can sort it out—'

'I've heard that before—' I paced away from him, too irritated to speak.

Felix muttered, 'It could have been worse. At home they would have executed me on the spot.'

Macon sat next to Felix. 'We're all counting on them being a bit more reasonable here.'

Felix blinked. 'You sure you want to be sitting there next to me, Macon?'

Macon rolled his eyes. 'I've sat next to people like you before. I've slept next to them.'

Felix gaped, and Macon's brows lowered. '*Next to*, not *with*!'

Felix laughed softly. 'You never know.'

Curiosity pricked through my irritation. I paced back over. 'Who were they?'

'Ravi and Julian.'

I blinked. 'What, the two Strikers?' Ravi had been the leader of the patrol that had found Felix and me trying to escape. He had teased Julian the whole way home, when he wasn't trying to terrify us with horrific stories of ways we could have died. At the time I'd felt sorry for Julian, but he'd put up with the teasing with a grin.

Macon nodded. 'They kept it quiet, but a few of us guessed. I was often rostered on a team with them, before they died.'

'How?' Felix asked, his voice quavering. I knew that they hadn't been caught, because there hadn't been a public execution.

'A building collapsed on Jules during a scavenging run. Ravi blamed himself.'

I stared at Macon. 'He didn't—?'

'Two weeks later. We found him hanging in the Strikeforce Common room.' Macon closed his eyes and leaned his head back against the wall. 'He smiled, the last time we spoke. I shouldn't have left him alone.'

We were quiet after that. I paced while the two men sat. Felix pulled leaves off the scrubby bush and shredded them. I hoped the Elders made a decision before the bush was stripped.

The male chicken crowed triumphantly somewhere nearby. *Why do males have to be like that?* It reminded me of something, and I strode back to the men. 'By the way, if Macon rescues my children, I'm coming too.'

Macon reopened his eyes. 'You're still recovering, and it's too dangerous. And they're *our* children!'

'I can look after myself! We killed the wild dog without you!' I put my hands on my hips. 'And you barely know *our* children. They won't go with you.'

Macon glared. 'Yes, they will.' But he looked uncertain.

'You need to know that telling me what to do only makes me want to do the opposite! That is, if you're really thinking about this marrying thing.'

Felix snorted. It took me a moment to realise he was trying

to stifle laughter. He put his hands up. '*Stop it*! You don't know what's going to happen yet!'

We jumped when the door to the meeting hall opened behind us.

The lead Elder emerged. 'The vote passed, five to four. You can stay if you choose. We'll let your children stay too, if you decide to make that journey.'

I drooped with relief and hugged Macon and Felix both at once. Horror spread across their faces, and Felix swiftly detached himself. I would have laughed in other circumstances.

Then the lead Elder smiled, like sunlight gleaming from behind a cloud. 'Below can be harsh if you don't fit in. I should know.'

As she pulled up her left sleeve, I saw a faded tattoo on her left elbow. The absence of wrist tattoos meant that she must be a similar age to my sire and many of the Councillors; she had been born and come of age before those tattoos had been introduced.

'You're from home!' I exclaimed. 'I *was* wondering ...!' I decided not to tell her I'd thought she was a spy.

'My name is Rana. They exiled me when I was a little older than you.' Her mouth turned down. 'I left behind four children of my body.'

'I'm sorry,' I said.

With visible effort, she put her pain aside. 'Come in, everyone's waiting.'

We filed back in. Most of the people inside were smiling, even the rat-faced Elder. We thanked everyone, and the meeting broke apart. Lily and Jon hugged me. Kayla introduced me to Alex, and I thanked her for her support.

Out of the corner of my eye I saw that the rat-faced man had approached Felix. I needed to learn his name. When Lily and her family left, I joined Felix.

Felix gestured to the man. 'This is Terry.'

I greeted him, and tried to mentally imprint 'Terry' over 'rat-faced man'. *Terry, Terry, Terry.*

Felix beamed. 'Terry and Raj have lived here for twenty-five years.'

Terry looked dour. 'One of the reasons I've never thought much of you Below people. Why don't you live and let live? Raj and me is a useful part of this village. There's nothing perverted about being how you are, Felix. Nothing at all.'

I blinked, but after a moment understanding bloomed. *Felix can live here!* I smiled at Terry warmly, and he smiled back. It made him look less like a rat.

Macon came up beside me, looking sombre. I turned to look at the direction he'd come from and saw that Rana was walking out of the Hall, wiping her eyes.

'What happened?' I asked Macon in an undertone.

'Rana asked me about the children of her body. Two are dead. One's alive. I think the other's a Barren, but the name isn't quite the same. Everyone else she asked about is dead.'

'Did you ask if she thought I should come with you?'

Macon's jaw took on a stubborn set. 'We disagreed.'

'Hah!'

'That doesn't mean you *can* come.'

'Bad luck. I'm coming!'

Terry grinned at Macon and me. 'Doesn't seem like you two need a wedding ceremony to me.'

Felix rolled his eyes and sighed. Terry laughed and clapped Felix's shoulder. 'I'm going now. Stop by our place and meet Raj, okay?'

Felix frowned at us. 'You two, stop fighting. Let's make some plans.'

We went to Lily and Jon's hut to plan. Lily hovered in the background and supplied tea, which we drank politely.

After the second cup, I glared at Macon and began again. 'How many times have you been on Parental Duties, Macon? You've never been with the babies; you don't have a clue!'

Macon frowned. 'I've done Parental Duties a few times. How much harder can the babies be?'

Lily coughed. She had her back to us, but it sounded like she was trying to cover a laugh.

'You'll need my help,' I said. 'How's it going to look if you turn up alone after almost two weeks?'

Macon shrugged. 'I'll think of something.'

'I know you've always been able to talk your way out of anything. But this is about *all* of us. They know you found us and sent Vin home so you could help us on a secret mission that doesn't exist. What are they going to think about that? Whatever you tell them, you'll need me to back you up.'

'Why would they believe you any more than me?'

I had to stop and think about that. I'd ignored my duties so many times, and betrayed them all by leaving. They'd trust me even less than they trusted Macon.

Felix looked up at us. 'It's not what she says—it's *her*,' he said. 'You did whatever it took bring her back—alive. And you did. What's more important than that?'

I found myself nodding along with Felix. 'And I got sick, and that's why we couldn't come back any sooner. It's the truth!'

Macon frowned. 'What about Felix?'

Felix made a face. 'I told you, I'm *not* coming back. Say I died from whatever Marri had. Or you had to kill me, I don't care.'

A shiver went down my spine. 'I don't like pretending you're dead.'

Felix looked worried. 'What if they sequester you again?'

I grimaced, and my stomach clenched. I'd been trying

not to think about that possibility. 'If the Chief Councillor is thinking of loosening the rules, like Macon says—they might let us go—'

'But I've just done whatever it took to bring you *back*!' Macon said. 'It's too risky. I'll think of something that doesn't involve you.'

I felt enraged but I looked at him calmly. 'They're my babies, I'm coming to get them.'

'*Marri*—'

Felix breathed out and sat back.

I turned to him. 'What?'

Felix shrugged. 'Nothing—' He glanced at Macon, and chewed his fingernails, refusing to meet my eyes.

I glared at Felix. 'You've *never* agreed with him about *anything* before!'

Macon was confused. 'But he didn't say anything—'

'I know how he works. Why don't you want me to go, Felix?'

Felix took a deep breath. 'Well, Macon's right. It's too dangerous. You'll be well looked after here. And what if—?'

'*What if* what?'

Felix's face closed. 'Never mind.'

'You can't leave it like that.' I ground my teeth. 'You *can't*.'

'*Fine*. I'm worried that you're, you know, because we—' He trailed off and glanced at Macon.

'I'm *what*? We what—?'

Macon laughed at Felix's discomfort. 'He's worried that you're pregnant, Marri.'

I stared at Felix. 'Why should that make a difference?'

Felix looked at the tabletop. 'I don't want to lose you, or our child.'

I felt as if I were back in sequestration, trapped in the carriage room again. 'You don't even know if there *is* a child! All we do is bear offspring—no one cares about us for any other reason. No exploring, no reading, just having children, children, children, without even being able to love them. I'm so sick of it!'

The men gaped at me. Their uncomprehending expressions made me all the more angry. I stood up. 'YOU CAN BOTH GET LOST! DON'T TELL ME WHAT TO DO! I DON'T WANT TO SEE EITHER OF YOU EVER AGAIN!' Lily turned around, her eyes wide, and I realised I was screaming.

I ran out of the hut and up to the dairy. I cried and hit my fists on the shed wall. Then I realised that the cows were making worried noises.

'Sorry, cows! It's not your fault,' I said to them through the wall. My breath came in great hiccoughs and I had splinters in my hands. I sank against the wall and tried to pick the splinters out. Lily and Jon's neighbour emerged from his hut, peered at me, and retreated. Stories about the insane woman from Below would go around the village tomorrow, confirming what everybody thought about us.

After a while, Lily came out. 'Deary me. What a mess! Come back inside, honey.'

She walked me back. The two men were stiff-backed at the table. Felix's eyes were red and neither of them would look at me.

'Sorry,' I said.

Macon said, in a low voice, 'Come home with me, then ... if you must.'

'Fine, I'll go,' I muttered. I could hardly say anything else. The two men left without another word.

We spent two days preparing, and I avoided Macon and Felix as much as I could. I helped Lily make me a proper bag. Someone gave me decent scavenged shoes and Lily and Jon's neighbour wove us made us hats woven from leaves.

The afternoon before I left, I returned from egg-collecting duty to find Felix at Lily's table, a cup of the local tea in front of him. An empty cup was opposite. I tried to back out of the door.

Felix pleaded with his eyes. 'Don't go.'

'Okay.' I sat heavily, and Lily poured the tea.

Then she said archly, 'I've just gotta run an errand.' She left and I stared at the plumes of steam coming from the dark tea.

'I came to apologise,' said Felix. 'I don't want you to leave like this.'

'I'm sorry I lost my temper,' I said, still looking at the tea.

'You're right, everyone tries to control what the women do, and they use childbearing as the way to do it. I shouldn't have tried it with you.'

My tears fell onto the table and I smeared them into the wood with my index finger.

Then Felix hugged me. I clung to him, crying into his shirt. 'Are we still friends?'

'You're my dearest friend. I mean it.' He kissed my head and sat down. 'But I release you from our partnership—if you want.'

'Maybe we aren't the best partners.'

'No, I don't think we are.' Felix coloured. 'You were right, those feelings didn't go away ...'

'Why would they? Why *should* they?' I patted his hand. 'But I'd be proud to bear your child. I won't take any stupid risks. I'll let you know what comes of it.'

'Okay.'

There was a knock. 'Come in,' I said.

Lily smiled as she entered. 'Ah, now you two look more friendly!' She sat beside me and poured herself some tea.

Felix took a sip from his cup and tried not to retch. The tea had steeped too long. He put the cup down. 'So—what's the deal with *him*? What's going on?'

I played with my teacup and gave him a guileless look. 'Who—the Chief Councillor? I don't know what he'll think about this.'

Felix rolled his eyes and Lily laughed. 'Don't play the fool, gal, we know you better than that.'

I muttered into the tea, 'I don't know what's going on with the Chief Councillor's son either.'

Felix patted my arm. 'You're released from your partnership with me. And ... I think he still loves you, in case you're wondering.'

'How do you know what's love and what's—a physical thing? Or because it was forbidden?'

Lily grinned. 'You been looking all gooey cow eyes at each other when you think no one's looking. And Kayla says she saw two people who looked mighty like you two kissing out under the old beech tree the other evening—you can *imagine* how excited she was—'

I blushed and looked sidelong at Felix. He raised his eyebrows, trying to hide a smile. 'Was that the night before the Elders' Meeting that Macon forgot to tell us about? He was *distracted*, he said—'

'Hmph!'

'You don't have to be with anyone, Marri. But I think you should at least talk to him—without losing your temper, if that's possible.'

'I'll try,' I said.

Lily hugged me. 'Don't rush it, honey. Seems you been hurt.'

I twisted my fingers together. 'True.'

'Whatever you choose, I hope you'll be happy. You're a sweet gal. We don't mind what you want to do. Live and let live.'

Felix smiled. 'I'll see you tomorrow.' After he left, Lily and I kept packing.

The next morning, we woke early and ate breakfast in silence. Outside the hut, Lily hugged me. 'We've become so fond of you, Marri. We miss you already.' The children cried.

'I'll come back. And you can meet my children!' I hoped that if you said something confidently enough, it would happen. 'I'll find a way to repay you—if I can—'

'No need,' said Jon.

Felix arrived and slipped a letter into my hand, written on a scrap of Lily's parchment. 'Could you give this to Frankie?'

'Of course.' I tucked it in my pack.

Macon walked up. 'Ready?' His posture was wary, like I was a wild dog ready to bite.

I smiled brightly, trying to demonstrate that I could keep my temper. 'Ready as I'll ever be!'

Macon raised one eyebrow. 'Right. Good.'

People had gathered to farewell us. Some had gifts of food, which we gratefully accepted. We waved to everyone and left.

We didn't talk at first. I hadn't seen the terrain surrounding the settlement because I had been so unwell when we arrived. Now we marched through undulating fields of plants. I had been told that the grains were an ingredient of the bread I had enjoyed so much. I fingered the golden spikes, admiring the neat way in which the grain stuck to the stalk.

We reached an old dirt road, which turned into a black, tarry road, all cracked and smashed. The land started to rise, and empty buildings dotted the hills. As we walked past one building, a flock of blue-black birds rose into the air, making agonised screams. *Argh! Argh!*

'Ravens,' said Macon. 'Scavengers like us. They're very clever.'

As the sun rose higher, I was relieved to have a hat and proper shoes. I drank water frequently; I didn't want to see my friend the giant ant again.

I can't say exactly when we entered the city again, but suddenly there were more buildings, and deserted vehicles appeared on the streets. I saw now that the buildings were massive versions of the huts in the settlement. I wondered how many tens or hundreds of people had lived in each. The staring broken windows were sorrowful eyes, looking in vain for the owners to return.

I jumped when Macon spoke. 'You and Felix are talking again?'

I nodded. 'We apologised to each other.'

'Good. He was upset.'

'I shouldn't have said all that. I was so sorry afterwards—'

'I was sorry too,' said Macon. 'You wouldn't be *you* if you didn't insist on doing crazy things. I can't stop you from taking risks—I'm not sure I'd want to.'

'You're crazy too. You wouldn't be here if you weren't.'

He grinned. 'Maybe that's why we were attracted to each other in the first place—'

There was an awkward pause, and his grin fell away.

'Pia must be worried about you,' I said, after we'd passed another set of houses.

'I feel bad.' Macon grimaced, and glanced at me. 'It's a partnership of convenience, but she's a nice person, and I wouldn't want her to worry—'

I took a few more steps before saying cautiously, 'It is?'

'She didn't want to risk another pregnancy right away. I wanted a rest from serious partnerships—Rilla and I were disastrous—'

I laughed. 'I couldn't imagine what you'd have in common with Rilla.' I adjusted my hat. 'At least I love Felix as a friend! But that was a strange partnership too. It wasn't like ... like ... you and me—'

Memories of our reckless meetings in corridors sprang

into my head. I looked out at the houses to disguise the fact I was breathing more heavily.

Macon blinked. 'It *was* a strange partnership? With Felix?'

'We ended it yesterday. Felix doesn't think it's right for him.'

Macon chuckled. 'He might have a point.'

As we were speaking, the blue sky turned grey, and fluffy clouds rolled over, obscuring the sun. I didn't mind; I was hot, and my eyes hurt less now that the sun was hidden. As the clouds darkened, fat drops of water fell from the sky, steaming as they hit the warm black surface of the road. The air smelled green and leafy and sharp.

I held out my hand. 'That's the most rain I've ever seen! How long will it last?'

'If there's a pattern to it, I've never worked it out. My father says the weather's much warmer than it was when he was young.'

'Wow! Look at it!' I opened my mouth to let rain in. It became heavier, until I was standing in a natural shower. I danced around.

Macon looked on, tolerant and smiling. 'You'll be sick of it soon.'

Though I hated to admit it, Macon was right. By nightfall, I had changed my mind. I was sodden. Rain ran down my face in rivulets and into my clothing. The hat had protected my face until the wind blew horizontally. At least the wild animals stayed undercover. I was relieved when we reached the Strikeforce way post, a stone building with 'TOWN HALL' on the front.

The Strikeforces had cleared the decrepit furniture and laid out supplies in a room on the first floor. We dumped our packs, and Macon started a fire. He looked at me anxiously, almost with embarrassment. I wasn't sure why until he said,

'We can take off our wet clothes and dry them here. We'll catch a cold otherwise.'

'Turn your back while I change.' I peeled off my wet clothes, and put on the spare clothes from my pack—they were slightly damp too. Steam came off me as I sat by the fire.

I turned my back and stared at the fire. The shifting orange flames were mesmerising. 'Your turn.' The wood popped and crackled as it burned.

'Done,' said Macon.

We hung the wet clothes and our emptied packs on the rotting, rusting furniture around the room. The windows clouded over with condensation. I levered one open and propped it with a stick of firewood, and the mugginess dissipated. I put my hand out of the window and found that the rain had slowed to tiny drops.

We ate dinner in front of the fire. It felt like a party, with bread, dried fruit, and a sweet cake. There were significant drawbacks to life in the supraterran settlement—it didn't have electricity or hot showers—but the food was *so much better.*

Macon unrolled his sleeping mat, and then paused. 'Use my mat. You've been unwell.'

'You've been unwell too.'

'You almost died.'

After some argument, I gave in. We lay down, me on the mat, and Macon on the floor, on two blankets. He was making a racket. *Clunk. Shuffle. Sniff. Clunk. Bang. Snuffle.*

'You sound uncomfortable,' I said into the semi-darkness. 'Let's turn this mat on its side. We can share it.'

'Okay.'

We turned the mat around, and lay back down. I lay on my side, my back to Macon. He lay on his back, staring at the roof. After a while, I turned on my back to see what he was staring at. The roof was beautifully patterned, like a crumbled white flower, but I couldn't see why it had *that* much fascination.

I poked him with my finger and rolled back over. 'You'll snore if you sleep on your back.'

'Can I lie behind you?'

'Sure.'

He rolled onto his side behind me, and put his arm over my arm. It was comforting, and I breathed evenly, tired from the day's walk.

I was on the edge of sleep when I became aware of a warm, insistent pressure against my lower back.

I opened my eyes, and rolled over. 'You seem to be, um, awake—?'

Macon pulled away from me. 'Can't help it. Sorry.' He began to gather his blankets. 'I'll sleep over there.'

I put my hand to his face and smiled. 'Don't move.'

He blinked. I sat up and pulled off my slightly damp top.

His eyes widened in comprehension, and he smiled, and started to take off his shirt too. He paused with it halfway off, his arms still in the sleeves. 'Are you *sure*, Marri love?'

My trousers were already around my ankles. 'Who asks that in a situation like this?'

'If you fall pregnant again—'

'It's almost time to bleed, if I'm not pregnant already.'

'If you're sure—'

I kicked my trousers off, and was pleased to see that he was undressing again.

We reached for each other.

Once we had caught our breath, he said, 'I missed you so much.'

'Which part did you miss most?'

'All of you.' He stroked the muscles down my back and I shivered. He kissed me and reached downwards.

'I need you, *now*.'

Afterwards, we lay naked on the sleeping mat, one of the blankets over us, my head on Macon's chest. My pain and worry had been purged. The fire cast reddish orange lights on the flowery ceiling.

I was drowsing when Macon spoke. 'I've never felt this way about anybody else. I love you.'

I kissed his shoulder. 'I love you too.'

'Remember that time I sat next to you at the evening meal, before our first partnership? I'd just joined the Strikeforces. We argued about how the tunnels were built.'

'Um—no? It sounds like me, though—'

'Your face lit up when you argued!' He laughed. 'It took me a few Month Parties to pluck up the courage to make an offer.'

'Am I that *scary*? Felix said that there was some kind of bet—!'

'You had a reputation for rejecting anyone who asked, even Councillors. I was worried you'd say no, but I was even more worried about losing the bet!' He laughed. 'For once, Rich and Leo were good for something.'

I bit my lip. 'I was so scared. I hated the Month Parties. I hated it all.'

'You were so awkward at first, but then—' I could hear from his voice that he was smiling.

I smiled too. 'I got over it—!'

'The next morning you said that you were surprised that I approached you. I always meant to ask why—?'

'You were so clever, athletic, confident ... I didn't think a future Councillor should be interested in someone like me—'

'Hah. I guess Father's plans aren't as secret as he thinks ...'

'He can't have been happy when you chose me—'

'Not the *third* time, that's for sure—!'

A chill went over me, and I held him. 'He won't let you go.'

He patted my hair. 'He's made me come to his office every

month since I was ten. I've always—well, mostly—been able to reason with him. You don't have to be so worried—'

I nodded. 'You said your sire knew you better than most ...' I thought, staring at the white ceiling pattern. 'What did you do at those meetings?

'He'd make me read books and discuss them with him. He has *a lot* of books. He'd set tests for me. Sometimes he'd have a treat for me, like hydroponic raspberries.'

Something else occurred to me. 'You call him *Father* sometimes. Rana noticed it too.'

'He asked me to. I don't know why. He's strange, but he's not a bad man ... he's trying to do the right thing—'

We were silent for a time.

Eventually I spoke again. 'You sound like you have *affection* for him. That's strange, too ... it's like how we broke the rules—secret meetings, forbidden emotional attachments—'

Macon laughed. 'I never thought of it that way.' Then he grinned. 'I mean, there were other reasons for us to break the rules—'

I couldn't help grinning back. 'Remember our second partnership? I was determined to be good, and then I saw you—'

His eyes glinted in the firelight. He caressed my shoulder, and gently stroked my breast and side. 'I don't think I was ever that determined to be good. Not really—'

I laughed and turned to him. 'Nothing's changed, then?' We kissed. Things took a natural course after that.

Later, when light first came and the birds started singing, we woke and made love for a third time. This time, it was slow and gentle, as we explored and reacquainted ourselves with each other's bodies.

Then we dressed in our clothes from home and ate breakfast. We didn't say much. I was filled with a rich warm happiness, like honey, which made words unnecessary.

After breakfast, Macon grabbed my hand with his hands. He looked serious, and I wondered if he was nervous about returning home.

Eventually, he spoke. 'I want to ask something. I'm not kneeling—but Marri, will you be my partner for the rest of our lives?'

It took me a moment to understand what he'd asked. I blinked. 'You're asking me to ... *marry* ... you?'

He beamed. 'I can't remember the words they said to use!'

I felt it was important to be honest—more than ever, right now. 'Does it matter that I might be carrying someone else's child?'

'You did your duty. So did I.'

'Of course,' I said, relieved. 'And I may not be carrying Felix's child—we only ever managed to do our duty once—'

Macon frowned. 'You still need to answer my question—'

I smiled. 'Yes. Of course.'

We did a silly dance, hugging each other and bouncing around the room.

Afterwards, I scratched my head. 'Is that it? Are we married now?'

'Maybe I need to do that kneeling thing too—'

I shrugged. 'If it's just between you and me, that's what matters. As far as I'm concerned, we're married.'

Macon was sober. 'I hope we live to tell the others.'

'Let's make sure we do.' I smiled, and felt more positive than I had in weeks, months, and possibly, years.

CHAPTER 16

Macon knew an easier and quicker route home, but it was still difficult to go back underground. The dark was a stifling blanket, and everything smelt dank and earthen.

Macon said that it always took a day or two to readjust. 'Then everything from the last few weeks will be like a dream—' He stopped. 'We're getting close.'

We ditched the gifts from the supraterran settlement: the hats, my shoes, some clothes, and the extra blankets. Then we ate the remaining supraterran food.

I shook the crumbs from our packs. 'I hope the Monster Rat finds these.'

Macon laughed. 'Me too.'

I rolled up Felix's letter and tucked it into the waistband of my trousers. I'd have to remember to get it out before I took them to the laundry.

Finally, I dumped my pack, and we stuffed my remaining gear into Macon's. I went barefoot, as I'd left my overshoes in the settlement.

Macon gripped my elbow. 'Remember, you came back voluntarily? And you've been sick for a week? And I looked after you? Felix ran and he's probably dead—'

I patted his hand. 'Luckily, most of that is true—so I won't have to lie. Except Felix's death, but they'll want to believe that, won't they? I hope they don't interrogate us with force.'

'They'd better not hurt you—'

'They can't hurt me if I'm pregnant. I still haven't had my monthly bleeds.'

Macon sighed. 'I wish you'd stayed behind. Felix was right.'

I shook my head. We reached a corridor with a large iron door at the end.

'That's the Strikeforce guardroom,' whispered Macon.

We kissed. Then I tried to look resigned, as Macon became stern and expressionless. He knocked on the door in a precise rhythm. *Bong, bang, b-bong, bong-bang.*

Someone on the other side said, 'But there aren't any patrols out now!' I heard a quick, muffled discussion, then a metallic grating sound.

'Come in?' said another voice, more hesitantly.

Macon opened the door and pushed me through. I hadn't seen a Strikeforce guardroom since the time Ravi and Jules had caught us. This one was long and narrow, with paint coming off the walls in big flakes.

Rich, Leo and Vin gaped at us. Their crossbows were pointed at our heads. I glanced at Macon, but he was impassive.

'Macon! And *Marri*?' said Rich. 'Vin said he lost you, Macon—it made no sense. We thought you must have died! Where's Felix?'

Vin looked confused. I willed him not to say anything. We'd agreed on a story that would fit in with what we'd told him, but it was flimsy.

Macon frowned. 'Yes, I got separated from Vin but then found them. They said they were on a secret mission from the Council. They had evidence, and it was only after I'd helped them on their way that I realised they were lying. When I caught up with them again, they were being attacked by wild dogs. I don't know where Felix is now—for all I know, he's dead—but I captured Marri.'

I watched them all carefully. The way Macon said it, it almost seemed convincing. I was impressed by his persuasive power, and angry that he hadn't used it to help me before.

Rich narrowed his eyes. 'Why did you take so long?'

'Marri had heat exhaustion. She wasn't well enough to walk for some days—'

I interrupted. 'I thought I was going to die!'

Macon glanced at me dismissively. 'You're a fool! You're lucky not to be dead.'

'I didn't realise—!'

Macon shook his head. 'When Marri recovered, she agreed to come home with me. I need to report to the Council and explain. I'll submit to any penalty.'

Rich and Leo's faces remained hard. Vin's crossbow wavered for a heartbeat or two, but he kept it trained on us. The hair on my neck rose. *Something's wrong.*

Rich shook his head, and a smile crept across his face. 'You can't report to the Council, Macon. The Council has been abolished.'

A rush of disorientation went through me, almost as if I had heat exhaustion again. Macon let go of my arm. 'What did you say?' He swayed on his feet.

Leo's face was grim. 'The new Leader will want to see you.'

Rich kept his crossbow high. 'I'm arresting you both. The Leader will consider your actions.'

Macon had turned so pale he looked almost grey. 'Who is it? Who is this *Leader*?'

Leo ignored him and took his crossbow. They emptied Macon's pack and searched through it, and then they made us strip. I was covered in goose bumps and humiliation. Leo stood behind me and patted my bare buttocks, grinning. 'Nice.'

Macon glared at Rich. Rich shook his head at Leo, and then looked back at Macon. 'Sorry.'

Why apologise to him? *It's* my *backside, not* his.

Vin picked up my clothes, and his brow creased as he held the waistband of my trousers. He shook them, and my breath caught. The letter stayed put, and I breathed out.

Maybe he'd seen my relief, but he kept searching. His eyes widened and he pulled the rolled-up paper from the lining. 'Look!'

Rich unrolled and read the note. His eyebrows went up. 'Well, well, well …'

Leo looked over Rich's shoulder. 'What does it say—?'

'It's a love letter. No names, but that's Felix's handwriting.'

Rat shit. 'He gave it to me,' I said. 'If I'd known it expressed any inappropriate affection, I wouldn't have taken it.'

Rich spat out a laugh. 'Nice try, Marri, but no man would write to a woman who can't read.'

Leo leered. 'Don't worry, we'll come back to this. In a lot more detail.' The goose bumps on my arms prickled.

Rich commanded us to put our clothes back on, and they tied our hands behind our backs. Vin pulled the cords around my wrists. I struggled. 'It's too tight!' Rich slapped me, so hard my teeth rattled, and they gagged me.

Macon said, 'I promised her she wouldn't be treated badly. Don't hurt her.'

Rich shrugged. 'That'll teach her not to break the law.'

'Sorry, Marri,' Vin breathed into my ear as he led me away.

As we passed through the corridors, people scuttled away or put their heads down and refused to look. Suze was the only person who spoke to me. She reached her hand out and gasped. 'Marri! Where have you been? Where's Felix? Why have they gagged you?'

Leo pointed his crossbow at her. 'Shut up, or I'll arrest you, and gag you too!'

Suze's face worked with rage and fear, but she ran. I turned my head to watch. She had propped her head on her arm against the damp wall and was weeping.

Ruddy oil lamps lit the Council Chamber. Maybe the solar generators weren't working, or maybe it was for effect.

Only one person sat at the Council Table. Conor's face loomed orange in the strange light. My gut clenched. *No. This can't be true.*

'Kneel before our Leader,' said Rich. I knelt. Macon looked like he was going to resist, but to my relief, he knelt too.

Conor leaned back in his chair, his legs wide. 'Look what the cat's dragged in! Where did you find them, Rich?'

'Macon brought Marri back. She had been trying to escape, Sir, but he persuaded her to return. Felix ran, supposedly. Macon says he's dead—'

Conor rose and gripped my chin in his hand, turning my head back and forth. I tried not to panic.

Conor let go. I wouldn't be surprised if his fingers had left bruises. 'That would be a pity.' He smiled. 'I've been looking forward to executing the filthy pervert—'

I couldn't stop myself from gasping, although the gag muffled the sound.

Macon was indignant. 'What happened to the Council? What happened to normal procedure?'

'*Silence!*' said Conor. He hit Macon's face. 'You will address me as Sir and only speak when spoken to.'

An image of Ramala's large, one-eyed, greedy cat, also called Sir, sprang into my mind. It was lucky I was gagged, because a hysterical laugh bubbled in my throat.

Conor slammed his fist on the table. *Crunch!* His next words killed any laughter.

'I have dispensed with the Council. They were corrupt and self-interested. One Councillor was a pervert. Others showed favour to their offspring. Some wished to weaken our resolve. They were endangering our society.' Spittle gathered at the corners of his lips, and he wiped it off with the back of his hairy hand. 'I shall sequester you and try you for your crimes. It will deter other would-be escapees or rebels.'

Vin piped up. 'Sir, are you sure?' His voice squeaked. I winced.

'*Don't* question my orders!' screamed Conor. 'Put these criminals away.'

As they dragged us up the stairs, Macon tried to reason with Rich. 'We came back as soon as we could. We tried to do the right thing. Why are you helping Conor?'

Rich glared. 'The rules saved us all. If we turn away from them, it'll be anarchy and death. And you two are rulebreakers—'

'Conor doesn't care about rules. He only wants power—'

Rich slapped Macon. '*Shut up!*'

'You know I'm right—'

Rich gestured at me with the crossbow. '*Shut up*, man. Or I'll shoot her.'

Macon backed off. His eye was swelling, and blood ran from his nose onto his chin.

As we neared the sequestration area, the stench of crap, urine and unwashed bodies wafted down the corridor. Jack emerged from the shadows holding an oil lamp. 'Not *more* of you!' he said. 'We've almost run out of space.' Then he held up the lamp and his jaw dropped. 'Macon! *Marri*?! I thought you'd escaped.'

Macon looked grim. 'We did.' He glanced at me, agony in his look. I knew he was wishing he had refused to let me come. Part of me was also wishing that I hadn't been so stubborn.

Jack removed the gag, and I licked my cracked lips.

'Separate them,' said Rich.

Jack was scornful. 'We don't put men and women together.'

'Don't regret bringing me back, *husband*,' I said to Macon

softly.

Macon smiled for a heartbeat. Then his smile faded. 'Stay strong, *wife*.'

Rich looked at us with narrowed eyes. 'What are they talking about?'

Jack shrugged. 'Beats me.'

Jack removed my bonds and thrust me into a dark, smelly carriage. There was no bedding, but to my surprise, another person already sat on the wet floor. The door clanked closed.

'Marri!' said the silhouette. 'Didn't you escape?' She came forward, coughing throatily. As my eyes adjusted, I saw it was Ramala.

'I came back for the children,' I whispered.

Ramala's eyes filled with tears. 'Oh, poor darling.'

'What are you here for?'

'Conor kicked Sir, so I called him a fucking slug.'

'Sounds about right to me!' I looked around. 'Why's it so dark?'

'The lights and the pumps are failing because anyone who knows how the generators work is probably dead. I'm sure we'll drown in a flash flood any day.'

A hopeful thought struck me in the gloom. 'Macon can fix the generators! Maybe he'll be okay!' Then I paused. 'I shouldn't have come back. Macon was right—'

'That stinking piece of rat crap Conor! I wish I'd killed him. And a few others too.' Ramala's hands shook. In the dim light, she looked ten years older; her face was no longer made to laugh.

'What about Felix?' she said then.

'Probably dead.' I closed my eyes. 'I have to lie down.'

I dozed on the floor. I was so tired that I didn't care about the cockroaches crawling on the damp carriage floor. Felix would have laughed.

A dragging noise woke me. Two men were pulling a heavy figure across the platform by the legs. A few electric lights had come back on. I peered as they dragged the unconscious man past. His muscular arms reminded me of Frankie. I bit my fist to stop myself screaming, and stood.

Cramps gripped my midsection, and blood ran down my leg. *Oh, that. Five days late. No baby after all.*

'My monthly bleeds,' I said to Ramala. She tore material from her shift, and I wiped my leg and wadded the cloth in my trousers.

I slumped next to Ramala. She looked at me shrewdly. 'You're disappointed.'

I shook my head. 'It's not a good time to bring a child into the world. It would have been complicated, in the circumstances, but—'

Ramala put her hand on my arm. 'I'm sorry about Felix.'

I laughed hysterically until I cried. Ramala put her arms around me.

'Sorry,' I said, once I'd recovered.

'Shock.'

'I would have liked to have borne Felix's offspring. But ... maybe it's for the best. There's a very small chance it might not have been Felix's—' I admitted after a time.

Ramala was horrified. 'Earth Above! If not his, whose?'

I didn't answer.

Ramala studied my face, and then crossed her arms. '*Marri*—! Not *again*!'

'Felix ended our partnership, before—'

Ramala shook her head. 'Can you two not keep your hands off each other and your pants on?'

I shrugged helplessly.

'What happened?'

I decided to trust her. Even if I was wrong, and she reported me, I was dead anyway. 'Felix tried to escape. I followed him to warn him they were after him—'

Ramala leaned forward. 'Tell me what you saw,' she said. 'It'll make things better.'

I couldn't tell her about the other settlement and Felix still being alive. But I told her about clouds, twisted skeletons, birds and feathers, orange fluffy animals, rain, ruined buildings and cars, wild dogs, and the sun sparkling on green leaves. She was right. Somehow, despite the stinking, cockroach-infested darkness, it made our prison seem more open.

CHAPTER 17

Two days later, I was woken from deep sleep and dragged to a small, dingy room, with a single bulb hanging from the ceiling. Knives, pliers, and other unfamiliar, unpleasant implements were propped against the wall.

The guards shoved me into a chair, pushed me in against the table, and angled a lamp so that it shone into my face. It looked like a repurposed hydroponic lamp. Sweat sprang up immediately and ran down my temples.

Leo was a black silhouette against the bright light.

'Were you trying to escape?' he said.

'No—not originally.'

'How do you explain your actions, then?'

'It all happened because I warned Felix that the Strikeforces were after him. I heard you and Rich in the boiler room, on the night of the Month Party—'

Leo's eyebrows rose. 'Where were you?'

'Behind the boiler. I'd just watched Felix escape and locked the door after him—'

Leo looked triumphant. 'That explains the door—!' Then he frowned. 'Whose idea was it to escape?'

No point in pretending. 'It was Felix's.'

'Did you help him?'

'I made a bag out of discarded pillow cases for him—'

'Who else helped you?'

I bit my lip. 'Nobody.'

'You don't want to rethink that answer?'

I put my chin up. 'No.'

Leo frowned. 'Let's try another question, an easy one. I don't want the boys to get nasty with you right away. Did you know Felix was a pervert?'

I didn't answer. Leo hit my face.

'Answer me! Did you *know* Felix was a *pervert*?'

My nose and lips stung. Blood dripped from my face onto the table, but I couldn't staunch it because my hands were tied. I spat the blood from my mouth onto the stained table.

'*Answer me!*'

'He's not a pervert! I didn't know anything until we'd entered into our partnership. I wouldn't have offered myself to him if I'd known—'

'You're lying. You were in a partnership of convenience.'

I mumbled through bloody lips, '*We did our duty*! It took a while to manage it, that's all. I wish something had come of it—'

Leo was scornful. 'Felix hasn't been able to do his duty with any woman. And Jack told us you had your monthly bleeds in sequestration.'

Tears mixed with my blood. 'We tried! Ask Neena and Jessie and Rilla!'

Leo slammed his hand down. 'You lying shit!'

'I'm not lying! Ask Macon too—'

Leo's mouth twisted. 'Earth Above, you didn't fuck each other in front of Macon, did you? *That's* perverted.'

I shuddered. 'Of course not!' I took a deep breath. 'When I was sick, up there, Macon was worried I might be pregnant. It was too early for morning sickness, but it was possible. I was five or six days late with bleeding—'

Leo looked at me narrowly. 'Really?'

'You can ask Macon.' I took another deep breath to calm myself. 'I wanted to have Felix's child. It's true that my partnership with him was—*unusual*, but I didn't care that he was

... *that way*. He is—was—my best friend—I've always helped him—' I blinked away tears. 'There's nothing perverted about him.'

Leo rubbed his chin, and noted something on a piece of paper. 'Where do you say Vin and Macon found you?'

'A large thoroughfare near the Black Line. Heath Station Plaza or Heath Platform—I can't remember the name. We were hiding from a giant rat.'

'A *what*—? Don't play games.' Leo stood, blocking the light.

I shrank back. 'Ask them! There was a rat the size of a cat! They found us and tried to send us back. Felix came up with the Chief Councillor story—'

'What happened then?'

I paused. *Keep it short, and as close to the truth as possible.*

'Macon believed Felix's story and sent Vin home. He took us aboveground, scavenged some stuff we'd need, pointed us towards the settlement and left us. We walked for two days, then got attacked by wild dogs—it was awful—the big dog bit Felix—' I started to sob.

Leo waited for me to calm down. Then he said, 'Why did Macon then find you and bring you back?'

'He must have been suspicious, and he tracked us. He heard me screaming and ran to help. I don't remember much afterwards. I was sick—heat exhaustion. I couldn't stop vomiting. I saw a giant ant and other crazy stuff—'

Leo snorted. 'First giant rats, then giant ants—?'

'The ant wasn't real. I spent most of the next week resting. I slept a lot.'

'Who suggested coming home?'

'Macon did—repeatedly, from the start. But when I recovered, I wanted to come home too. I only left to help Felix.' I looked away.

'You seem to be on good terms with Macon now?'

'He saved my life. I was sick, I thought I was going to die.'

'Now I'm going to ask again. Who helped you with the escape?'

'I told you. It was just me and Felix—'

'We know that at least one other person was involved.' I couldn't stop myself from flinching. Leo pounced at my expression. 'There *was* someone else! Was it Macon?'

'*No!* He didn't know anything about it!'

Leo cracked his knuckles. 'Are you *sure?*'

'I wasn't allowed to talk to Macon! I didn't *want* to. I never wanted to see him again—!' *True at the time.*

'But you've disobeyed orders before? Haven't you?'

'Not this time. Even if I'd wanted to see him ... which I didn't ... I knew I was being watched—'

The table was covered with a dark red-brown stain. Leo smiled as he saw me look at it. 'If you lie again, I'll cut Macon's fingers off in front of you.'

'It wasn't Macon. It *wasn't.*'

'Who, then?'

'No one.'

'Right, that's enough.' Leo motioned to the guards. One untied my arms and the other held me down. I screamed. Meanwhile, Leo stood, and held my hand in his. 'Such a shame to damage such a perfect hand. But—'

He gestured to one of the young men. *Snap!*

I cried out with the sudden, searing pain. 'It's true!'

They broke the next finger on my left hand and let me sit down.

'There's eight more fingers to break if you keep lying—' Leo said, still standing.

How to tell the truth but keep Frankie out of it? 'Felix told one other person about his plan. They didn't think it was a good idea. He ... didn't want to participate.' *Crap. I said 'he'.* The pain was making it hard to think. I squeezed my eyes shut and leaned forward.

'That's better. Who was it?'

I kept my mouth shut.

Leo leaned closer. 'Shall I get that fat Barren you're sharing a cell with and get the boys to break her? The fingers are just the start. You don't want to know what they do next—'

Vomit rose in my throat, and I swallowed. 'Okay! It was … it was …' I shut my eyes. *I might be able to stay silent if they tortured me, but if they torture anyone else because of me … Forgive me, Frankie, Felix.* 'It was Frankie. The Barren. He stole a map but he didn't want to escape.'

Leo smiled. 'That's better, Marri.' He patted my head. 'Good girl.'

They repeated the questions again, in a different order. I hoped my answers were consistent, but I was horribly unsure. Leo seemed fixated on the idea that Macon had helped us escape. The only positive was that he didn't ask much about Felix's supposed death or my recovery from heat exhaustion.

When they dragged me back to my carriage room, I collapsed against Ramala, and she caught me. My nose and lips were still bleeding, and I wiped them with my sleeve.

'Did they *hit* you?' she said.

I nodded. 'And two of my fingers are broken.' I held out my hand. My injured fingers were already swollen and crooked.

Ramala's eyes widened. 'Those cockroach shits!'

'It could be worse. Leo threatened to torture other people in front of me.' I sank to the floor, sobbing. 'Ramala, I betrayed Frankie. I betrayed him!'

She sighed. 'I hadn't seen him around for at least a day before I was sequestered. I'm sure they already know—'

I lay in a foetal position on the floor. It was hard to sleep because my hand was throbbing.

Fred, the violent man who'd propositioned me before my partnership with Felix, was on warden duty. He laughed as he passed. 'You finally got what you deserve. Keep quiet, or I'll add to it.'

After five days in the stinking, cramped cell, Jack told me that my trial would be held that afternoon. 'I'm sorry,' he said, not meeting my eyes.

'Thanks, Jack,' I said. He was the only decent warden. The other two, Fred and Marvin, had begun waking us in the middle of the night and strip-searching us without any reason. The only time I'd left the cell was for interrogation. We weren't even taken to Lionel's Lights. I was almost looking forward to the trial so I could get out of the cell. *And ... I'll see Macon.*

When the guards came after the lunch bell, Ramala embraced me, crying. 'Good luck, Marri.'

I couldn't reply. Everything felt unreal, as if I'd had a Month Party drink, but in a bad way.

They tied my hands behind my back, and my broken fingers throbbed. The guards had to half-drag me because my legs had cramped.

The Council chamber was crowded. The main table had been removed, and a central circular area had been cleared, with guards around it. Pia was in the front row of the crowd, her eyes swollen and red. Nobody else would look at me when I passed my eyes over the crowd, not even Pam.

I gasped when I saw Macon. Like me, he was filthy and blood-spattered, but he also had a stubbly half-beard. His black eye had faded to spectacular greens and yellows. I peered at his hands. *I think he still has all his fingers, at least.* We were conducted to two seats in the centre. Guards stood beside us, crossbows at their sides. We quickly glanced at each other, and then looked away again.

Conor entered, his face shining with sweat, and sat at a large square table. *Bang bang bang!* He hit the table with a hammer, and I jumped. Everyone fell quiet.

He stood and read from a piece of paper. 'These two people are charged with treason. Macon is charged with aiding and abetting this woman, Marri, to escape, along with another. Marri is a destructive presence in our community. She is charged with attempting to escape, with assisting a known pervert to escape, and with failing to share herself.'

Then Conor looked at Macon. 'Did you help them plan this escape?'

'I didn't. I asked them to return.'

Conor looked at me, and I treated it as an invitation to speak. 'It's true. Someone who's planning to escape doesn't come back—'

Conor's face was covered with dislike. 'Can anyone else comment? This pair conducted a notorious illicit liaison. They've concocted this account.'

Vin stood forward, his voice wavering. 'I was there, Sir—'

Conor's eyes narrowed. 'Speak,' he commanded.

Vin cleared his throat and walked into the circle. His hands shook. 'Um, what they said is true, from what I saw. Macon and I found them hiding in a Fast Mart. We tried to persuade them to return, but they wouldn't. Marri screamed at Macon to shoot her, she was crazy—' He glanced at me. 'She didn't want him there. They could barely speak to each other politely. I thought she might punch him in the balls—sorry, I mean ... the *delicate* bits—'

A small nervous laugh went around the room.

'Silence!' said Conor. *Bang* went the hammer. 'Keep going, Vin.'

'Felix told us they were on a secret Council mission. Macon

and I believed him. Macon promised he would come back after a day. And yeah, I came back alone.'

Conor looked mildly disappointed.

'Thank you, Vin.' He turned to Leo, who was nearby. 'Does this accord with the interrogations?'

'Pretty much,' said Leo.

Conor turned back to Macon. 'Why didn't you return after a day, Macon?'

'I can explain,' said Macon. 'I realised after I'd helped them on their way that their story didn't make sense. I felt so stupid—' He cast his eyes down. 'When I found them, wild dogs were attacking them. Marri suffered heat exhaustion and collapsed. She almost died. She insisted on returning home as soon as she had recovered—I was worried she wasn't well enough, and that she was pregnant with Felix's child. I promised her I'd talk to the Council to make sure she wasn't treated harshly—'

I said in a loud voice, 'Everything he's said is true.'

Conor's lower lip stuck out. 'Do the interrogations agree, Leo?'

Leo paused, and I held my breath. But then he said, 'Macon and Marri told the same story. I don't think they could separately come up with giant ants—'

'I will decide Macon's fate.' Conor leaned back and stared at the roof. Then he pronounced his sentence: 'Macon will be released. However, his behaviour in siring three offspring with a dangerous law-breaker shows that he is disloyal. He will be reduced to the status of a Barren, or below, unless he proves his loyalty to me. He will not be on the Strikeforces again.'

The audience was still, but I was relieved. Not good, but Macon *lived*. I shot a glance at him and saw his jaw was clenched. *Stay quiet for our community and our children. Please ...*

Then Conor turned to me. 'The charges against Marri are

more serious. First, she tried to escape. Secondly, she assisted the known pervert, and entered into a fraudulent partnership with him—'

I was indignant. 'It wasn't a fake! I told Leo, we did our duty! It's not my fault that nothing came of it!'

Malice shone in Conor's eyes. 'Felix conducted relationships with other males. This letter is in Felix's handwriting.'

He brandished the letter they'd found on me, and read it in a horrible falsetto voice:

'*I'm sorry I left you. I wish you'd come with us. I will love you forever.*'

My blood turned to ice when Conor commanded Rich, 'Get Frankie.'

They dragged him in. He could barely walk, his eyes were blackened, and a front tooth was missing. I was not the only person to draw my breath in horror.

Conor eyed Frankie with distaste. 'Frankie has confessed to perversion with Felix. He said your partnership with Felix was false and that Felix intended to escape. He will be executed.'

Frankie raised his poor, battered face and saw me. His face froze with horror, and he began to cry. *Sorry*, he mouthed.

'No, Frankie,' I said aloud. '*You* don't need to say sorry to *me*—' They had *tortured* this kind man who Felix loved. I had informed on him. My heart burned.

'Be *quiet*, woman,' said Conor. 'You have also been charged with failing to share yourself. Your partnership with Felix was a sham, and you had three offspring with Macon. You *know* that we need to share to rebuild a genetically diverse population. You've broken the rules over and over—'

Despite my bound hands and cramped legs, I stood. My vision had gone red. I turned around to face everyone. My voice shook with anger as I said, 'It's true that Felix was born with a love of men. He didn't ask for it. It brought him pain, as well as comfort. He was ashamed, though I don't think he should have been. Even so, we did our duty—we did! I'd be proud to bear his child; I wish something had come of it.'

I knew I was making things worse for myself, but I couldn't stop. 'I never forced anyone to do anything they didn't want to do—nor did Felix. Our actions came from *love*. I helped Felix escape because he was my friend. I've been punished for what Macon and I did, but I don't regret it. I'll always love him, no matter what!'

There was a shocked silence.

Behind me, Conor said, almost blankly, 'You're a fool— you've admitted the charges against you.'

I didn't care: I needed to say something. It brimmed over.

'This society isn't loving. It's a *lie*! Conor broke the rules too, and no one did anything about it. It's not sharing if you're forced, that's our rule. When I was sequestered, he raped me—and he tried to do it again—'

'BE QUIET!' screamed Conor. I supposed he was so arrogant that he hadn't realised what I might say if I had nothing to lose. Perhaps he really had believed that he was doing me a favour. He shook with rage. 'Guards, restrain her. Gag her. Don't listen to this lying piece of rat crap!'

The guards raced forward. I tried to bite Rich's arm, but he hit me in the face. I fell to the ground, my ears ringing and my head spinning. My left hand throbbed with pain. Rich put his knee into the small of my back, and tied the gag so tight I could barely breathe.

While the guards were attempting to restrain me, and while others were taking Frankie out, Macon stood, and strained against the bonds holding his wrists. 'STOP! LEAVE HER ALONE!'

Rich and the other guards paused.

Macon turned to the crowd and said, 'The question I ask

is *who* judges this man Conor? Can he rule on his own conduct? He abuses Barrens, he's raped a woman and he tortures people! You should be judging him, not Marri—you have to let her go!'

Rich stopped grappling with me. He walked over and held his crossbow to Macon's head. 'Stop talking, man. *Stop* it! What under the Earth has happened to you—?'

Macon ignored Rich and his crossbow, and looked at me. 'Marri, I kept my distance after our son was born because my sire said he'd hang you if I came near you again. I'm sorry I didn't stand up to him. I love you too. You're my partner for life, remember?'

Oh, my poor love. That's what happened after Tomas. Pride, fear, distress, love, sadness, and regret warred within me. *You silly, brave man. We're both going to die. Why can't I keep my temper?*

Conor leapt up, puce with rage. 'Gag him too! *Now!*' The guards obeyed. It took three men to hold Macon down.

Everyone sat silently while Conor's face turned back to cherry red and he composed himself. *Isn't anyone going to speak out? Can't they see that Conor gagged us because we spoke the truth?*

Eventually, Conor banged his hammer on the table, and pronounced his sentence:

'I have revised my sentence against Macon in light of what he has just revealed. He has continued his unlawful liaison this woman. Felix, Marri and Macon were and are dangerous perverts who threaten our goal of creating a diverse new society built on love and sharing.'

I wanted to laugh. *Why is nobody laughing?*

'I sentence these people to immediate execution. They refuse to observe our rules. These elements must be expunged.'

He walked out.

Some people were weeping. Pam had fainted, and someone was trying to rouse her. I wasn't faring much better; the guards had to carry me back to the cells.

I had expected that sentence for myself, but I was heartbroken for Macon. *It's my fault. I couldn't keep my mouth shut. He can't help our children now.* I was filled with unutterable sorrow.

When I was returned to our carriage room, Ramala tried to talk, but I lay and stared at the roof instead. I retreated to a place in the back of my mind. I had been there before, when I was sequestered the first time, after Conor.

Tears rolled into my ears, and pooled there. I didn't wipe them away. I couldn't stop blaming myself. If I'd been better at following the rules in the first place—if I hadn't run away—if I hadn't told Macon I wanted to free our children—if I hadn't insisted on coming as well—if I hadn't lost my temper during the trial—the list went on.

The next time Jack was on shift, he looked in the window and pleaded with me to eat.

I looked at the roof. There was no point eating, or speaking.

CHAPTER 18

The day before my execution, I was in despair. I'd barely moved since the trial, and I hadn't spoken or eaten.

Ramala kept trying to talk to me, though I never responded. After lunch, we heard shouts and scuffling even from our cell. Ramala rushed to the grimy windows and wiped them with her sleeve. 'They're bringing in *Peter*! He's fighting like a crazy man.'

A spark of interest kindled in me. *Peter*? Suze's current partner?

'He's kicked a guard in the balls!' she reported gleefully. 'He's trying to kick Jack!'

Sudden silence. My interest burned more strongly. I waited.

'Crap, a guard knocked him out,' said Ramala. 'They hit him hard. I hope he's okay—'

She stroked my hair back from my face. I'd seen Lily comfort her children in a similar way when they were distressed. *I'll never get the chance to pat my children's hair like that.* Tears rolled down my cheeks, and Ramala sighed.

Then we heard a high-pitched shriek, and more shouting.

Ramala peered out. 'Marri, you've *got* to see this! It's *Suze*!'

I couldn't resist turning my head when I heard a furious screech. 'She just clawed Jack!' said Ramala. 'He's so tall that he held her back, but—!'

My head spun, and glittering lights swum in my vision. I crawled slowly to Ramala, and leaned against the window ledge. My voice was croaky with disuse. 'Have they arrested her?'

Ramala started when I spoke. 'Marri! Thank the Earth you're back to yourself! She's trying to rescue Peter—?'

Suze shouted, 'Let him out *now!*'

Jack held Suze at arm's length. 'Go back to your room, Suze—!'

'How can I leave him here? Tell me that!' shrieked Suze, still trying to hit Jack. She was stronger than I had realised.

Jack pushed her away. 'Please, Suze. They'll arrest you—'

'I don't care!' Suze collapsed and grabbed Jack's knees. 'Just let me talk to him.'

Jack pulled Suze up, and they disappeared in the direction of the other cell block. A little time later, they came back. Suze was sobbing convulsively, while Jack half-supported her. Ramala and I looked at each other in horror.

As they passed our cell, Jack stopped and stared at me. 'You're up! Do you need some food?'

I shook my head. 'Is Peter ... okay?'

Suze's eyes were swollen and red. 'He's unconscious.' She stared through the window. 'Earth Above, how long since you've had a shower?'

'They don't wash us,' Ramala snapped.

Suze glared at Jack. 'You're not going to treat Pete like this, are you?'

Jack looked away. 'This isn't a Month Party, Suze.'

'No.' Suze pointed at Jack. 'I need to tell Marri something.'

Jack tried to grab Suze's arm, but she shoved him away. 'I'm a free woman. I can talk to her if I want.' He relented.

Suze looked me in the eye, her chin up. 'Pete told Conor he wasn't fit to be leader. He demanded that you and Macon weren't to be executed. That's why he got sequestered.'

As it sank in, I choked with emotion and put my head on the floor.

'You're kidding!' said Ramala. 'He's so brave!'

'Brave fool,' I sighed.

Suze's eyes shone with unshed tears. 'I thought you should know, Marri.'

I pushed myself into a kneeling position. 'Thank him from me.'

Suze sighed. 'You're a good woman, Marri—'

Self-loathing bubbled within me. 'I'm an idiot. I wish I'd kept quiet. For Macon's sake, and my own—'

Suze crossed her arms. 'Most people don't say what they think—we're too scared. If more of us were like you and Pete, things would be different.'

'If I hadn't lost my temper, Conor wouldn't have sentenced Macon to death.' I bowed my head, remembering how Macon had railed against Conor at our trial.

Suze patted my hand where it gripped the bars. 'Everyone knew you'd be sentenced to death. Macon was always going to try to join you—that's not your fault—'

'I agree,' said Ramala.

'So do I,' said Jack, and we all turned to look at him in surprise.

Suze's friendly face hardened as she looked at Jack. 'How can you do this job, Jack? I thought you were one of the decent ones—'

'So did I,' muttered Ramala.

Jack's cheeks darkened, but he rounded on Suze with surprising vehemence. 'They're going to enforce the rules properly. I'm sick of people not being treated equally. Surely you understand!'

I nodded. 'I remember when we talked, that time in the corridor. I was the only one to be sequestered after Macon and I were caught.'

Jack spread his hands. 'My sire was a hydroponic technician. No one helped me get out of work, or got me a nice job.

This job was a step up for me.'

Ramala snorted derisively. 'Awesome job, Jack!'

Jack thrust out his lower lip. 'Let's say I quit. Only Fred and Marvin would be left to look after the prisoners.'

Suze noticed my shudder of distaste. A grimace of horror spread across her face, and her mouth worked, but she had nothing to say.

'Leave it, Suze,' I said. 'I don't want you to be sequestered too.'

Jack looked at me approvingly. 'Marri's right. Our society needs to be reset—recalibrated. It's a pity people have to suffer for it, but that's how things are—'

Suze bit her lip. 'I'd better go.' She looked at Jack. 'Can you tell Pete I visited?'

Suze's shoulders drooped as she trudged away.

Once she had gone, I was consumed with the execution tomorrow. *Who will be first, me or Macon? I can't think what is worse. I must be strong for him, whichever it is.*

I tossed and turned that night. In my dreams, I chased someone or something through the tunnels, but I couldn't catch it. Sometimes it was Macon; sometimes it was the children; sometimes it was the Monster Rat, its eyes glowing like red spheres, its teeth ready to rip out my throat. Every time, I woke up sweating. I couldn't sleep any more.

As I lay awake, I remembered something I hadn't thought about for years. I had been sitting next to Rilla in class when a bug wandered across the floor. One moment it was walking, the next it was squashed under her finger. The swiftness of that transition from life to death had horrified me. That was going to be me tomorrow.

The next morning, I didn't want any breakfast. I drank a little water.

Jack knelt and whispered. 'He asked me to tell you that he loves you. And that you are still—*married*? I don't know what that means.'

I said, 'Tell him I love him too. That we'll live on—in a way—in our children, and I'm glad we put everything right between us before—' I choked. Ramala cried, quietly.

Jack said, 'I'll tell him.'

I lay down, closed my eyes, and breathed slowly, trying to clear my mind. I wanted to look brave.

When they arrived, the guards gagged and bound me. I could barely walk, and they carried me the short distance to the execution area.

The execution platform had featured in my nightmares since Petra was hung. In my dreams, the roof had been higher, and the shadows had concealed lurking black hands which grabbed my throat. I wondered if I'd had a premonition about my death, and shivered.

A large crowd was gathered in front of the scaffold. The noose swung gently in the breeze from a ventilation tunnel. As I was brought past, conversation stopped, and there was a collective gasp. But I caught a perverse look of pleasure on Jessie's face. She wasn't the only one to be enjoying the drama—Seana and Paul looked excited too; the atmosphere reminded me of a Month Party.

I couldn't believe this was really happening. I sagged, but the guards pulled me up. Cam snarled, but the other guard, Flynn, supported me. I was astonished to see that his eyes were damp.

Macon was paraded in front of the crowd next. He was bruised, dirty and thin, and had also been gagged. We stared at each other. I tried to stand up straighter. *Be brave. For him.*

Boom! Boom! A drumbeat sounded. Conor marched out,

wearing a pompous red suit the colour of blood. I wondered where they'd found the red material. I had enough spirit to notice that Conor's suit clashed with the pink of his face. I wished I wasn't gagged so I could tell him. *No reason to keep my big mouth closed if I'm going to die anyway.*

Rich emerged behind Conor, his face in grim lines. He looked down at the ground, his hands shaking.

Conor read from a script. 'We are here today to see the execution of two notorious criminals. Let them be an example to all who would think of rebellion. Rich will conduct the executions.'

My mind wouldn't stop processing what was happening, right to the end. *The Chief Councillor never needed a script. He wore the same clothing as the rest of us. Rich doesn't look happy with his new job.*

Rich didn't move right away. He consulted a piece of paper, and chewed his lip. *Is he going to speak too?*

I jumped—Suze was stepping forward from the crowd, almost to the gallows. Her hair stood out in long crazy curls, and her top was crooked. Her eyes were still swollen and red. Some unkind people in the crowd sniggered. She ignored them. 'Sir, I would like to say something before the executions.'

Conor looked at her quizzically. 'You want to speak, Suze?'

Suze ducked her head. 'May I?'

Conor gestured. *Be my guest*, said his hand.

Suze stood next to Conor and turned to the crowd. 'Yesterday, after seeing Marri in sequestration, I realised something. We need to change our society, and sometimes people get hurt in the process. What will happen next is difficult, but necessary, so that the society I love isn't ruined.'

I was puzzled and betrayed. *Do you have to rub it in?*

Conor smirked, and stroked his chin. He signalled the guards.

The guards pulled at my arms, and Rich moved towards the gallows. Macon strained against his ropes, and his guards pulled him back. My legs had gone to water and I couldn't walk. Flynn and Cam grabbed my elbows and hoisted me onto the wooden platform. They removed the gag. I licked my lips, and wondered if I could speak.

Suze spoke instead. 'Someone needs to do something about the criminals in our society. *I have had enough.*'

She reached under her loose top and drew out a pickaxe, the kind used by Strikeforces to clear debris. The honed edge and sharp point shone. She turned and brandished the axe in my direction.

I mouthed 'Suze—!' but no sound came out. I cringed, and there was a muffled shout from Macon.

Then, with a swift movement, Suze pivoted, and swung the pickaxe high, right into Conor's neck. As I had noticed yesterday, she had a surprising strength. He put his hands up to protect himself, but it was too late. I gasped with shock as the axe made a revolting *crunch*. In sequestration I had dreamed of killing Conor, but I was unprepared for the reality.

By chance or design, Suze had hit a large blood vessel in the side of Conor's neck. Blood spewed from his neck in rhythmic gushes, soaking into his red suit. He reached out to grab Suze, a look of disbelief on his face. Then he gave a horrible bubbling gasp, and grasped at his throat and his chest, and fell to his knees.

A woman wailed. The sound released the guards from their shock. A thrumming set of twangs, and a crossbow bolt stood out of Suze's chest. She looked at it and sank to the ground. Darker blood spread where the bolt had hit, mingling with Conor's blood. The pickaxe fell from her hand and clattered to the floor.

Rich put up his hands and shouted. '*Stop!* No more! *Put the crossbows down!* Keep calm!'

The guards lowered their crossbows, and all was quiet. Conor fell forward. His gasping gurgles slowed, and stopped.

Rich checked Conor's pulse, then moved towards me. I tried to run.

'Stop, you stupid woman, I'm not going to hurt you,' he said. To my surprise, he loosened the cords around my wrists, and I pulled my hands free.

I rushed to my kind, tactless, brave friend Suze. Dear Suze, who had turned out to be better than any of us. No one stopped me. She looked up at me. She couldn't speak, and bloody froth bubbled from her mouth. But she smiled, her teeth red. There was triumph in that look. I held her to my breast.

'Suze, no, no, no! *Suze!*'

She gave two rattling breaths, and died.

CHAPTER 19

As I held Suze, Rich told the crowd to leave the platform area. To my surprise, almost everyone obeyed. Someone was keening, a dreadful rising wail. From a distance, it looked like Rilla. I was glad when she was escorted out.

I felt a hand on my shoulder. It was Macon: Jack had untied him. I hugged him, crying. I could feel his ribs and the ridges of his shoulder bones through his shirt. He didn't flinch, even though I was filthy and covered in blood. He hugged me back. I was shivering.

Rich told Jack to release all the people in sequestration. I let go of Macon and pulled at Jack's sleeve. 'Let Peter out first.'

Jack nodded, and went to the train carriages.

Peter ran to Suze's body. After a moment of hesitation, he knelt and held her, crying.

Some of the freed people spat at Jack, but most ignored him. Others threw angry looks at Rich. Rich had picked up a spare crossbow and had it half-raised across his body in warning.

When Ramala saw me, her face broke into a smile. 'I didn't believe it!' she said, hugging me. 'I couldn't believe it when they told me!'

I looked for Frankie among the freed people. Macon's arm was tense where I was holding it, and he scrutinised the faces of everyone who emerged.

'I don't see Frankie.' I frowned. 'Who are *you* looking for?'

'I was hoping—that they'd sequestered the Councillors. Surely they would have been useful? But—I don't see—'

I squeezed his arm. 'I'll ask Jack.'

Jack shook his head. 'They just said the Council was gone and that Conor was the new Leader—but I'm guessing—'

I nodded. 'What about Frankie? The Barren guy who did deliveries?'

Jack frowned. 'He's alive, but only just. He got that cough that's going around. A few people have died. I'll see if the medics and Barren midwives can help him.'

I dreaded the answer, but I needed to know. 'Who's died—?'

'Remember Mack, the mushroom guy? He was the first.' Tears filled my eyes, and I bowed my head, remembering how he'd saved me from Conor.

I walked back to Macon. 'Frankie's alive, but Jack says there's no Councillors here—'

Macon's face fell. He held my hand tightly. 'Somewhere else, maybe?'

I shook my head. 'Not that Jack knows.'

He looked away. His grip on my hand had become almost painful, and I tried to shift my fingers without removing my hand.

Jack came up. 'Do you want to see Frankie?'

I smelled Frankie's cell before I saw it. The cell was more cramped and filthier than mine, with puddles of excrement and blood on the floor.

Frankie was curled in the corner. He coughed, a wet, unpleasant sound that made me wince. I stepped gingerly over the puddles, knelt, and put my hand on his shoulder. He was burning up, and his bony, bruised face was covered in sweat.

'Marri! Am I dreaming? I thought they'd killed you.' Frankie's normally tanned face turned paler as his eyes focused on me. 'Blood everywhere! Are you hurt?'

'Not my blood.' I squeezed his shoulder. 'Felix is alive. I left him above ground.'

Frankie's eyes widened. 'He's *alive*? He's alive!' Tears carved tracks down his grimy face.

'I'll write to him. I'm sure he'll come home to see you.'

'Thank you,' said Frankie. Then horror filled his eyes. 'I told them about the escape! I wish they'd killed me!' He put his hands over his eyes, and I gasped. They'd broken all his fingers and pulled out some nails.

I cried. 'I told them about you helping us too. I'm sorry. I don't blame you. I promise I don't. I hope you don't blame me—'

A Barren midwife pushed past me. 'We need to get him to the medical room.' I hadn't heard her arrive, but I got out of the way.

Macon was waiting outside. 'Let's go see the children,' I said.

He stared. 'Are you *insane*?'

His disbelief stung me. I thought he'd understood how I felt about them. My voice broke. 'Our children. I want to see them!'

Macon sighed. 'You're covered in blood and crap. You stink like ten toilets. If any children saw you, they'd run screaming.'

'Oh. I forgot,' I said in a small voice. 'Do you think we could have a shower—?'

I had to sit on a chair in the shower. The cramping in my legs eased as the warm water flowed over me. It was indescribably wonderful to remove the blood and filth, although some dirt was ingrained. I felt I was turning into a real human again. Someone had found us clean clothes. Macon was shaving in front of a nasty greenish mirror. I checked to see no one was looking, then kissed his smooth cheek.

We sat in the communal eating area and ate slowly. Someone had smeared mud over the picture of the Chief Councillor, and his painted eyes had been hacked out. I saw Macon's eyes move to the mural, and then flicker away.

As we finished our meal, there was a rumbling crash. A smoky smell filled the room and Strikeforce men ran into the dining room with crossbows raised.

'What's going on?' I said.

Two Strikers went to the Barrens serving food. 'Don't move! Sit on the floor with your hands on your heads!'

The Barrens did as they were told. I cowered next to Macon, shaking, and he put his arm around me. As a Strikeforce man ran past, Macon grabbed him by the elbow. 'Sam, what's all this about?'

Sam, a middle-aged, balding man, stopped. 'Hey mate, glad you're not dead! Some of the Barrens are rebelling. Don't worry, we won't let them get here. They're cornered now.'

I pulled at Macon's elbow. 'The children.'

We hurried to the children's rooms. There were no signs of rebellion there, although Strikers stood on guard everywhere. I skirted widely around them.

When we arrived at Lilah's room, she ran to me and hugged my legs. She said accusingly, 'You haven't been here for *ages*, Marri!'

I knelt. 'I'm sorry. I wanted to see you, more than anything, but I couldn't come.' I stroked her bright red hair. 'I've got something to tell you, but it might be difficult for you to understand. You know how women have babies? You were *my* baby. I carried you in my tummy.'

Her grin of triumph astonished me. 'I *thought* you were my mother, even though they told us not to think about that. I could tell from how you looked at me.' I was momentarily struck dumb.

Macon stood to the side, shifting his feet. Lilah looked up at him when he moved. 'And are you ... my *sire*? They said he was a Striker. They said he had red hair too.' She inspected his hair suspiciously, and jumped from foot to foot.

'Yes. Hello.' He waved his hand in a small gesture.

Lilah smiled. 'Do you know something?'

After a long pause, he said, 'What?'

'My special cart rescues people. It was going to rescue you and her.' She pointed at us.

'Oh,' he said. 'Good.'

'John told me you were dead. He's *wrong*. Ha! I'll tell *him*.'

She went to run away, but I gently caught her arm. 'Lilah, can we visit again? Would you mind?'

'Sure, Marri! But I've got to tell Marla 'bout this!' She raced away.

We pushed through the curtains to Cady's room. She didn't seem to understand when I explained that I was her birth mother, but she asked me to hug her. From my arms, she demanded that Macon hug her too. He put his arms around me as I was holding her. Internally I winced. *Could he be any* more *awkward?*

Macon was almost tearful when he met Tomas, although he later tried to pretend that I had imagined it. I tried to pass Tomas to him, and he backed away, his hands raised.

'What if I drop it?'

All the women in the babies' room laughed. I sighed. 'I can't believe that a man who doesn't flinch when Rich holds a crossbow to his head is scared of a baby.'

He backed away further. 'I'm not scared! And that's totally ... different—!'

When we returned to the main thoroughfare, Sam the Striker told us that the Barren rebels had been subdued. He shook his head. 'It's all the fault of that rat Wilson. He talked them up big and proper, told them he was going to be the new Chief Councillor.'

Apparently, they'd managed to set fire to the Month Party room, which had partly collapsed, killing two Barrens and a Strikeforce man, but also putting out the fire. Wilson had been sequestered. I found out later that the limping Barren who'd brought my morning meals during sequestration was one of the Barrens who'd been killed, and couldn't help feeling a pang of sadness.

We were exhausted, and decided to sleep. Neena stood at the doors of the communal sleeping quarters, her face serious and her hands over her pregnant belly.

'Macon. I've been waiting for you.'

'Should I leave—?' I asked.

'No, stay—' She and Macon spoke simultaneously. I moved closer to Macon.

Neena patted her stomach. 'Jack said you wanted to know what happened to the Councillors—'

'Are they dead?' asked Macon.

Neena closed her eyes for about two heartbeats before answering. 'Yes.'

'How?'

Neena's face fell. 'They were shot with crossbows. We'll arrange for the bodies to be cremated.'

Macon took a step backwards. 'Thanks for letting me know.'

'I wish it had been otherwise.'

After she left, I led Macon to the nearest vacant sleeping quarters. He sat heavily on the bed, his head in his hands. I drew the curtains and patted his back, unsure what to say. I hadn't cried when my own sire died—there was no reason.

Macon's eyes were reddened when he raised his head. 'In his own weird way, he had affection for me—'

'I'm sorry, love—'

'Thanks.'

We lay down. We had survived, but it didn't feel like a victory. I put my head on Macon's chest and held him, while he patted my hair. We fell asleep.

We learned the next day how the coup had unfolded. Conor had talked about a quarter of the Strikeforces into joining him. He had invited each Councillor to a remote corridor for a private meeting, where the Councillors were shot, and their bodies hidden in a side room. Adam had been tortured. They'd also executed the Commander of the Strikeforces after he'd protested.

For about a week after Conor's assassination, there was a strange lull in the tunnels. Perhaps the funerals dampened everyone's mood. The Councillors were cremated first, and we attended the Chief Councillor's funeral, then Adam's. After that, funerals were held for Suze, Conor and the people who'd died in sequestration or in the short uprising. Almost everyone attended Suze's funeral. Someone had drawn Suze's birth-mother symbol on her urn, a swirly pattern like a supraterran flower. I wanted more than that. I picked up a piece of burnt wood from the floor, and scraped 'Suze' on the urn. Then I wrote 'A Brave Woman'.

As we left, Peter sat by Suze's urn. I wanted to say that I thought Suze had loved him, and to thank him. But he didn't raise his eyes, and I didn't want to intrude.

After Suze's funeral, we had a public meeting. Macon and I told anyone who wanted to attend about the supraterran settlement. Some of what we had seen was difficult to describe. How do you explain cows to people who have only seen rats and cats? We didn't know the answers to some questions, and I suspected that some people didn't believe us.

Conor's remains were put in an unmarked urn, and it was placed with the other unmarked urns without ceremony. I heard later that Ramala had suggested his remains should be tipped into the cesspit. I was glad we hadn't done that. We did not treat him with disrespect, but nor did we treat him with deference: he was treated as a Barren who had sired no children, although of course he had sired many.

The solar generators kept breaking down. Macon had to fix them every time at first, although he said that the people he was training were progressing well. We had to use lamps a lot. The hydroponic plants were not doing well because of the generator failures. The pumping system was struggling too. A flash flood in one of the storage tunnels ruined a stash of food, and a woman who had been walking down the tunnel at the time drowned.

A Strikeforce messenger was sent to the settlement Above to explain why the Strikeforces were late in delivering the goods we usually swapped for food, and to tell Felix what had happened.

I felt adrift, with nothing to anchor me to my life before. The only thing that remained from our old life was the weekly session at the Lights. There were no Month Parties, because the room was still unsafe. There were informal parties in another abandoned tunnel, but both Barrens and non-Barrens attended, and to my shock, some people were apparently taking several partners at a time. Nor were there weekly talks by the Chief Councillor, although the hacked-out hollows where his painted eyes had been still watched me reproachfully as I ate meals.

Everyone now ate together, although a few non-Barrens still refused to sit next to Barrens. On the other hand, some of the Barrens said that they should eat first, and non-Barrens should wait until they were finished, so that we would know what it felt like. Food was scarce. The mushroom beds were not well cared-for now Mack was dead. We hadn't been self-sufficient for a long time, but the Strikeforces were so disorganised and decimated that the trades with the supraterran settlement were difficult to complete.

After the Barrens protested and refused to do their duties for three days, Wilson the rebel Barren was released from sequestration. The man's sudden prominence confused me. I'd never heard of him before, although he'd apparently stoked the boilers for fifteen years.

Two weeks after we had been released, I said to Macon, 'Do you remember the rain on the way back here?'

Macon gave me a rare smile. 'The rain that you liked at first, and then hated—?'

'Remember how the air felt before the rain fell? It felt ... full ... like it was pressing on my ears. And I'm getting that feeling again now, but not in my ears.'

Macon's face fell, and I felt bad for chasing away his smile. But then he said, 'I feel it too. A build-up of pressure.'

'I wonder why we're getting that feeling?'

We found out the next day. A group of Barrens cornered Jack and beat him badly. We went to visit him, but he was still unconscious. Talla was worried that he would never wake again. After four days, I was relieved to hear that he'd come around, although he was still badly wounded.

The mood in the tunnels worsened after that. Some Barrens openly strutted around the corridors, boasting about Jack's injuries, but nothing was done about it.

At the dinner table, a stocky Barren man with burned hands glanced quickly at us before he spoke, his blue eyes like knives.

'Jack won't be the last to be beaten. Mark my words.' As he bent his head to eat, he smirked at his plate. I bit my lip, and looked at Macon. Macon's eyes narrowed.

Another Barren cracked his knuckles and grinned at our apprehension. 'You're right, Wilson. Too right.' With a prickle of fear, I realised the stocky man was the rebel responsible for the riot and fire after our release.

Paul, who was opposite us, stood abruptly. 'I don't have to listen to talk like that from you, Barren cockroach.' He strode away. Later I saw a huddle of men in the corridor, with Paul at their centre. 'It's only justice,' whined a boy with a few wisps of hair on his chin. 'We can't let them get away with it ...' Someone indicated that I was watching and they all quietened and moved away.

I told Macon what I had heard, and he told the Strikeforces, but they said nothing could be done unless any actual threats or violence were witnessed.

A few days passed, and I began to hope things had calmed down. But one evening after dinner, a mob of non-Barren men beat old Bran the Registrar. He died the next day, and I sobbed, thinking of that poor frail man cowering under blows.

Bran had been popular across the community, Barren and non-Barren. Phil the Strikeforce man called everyone together as the Chief Councillor had always done. We wondered if he was setting himself up as a new Councillor. But his speech was short.

'The beatings will stop. I'm not the Chief Councillor, and I've no wish to be, but I'll hang any arsehole I discover beating anyone after this.' He looked at Wilson, who stood at the front of the crowd, arms crossed. 'Even you, Wilson.' Wilson snarled, but Phil had ten armed men behind him.

The beatings ceased, but tension bubbled under the surface.

Shortly after Bran's death, Neena and Peter approached us to suggest that the Council should be reconstituted, but that the ten members should be elected. Our description of the Elders had inspired them. We agreed; we felt that it was important to have leadership again. Eventually we came up with a list of ten people and provided it to Neena.

A few days later, Macon and I were eating breakfast when a serious group approached us. *What's going on?* I tensed, my body fearing sequestration.

In fact, we'd been nominated to sit on the new Council. The new Councillors included women, and three Barrens: Ramala, Frankie and Wilson.

Macon laughed when we returned to our cubicle. 'So my father got what he wanted for me, after all.'

'You were *always* going to be nominated.' I kissed his cheek. 'They want to keep you, as any sane person would—'

After some thought, we accepted the Council nominations on a temporary basis. We were clear that we would leave once our society could cope without us.

Three days later, the messenger from the Strikeforces returned from the settlement. To my surprise, he was accompanied by a tanned supraterran man. The man stared at me.

'Marri!' he said. My jaw dropped when I realised it was Felix.

'You're looking very well,' I said. There was a pause. 'Don't worry, I know I'm not looking well at all.'

'I heard what happened. I'm sorry. I wish I'd never written that letter—' His hands were clenched.

I grabbed Felix's arm. 'Frankie doesn't see it that way. Nor do I!' I sighed. 'If anything, Frankie blames himself for not coming with you.'

Felix looked unconvinced. I glared at him. 'Don't make sad cow eyes at me, Felix! It's not your fault—'

Felix blinked. 'Did you just say I had *cow eyes*?'

'I'll call you Buttercup if you don't cheer up. I'm taking you to Frankie.'

We went to the medical area. Frankie lay on a bed, staring at the water-stained concrete ceiling. Felix gasped as he saw Frankie's injuries.

Frankie turned at the noise, and his face lit up. 'Felix—!'

'Frankie,' said Felix, lingering in the doorway.

'I'm so sorry I didn't come with you ...' said Frankie, and started to cry.

Felix winced with pain. 'No, I'm sorry—'

He still didn't move towards Frankie.

'Get in there, Buttercup.' I pushed him. 'He's tied up with guilt; I've had to drag him here.' Felix glared, but I didn't care. It was better than the stupid shy act. I shoved him again.

'Guilt about what?' said Frankie, smiling through his tears. 'Did you meet a handsome supraterran man?'

'No!' Felix frowned. 'It's my fault. You being hurt, her being hurt, everything—'

'And I was worried that you didn't want to come in because my good looks have been ruined—' Frankie's tone was joking, but I sensed a genuine current of worry underlying his words.

Felix sat on the edge of the bed and stroked Frankie's battered cheek. 'You look as gorgeous as ever.'

Frankie gave him a smouldering look.

'My work is done,' I said, smiling, and left.

The next day, Frankie moved out of the medical rooms and into a couple's room with Felix. To my surprise, no one said anything. Felix and Frankie didn't hug or kiss in public—maybe they were too used to sneaking around—so everyone pretended nothing was happening. I hoped they wouldn't have to pretend for long. I had never seen Felix so relaxed, and it was wonderful.

However, I couldn't help contrasting Felix's happiness with my own situation over the next few months. Macon and I were constantly busy, and stressed by our roles on the Council. Nights provided no relief. Macon suffered from terrible recurring nightmares, and I was guiltily relieved when he had to fix a solar generator because it gave me a break from his thrashing and shouting.

Most nights, I lay awake worrying. The vision of the crossbow bolt entering Suze's body kept coming into my mind, whether I wanted it to or not.

I began to check on our children, to make sure that no one had beaten them or taken them away. One night, I checked ten times, and felt dreadful the next day. I tried harder after that to restrain myself from checking them, but terrible visions of the things that might happen to them would not stop crowding into my head.

A few weeks later, as I pushed through the curtains to our cubicle, I jumped when Macon sat up and glared at me.

'*What* were you doing?'

'Checking on the children.'

'Didn't you check before bedtime?'

I nodded.

'How many times tonight?'

'Only twice.'

He scowled. 'What's going on?'

I sat down. 'I don't know.'

'You're not happy.'

'No.' I hadn't acknowledged this before.

'Why?'

I started to cry. 'This isn't working. You, me, this whole place.'

'This place is a pile of rat crap, but how could you doubt me? I told you I loved you in front of everyone. For the Earth's sake, what *else* do I have to do?'

'We don't talk, we don't kiss, we don't have sex. We do our

jobs, see the children, sleep, and that's it. You're always in a bad mood. Maybe you don't want an ongoing partnership?' I bit my lip. 'The old Council would have begun to consider whether we should be split up by now.'

'I love you! But I've been worried—'

'About what?'

'Food, our children, a Barren rebellion. Also, Tomas is so young, and you're still unwell. I don't want you to fall pregnant.'

'Why didn't you tell me?'

'I don't know, I wasn't sure how you felt—'

I shook my head and pulled the box from under our bed. I pushed away his experimental machines, and drew out a woollen woven bag. I took out some dried leaves and brandished them at him.

'What are those? They look supraterran.'

I was smug. 'They're from Lily. Felix brought them. If a woman boils one of these leaves in water and drinks the tea every morning, she won't get pregnant.'

'Why didn't you tell me?'

'You've been so grumpy, it's been difficult to have a proper conversation.'

'That was a big mistake. Have you drunk that tea?'

I grinned. 'Every day since Felix arrived.'

He smiled broadly. 'Oh well, in *that* case—'

After that, I was left in no doubt that Macon still liked me. I had no trouble getting to sleep, nor did I wake to check on the children again.

But there were still difficult times. We had quirks which hadn't been evident in our previous brief partnerships. We had to get used to the idea that our relationship didn't have a fixed end.

We also had to get to know our children. Macon was afraid he'd lost his chance. I still had trouble letting them out of my sight, but I couldn't shake the sense that this desire was self-ish. We began taking them out of care for a time, sometimes eating lunch together. We ate in the communal area once, and a few people complained that it put them off their food. However, after we had visited our children several times, we noticed that others were quietly visiting their offspring too.

Tomas fascinated Lilah and Cady; they had never seen babies in their age-segregated classes. Lilah loved to cover her eyes with her hands, and then remove her hands and shout 'Boo!' Tomas thought this was hilarious. His chuckle was a thing of wonder. Macon and I couldn't help laughing every time we heard it.

It was lucky that we had the joy of our children to sustain us, because the Council had a difficult job. Some wounds never heal fully. My fingers were still scarred and crooked, just like our society. Our first task was to work out what to do with those who had participated in the coup. Anyone who had assisted Conor in killing Councillors was put on trial and juries decided their fate.

Leo's jury decided that he should be hanged. I knew Leo was a torturer, but having almost been hung myself, I felt a terrible sympathy, even for him. Surprisingly, Rich was exonerated. He argued that he had saved our society from falling apart after Conor's death, and managed to convince his jury that he had acted with good intentions. Ramala and Wilson were furious.

Then the Council had to decide what to do with people who had been involved with Conor's regime in smaller ways. These people had helped Conor, but some had shown small kindnesses and expressed misgivings. Wilson wanted *anyone* who had not spoken out against Conor to be sequestered and tried. If they couldn't justify their failure to act, he believed that they should be exiled or executed. Luckily no one else agreed, and instead we decided that only people who had an official role should be put on trial.

Then Wilson argued that those who had an official role should be presumed to have been in the wrong. I disagreed. 'We don't know why these people did what they did. They should be allowed to explain.'

The Council had an even number, a mistake the supraterran settlement had not made. I was worried that the vote would be split evenly, but Wilson's proposition was rejected. Five Councillors joined me, including Ramala. I suspect she remembered Jack explaining why he'd stayed as sequestration warden. Jack still had a bad limp from his beating, and a scar down his face. I felt he'd been punished enough.

Many Barrens weren't happy with the result of the vote, and again refused to do the jobs they had always done. We tried to organise others to do them instead, but the non-Barren population resented it. There was an impasse, and garbage built up because no-one would take it away. Eventually the Councillors, both Barren and non-Barren, cleaned up together.

Macon and I often stayed up late, worrying about food and the anger and tension in the corridors.

One night I said, 'Love, I think it's time for us to leave this place.'

I had packed bags for us weeks earlier.

Macon was privately conflicted between his sense of duty and his love for our children and me. 'Maybe we should leave in a few weeks' time?' he said. 'In two weeks, it might be better.'

'You've been saying that for months,' I reminded him.

He was glum. 'You're right. It's just—'

'You're too good for down here. I think everyone should be given the chance to leave.'

I raised it at the next Council meeting. 'Our society is broken. We don't know if it will ever heal properly. Everyone should be able to choose to stay or to try their luck above ground—even the children. I can't promise that everyone— or anyone—will be welcomed into the supraterran settlement we found, but there are other areas or settlements where people can go. In any case, Macon and I are leaving.'

Neena frowned. 'Aren't you giving up? You're quitting.'

A year ago, I would have reacted angrily. But now I thought before I answered.

'We didn't return immediately to the supraterran settlement because we care about this society and wanted to help. Macon's trained people up. We've sat on the Council.'

Neena nodded. 'You have.'

'But I—we—want a better life for our children. Maybe a new society can grow out of this one, but that's for other people to do. We've suffered too much down here. There's a place for us Above, and we're going to take it.'

There was a long session of bickering. Wilson and Neena became adamant that no one should leave. Macon stood up. 'Enough. You can't force people to stay.'

He held out his hand to me, a gesture which would have been unimaginable a year before. I stood and took his hand. Frankie joined us. We walked out.

After the door slammed, Frankie stopped, and held his finger to his lips. Then he tiptoed back to the door, and put his ear to it. We moved closer. Ramala was shouting at Wilson. A cacophony of voices erupted. Frankie gestured, and we moved quietly down the corridor.

When we were halfway to the sleeping quarters, Frankie batted his eyelashes at Macon. 'Aren't *you* a popular man—?'

Macon looked shocked. 'Am I?'

'Neena and Wilson want to lock you up—they need your

knowledge.' Frankie shrugged. 'Ramala was arguing against it. So was Peter. He said Suze wouldn't have wanted it.'

Macon grabbed my arm. 'We've got to leave now!'

Strangely, I felt galvanised. The moment I'd feared had arrived, and I was ready. 'It's lucky we're packed. I'll get the children.'

My body buzzed. I couldn't walk quickly enough. I collected Lilah, Cady and then Tomas.

As I picked up Tomas, a woman sat up in a nearby chair. It was Jenn, the one who'd let me cuddle Tomas so long ago.

'Marri,' she smiled. Her gaze grew sharper, and her smile dropped away. 'What's going on?'

I pulled Lilah and Cady to me with my free arm. I didn't know Jenn well. I hoped I wouldn't regret what I was about to do, but I was relying on the fact that she had let me have that cuddle.

I whispered, 'Don't tell anyone. We're leaving.'

She whispered back. 'Can I come? And my two children?'

'You could ask the supraterran settlement to stay. I don't know what they'll say, though ...'

'I'll take the risk,' said Jenn. 'Anyway, I'll feed Tomas for you.' She collected her children: a ten-year-old and a small female baby, younger than Tomas. I waited while she stuffed clothing, nappies and supplies in a bag.

We took the children to Macon's and my room.

Macon looked up from the pack he was fastening, and his face lit up. 'Jenn! Are you coming too?' I was dismayed when they embraced. They must have been in a registered partnership once, to have that kind of familiarity with one another.

'Someone has to feed Tomas,' Jenn said, patting my arm. I think she sensed my jealousy.

Felix and Frankie joined us, packs on their backs.

We were poised to leave when Ramala poked her head

into the partitioned room. We froze. She took in the jumble of people, children, and bags.

'I was going to tell you to leave. I should have known that you'd figure it out. Go now—while they're still debating. I don't want to see you locked up again, girl.'

'Thanks, Ramala. Come with us!'

'I'm too old and fat to go traipsing across the surface. But go well.'

We embraced, and I kissed her.

'Why are you crying, Mama?' said Lilah.

'This lady has been kind to me. We're saying goodbye because we're going on a big adventure.'

As we hurried through the Upper Level, people stared. It must have been clear that we were leaving, but no one spoke. We reached the Strikeforce guard room where Rich had caught Macon and me. Vin was on guard there, alone. None of us had spoken to him since our sequestration.

'What's up?' he said in a dull voice, but he didn't move. It appeared that he hadn't been told to stop us.

'We're leaving,' said Macon. 'You can leave too if you want.'

'I'll think about it,' said Vin, looking happier. He opened the door. As I passed through, he said to me, 'I'm sorry. About what I had to do to you. About all of it.'

'It's okay. Good luck with everything, right?'

'What will you do up there?'

I shrugged. 'I don't know, Vin. We'll take our chances.'

ACKNOWLEDGEMENTS

I never thought I'd write a novel. However, this novel decided that it must be written regardless of my plans, and kept me up many a long night. Nonetheless, it could never have been written without the help and suggestions of many other people.

Special thanks are due to Caroline Heske, Liezel Van der Linde and Esme Foong who have consistently helped me and encouraged me from the beginning. Other people also made helpful suggestions along the way, including Laurence Mandie and Vanessa Griffiths, who encouraged me to show not tell; Hannah Robert, who helped me refine plot details and confirmed that families came in many forms; Lorenzo Warby, who reminded me of Malthus and put me on to Stephanie Koontz's book on marriage, *Marriage: A History—How Love Conquered Marriage*; Pamela Johnson, who put me on to *The World Without Us*; and to Michael Brand and Jeremy Gans, who both persuaded me to reconsider some stylistic and plot aspects for the better. I am also very grateful to Liz Kemp from Writers Victoria for a thorough and very helpful manuscript assessment, and to Susan Prior for reading a first draft and suggesting edits to the first chapter. Also thanks to Rebecca Lim who gave me advice on pitching the manuscript and on the writing industry generally (thanks Matthew Bell for putting us in touch and generally being encouraging).

I had many beta readers, including the people mentioned above, but also many family members, friends and former students: Dad, my sister Helen, Taisia, Matt and Dan, Doug and Sharon, Heath Gibson, Riaan Louwrens, Natalie Heath, Tyrone Louw, Ilana Singer, Stephanie De Souza, Bronwen Ewens, Florence Wong, Kat Dizdar, Suzanne Huynh, Jim Belshaw and David Spence, among others.

Michael Jordan designed my fabulous website, and Terry Rodgers did my fabulous cover. Thanks guys. You're extremely talented.

I am very grateful to Helen Dale for introducing me to Ligature Publishing and for editing the final manuscript. Special thanks to Matt Rubinstein of Ligature for taking me on and polishing the manuscript until it sparkled.

Finally, thanks to my long-suffering husband and to my children. Love you lots. You are my life.